ROGUE ROYAL

CLUB ROYAL, BOOK ONE

ELOUISE EAST

CONTENTS

DEDICATION

To Renee,
For pushing me to step outside my comfort zone

SUTCLIFFE ROYAL FAMILY

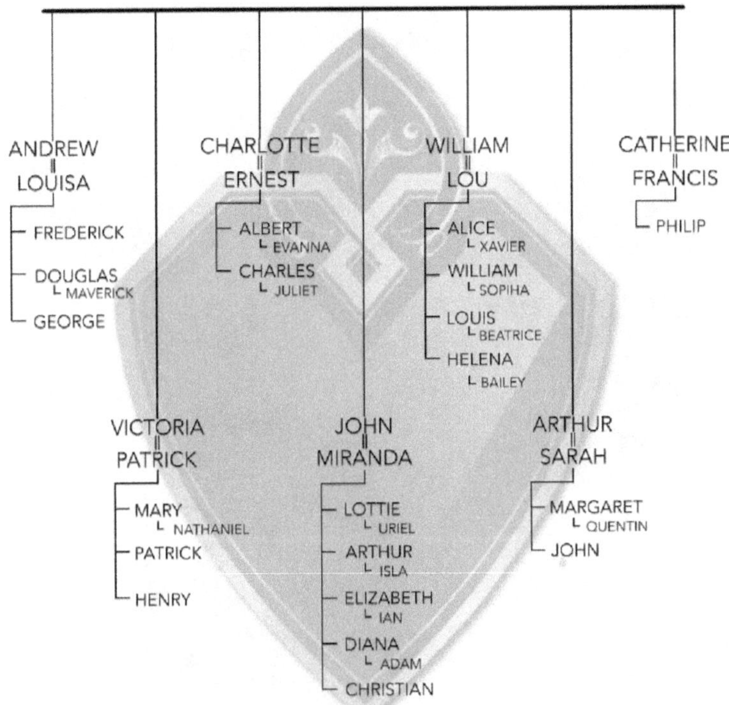

LIST OF CHARACTERS
(ALPHABETICAL ORDER)

Albert, cousin, Charlotte and Ernest's child

Alice, cousin, William and Lou's child

Andrew, King of England, Douglas's father

Arthur, cousin, John and Miranda's child

Bert, Maverick's boss

Charles, cousin, Charlotte and Ernest's child

Charlotte, Douglas's aunt

Christian, cousin, John and Miranda's child

Clarice, Club Royal's receptionist

Damon, Frederick's best friend

Douglas, second in line to the throne

Eddie, submissive at Club Royal

Elizabeth, cousin, John and Miranda's child

Eric, Douglas's bodyguard

Ernest, Charlotte's husband

Frederick, heir to the throne, Douglas's brother

Gareth, Maverick's ex

George, third in line to the throne, Douglas's
brother

Harvey, working with Talon, bad guy

Henry, cousin, Victoria and Patrick's child

Jeffery, Maverick's father's boss, Bert's brother

Katrina, Douglas's best friend, Domme at
    another club

Kendal, submissive at Club Royal

Lou, William's wife

Louisa, Queen Consort, Douglas's mother

Maverick, social media manager

Nico, Maverick's ex

Oliver, Club Royal bartender

Patrick, cousin, Victoria and Patrick's child

Portia, Queen Louisa's assistant

Quinn, submissive at Club Royal

Randall, King Andrew's assistant

Ronald, Maverick's father

Talon, bad guy

Tex, Zara's girlfriend

Umar, submissive at Club Royal

William, Douglas's uncle

Xan, submissive at Club Royal

Zara, Maverick's best friend

ROGUE ROYAL

DOUGLAS

"What in God's name do you think you're doing, Douglas?"

His father's voice echoed around the large sitting area, and Douglas kept his eyes lowered despite inwardly seething, once again, against the injustice of having his life mapped out for him and caught on camera for the entire world to scrutinise.

"Do you have nothing to say for yourself? I've heard plenty from Eric."

His father—Andrew Alexander Charles Sutcliffe, King of the United Kingdom of Great Britain and Northern Ireland —wouldn't like what Douglas had to say, so he stayed silent. Eric was Douglas's bodyguard, and Douglas had told him to always tell the truth regardless of how much trouble Douglas would get into. He didn't want to put Eric's job at risk for being untruthful.

Douglas flicked his gaze towards the other person in the room, who stood a step behind him, hands clasped around a tablet, which undoubtedly held Douglas's transgressions.

"What's the damage, Maverick?" Andrew asked.

His mother, Louisa, reclined in an elegant antique armchair that appeared designed to be uncomfortable and unbecoming. The old-fashioned fabric, though well-maintained, was...old. It reminded Douglas of something his great-grandparents would have used. Come to think of it, it almost certainly was the same piece of furniture.

"The media have published several photographs of His Highness in a compromising position. The focal point appears to be on who the unidentified man was and not so much on His Highness. Despite the...position of His Highness, no private areas were visible. I believe this should blow over—" Douglas couldn't help it if a snort escaped at those words. "—within a few days due to the...regularity of the incidents."

Douglas clenched his jaw and fisted his hands, which were resting behind his back. He hated being the focal point of their discussions, especially when they spoke as if he was not in the room. All he'd wanted was to let off a little steam somewhere other than Club Royal after the shitty week he'd experienced, but he ended up trying to help someone instead. Now, he was standing in front of his parents, being reprimanded for something he didn't do—well, kind of. Granted, he could've told them the truth of what he was doing, but they wouldn't agree with it. He was willing to take the heat of a few rumours. Didn't stop him from moping about it like a teenager, though.

The guy he'd tried to help had been slender and beautiful in his skinny jeans and shimmering tank top, but what had made Douglas glance twice was the makeup accentuating his features. If the guy—whose name he had no idea about—had told him he was an ethereal fairy goddess, Douglas would've believed it. But that wasn't why he'd tried to help—he'd wanted to get him away from his asshole friend, who he believed had been trying to pimp the guy out. Unfortunately, as they were leaving the bar through the back alley, the guy had dropped to his knees, dragging Douglas's waistband with him, then wrapped his shiny pink lips around Douglas's cock. All thought had fled, especially when he'd seen the evidence the guy had left behind...and was waiting to be washed away.

He had never intended for the guy to do it, but he felt his dick twitch at the image of the guy on his knees, and he breathed shallowly to calm his libido. The fucking paparazzi were to blame for his leftover simmering desire. Bloody arseholes. Once he'd put the guy in a taxi home, he could've gone back into the bar again and found someone to help him out with his...issue.

"Douglas, from tomorrow, you will spend every spare evening working at the club until I say otherwise." His father sighed and shook his head. "You would've thought with everything we have taught you at the club, you'd know restraint. Unfortunately, it doesn't appear to be the case. Some extra tuition may be beneficial. Go to bed, Douglas. You have duties to attend to tomorrow, and now, a new evening routine to get used to."

Dismissed, he pivoted and stormed away until a quieter voice brought him back.

"Goodnight, sweetheart."

He returned and kissed his mother on both cheeks, her porcelain skin cooler than usual, and inhaled her honey-suckle scent that always reminded him of his childhood. Sending her a small smile, he left the room, marching down the exquisitely and expensively decorated corridors towards his bedroom. It wasn't often he stayed within the walls of Windsor, but, as his father had reminded him, he had appointments to uphold the following day.

Aware of the footsteps following him, he ignored them as best he could. He would deal with "Storm Maverick" when he was safely ensconced behind closed doors.

He slapped his hand against his door, then twisted the handle to open it, wanting nothing more than to slam it in Maverick's face but knowing he shouldn't. His sitting room, with a dark wooden floor, was more neutral and modern than the principal areas of the castle. His space had white, cream and brown fabrics and dark brown walls. The fireplace, although never used, was a focal point, with a large circular mirror hanging above it.

With a sigh, he dropped into an unyielding but comfortable white sofa, repositioning the cushion to his side before crossing his legs and glaring at Maverick. The man, who had been a part of his life for the last two years, sat opposite him with a blank expression, his wavy, dirty blond hair framing his square face. Maverick crossed his ankle over his knee, supporting the tablet on his legs while he tapped on it.

"This is not part of my original job description, you know."

Maverick's voice was low and deep, and if Douglas hadn't seen his face, he would've said warm as well, but there was no emotion showing. Douglas pursed his lips and linked his fingers over his stomach while trying to stop them from trembling.

"Being in the limelight was not optional for me. I didn't get a job description before they gave me the job." Douglas shrugged. "Get over it."

Maverick shifted his gaze to Douglas's without lifting his

head, those steel-blue eyes spearing into him as if laying all his secrets bare. It was only Douglas's training that stopped him from recoiling from the intense stare. When Maverick lowered his gaze again, Douglas exhaled silently.

"Tomorrow, you have three appointments arranged. The first is at ten o'clock with the children's charity you wished to visit. You will have an hour and a half there, and we should be able to get some decent photos to mitigate the damage you have done tonight. Unless, of course, they contact us to cancel, which is highly likely."

Douglas stood, heat seeping into his cheeks at the possibility of his favourite charity not wanting to be associated with him. He paced in front of the marble fireplace, working off his embarrassment.

"At one o'clock, you are to meet with the Secretary of State about your request for more information into the benefits sector." Maverick scratched at his cheek, the continually present five o'clock shadow making the move audible, and Douglas flicked his gaze away, continuing his pacing. "Then, at seven o'clock, you are to join your parents for dinner with your brothers."

Douglas halted, resting his hands on his hips and staring at the ceiling. "Don't forget my punishment. Doesn't that need to make it onto the itinerary?" It wasn't a question, though it came out sounding like one. He couldn't help but snap, even when he knew it wasn't Mav's fault. Again, his default setting appeared to be a teenage tantrum when someone embarrassed him, which was humiliating enough. He couldn't seem to stop it.

Maverick was right on one front—he was doing more than his social media manager job title. Somehow, over the last two years, he had become more and more involved in the day-to-day schedule of Douglas's life and was now in charge of his appointments as well as the social aspect of his appearances.

"Inputting it now." Maverick stayed silent for several seconds before standing. His unwavering personality appeared much bigger than his height and muscle mass advertised—he was four inches shorter than Douglas but the same breadth in their shoulders. "I have you starting at the club at ten o'clock."

"Wonderful." Sarcasm was Douglas's best friend. He faked a smile, which dropped quickly.

He didn't mind being at the club, except after the week he'd been through, but he preferred to be playing instead of "working." By being one of the Dungeon Monitors, he needed to keep an eye on everyone who played within his allocated area instead of only who he was playing with. He enjoyed watching others when they played; the ecstasy and care being given was a beauty to behold, but he preferred being part of the scene. Although Dungeon Monitors could take part, Douglas refused because he didn't want his attention to waiver from his job.

"If there's nothing else, I'll leave you to your evening."

Maverick bowed his head and strode to the door. His dark grey trousers fitted him nicely, and the white shirt with a dark grey waistcoat left next to nothing to the imagination. Douglas wasn't dead. He knew a gorgeous man when he saw one, and if they had been anything other than what they were, he would've tried flirting with him.

"Goodnight, Maverick."

"Goodnight, Your Highness."

That was another thing about Maverick. He refused to

use Douglas's given name, speaking only his title as if he wanted the distance between them to be clear.

Douglas threw himself on the sofa again, staring at the large circular creation on the ceiling. His mind, however, was on his father's words. And Maverick's. He wasn't sure whose words cut him deeper. Needing a distraction, he rose and exited the room, dashing down the corridor to Frederick's room. As far as he knew, his brother was staying at the castle for a few days, having his own duties to navigate. As the heir to the throne, Frederick had a lot more on his shoulders than Douglas did.

He knocked on his brother's door, and Frederick shouted for him to enter.

Frederick's sitting room was similar to Douglas's, except he had chosen more regal-looking furniture in white and blue tones. His sofas and chairs weren't half as comfortable as Douglas's.

"To what do I owe the pleasure of your company this evening?"

His brother was the quintessential movie star, dream man for many women out there—and men, too—with his short black hair, ice-blue eyes and barely-there stubble. To top it off, he was a genuinely pleasant person, and someone Douglas tried to emulate, though rarely succeeded.

Douglas hugged his brother, clapping him on the back, and huffed. "Got into a bit of trouble. I'm working at the club every evening for the foreseeable future." He reclined in one of the uncomfortable armchairs and shook his head.

Frederick narrowed his eyes at him. "What did you do this time?"

Douglas winced and rubbed his mouth. "I might've got caught with my pants down."

"Literally or figuratively? Why I need to ask that question is beyond me." Frederick sat in one corner of the sofa, crossing his legs and resting his arm along the back of it.

Douglas said nothing, which was answer enough. "They took it out of context, not that anyone cares. I wish Father wouldn't berate me in front of people outside of the family."

"Most people would wish their parents wouldn't berate them at all. You give them too many opportunities to do it. We've had this discussion more times than I can count."

"I know, but I don't mean to. I hate being under so much scrutiny."

"We don't have the luxury of hiding under the radar, Doug. Everything we do will *always* be open to the public. Even more, if it's something we shouldn't be doing."

He understood what he wasn't saying. Douglas was the primary cause for concern within their family, and he had never been one to shy away from doing what he wanted. It was why they had brought Maverick onto his staff in the first place. His parents had hoped with some structure and guidance, Douglas would make better choices and could become a valuable member of their family.

In the beginning, he had tried his hardest, but the constraints chafed uncomfortably, and before long, he had snubbed the idea, reverting to his original ways with a few additional duties. He couldn't stop what he was doing; it was too important in his eyes. Unfortunately, Maverick had to pick up the pieces. He cared what the public had to say about him, but he refused to change who he was because of *what* he was.

"Father will remove the restrictions soon, I'm sure. Keep out of trouble for the time being."

Douglas sighed. "I don't do it on purpose, you know."

Frederick grinned. "Are you sure?"

Douglas's mouth twitched. "Positive."

"Hmm. I'll let you believe that." He cleared his throat. "How did Maverick take it?"

Rolling his eyes, he wandered to the window, peeking out into the darkness. "How do you expect?"

Frederick chuckled. "I can imagine you're going to turn him grey before he's forty."

"He's doing more than he should be."

"Well, stop giving him work to do, and he won't need to do it."

Douglas waved him away. "I don't mean that. He was hired as a social media manager, but he's overseen my schedule for the past year or more. It's not in his job description." And if Maverick hadn't mentioned it off-handily earlier, Douglas would've never thought about it, but now that he had, he was concerned Maverick was working too hard. Though why it concerned him, Douglas had no clue.

"Hmm. I'll speak with Father. Hopefully, they are reimbursing him for the extra workload." Frederick sniffed. "They should give him a medal."

Douglas frowned and glanced over his shoulder. "What for?"

"Dealing with you."

Douglas raced across the floor and pulled Frederick into a headlock. "That's not nice!"

They tussled and scrapped for several long minutes, reminiscent of their early years when they had more freedom, then lay prone on the floor, breathing heavily and extremely ruffled.

"Keep your head down, Doug. It will die down as it always does."

Rising to his feet, Douglas reached out a hand to help his brother. Frederick pulled him close, clasping the nape of Douglas's neck and rested their foreheads together for a moment. Most people would see this as more affectionate than siblings usually were, but Freddie, Douglas and their younger brother, George, were extremely close and showed it in their behaviour—only in private, of course.

"Thanks, Freddie." Douglas placed his forefinger under Freddie's chin and slid it forward in a move him, Freddie, George, Patrick, Henry and Christian did with each other—a reminder to keep their chin up no matter what life threw their way. They weren't called the Scandalous Six for no reason.

Freddie reciprocated. "Get some rest. I'll see you for dinner tomorrow night."

Douglas trailed back to his rooms, his mind whirling with the many infractions the media had accused him of—most of which weren't true.

Sighing, he strode into his bathroom, hardly acknowledging the tiled floors and large jacuzzi, and instead shuffled to the enormous shower at the opposite end of the room. It was the thing he loved most about his rooms at Windsor.

Stripping, he threw his clothes in the basket and stepped into the shower, sliding the door closed behind him. He switched it on, and hot water cascaded over him. Closing his eyes, he allowed the heat to seep into his muscles, removing the tension that had accumulated over the hours since the alleyway.

Dropping his gaze to his cock, he saw the remnants of the lipstick, and he grew hard. He shouldn't feel like that when the guy hadn't known what he was doing, but Douglas was only human. Biting his bottom lip, he fisted his shaft, groaning as sparks of fire lit in his groin. He stroked his hand higher at an agonisingly slow speed, twisted under the head, swiped his thumb across his tip, then thrust his dick through the grip, twisting again at the base. This was his type of foreplay, the slow but steady climb to the brink with his knees trembling, his spine straight, and his whole body clenched in need. The demand to go faster, but the denial of the craving, shooting red hot spikes along his nerve endings.

When his body couldn't take any more, he closed his eyes and pictured the man on his knees, his pink lipstick smudging along Douglas's cock as he lifted his head, and Douglas bellowed his release into the shower where the water washed away the evidence.

He sagged against the cold tiles, panting, then cleaned and dried himself, wrapping the towel around his waist. His reflection stared back at him, accusing him. Why couldn't he be like Freddie? Their parents didn't care Douglas was gay, which was a blessing, but why couldn't his life be quieter like George's? George was younger than him by four years, but as third in line to the throne, he kept away from the limelight more than Freddie and Douglas could. He attended major events and had his own charities and duties he focused on, but mostly, he kept to himself.

If Douglas could have, he would've changed positions with George.

He scrubbed a hand through his damp hair and sighed. Nothing would change. He needed to get over it, as he'd said to Maverick.

Shame he couldn't.

2

MAVERICK

averick clutched the tablet in his hand and blew out a breath, rubbing at his temple with his free hand. The room they had allocated him at Windsor was several corridors and hallways away, but his feet took him there without issue. It wasn't often he used the room, but the king wanted Mav to be close at hand when things like this happened. Which was more often than Mav was happy about.

He would've loved to return to his apartment, where he could relax and stop thinking about the bane of his existence. Being pissed off and tired was not a delightful combination, and he found himself dialling his boss, regardless of the time. If Mav had to be awake at two in the morning, then so did Bert.

"Hello?"

The sleep-filled voice didn't make Mav feel bad. How could he feel bad about the person who was holding this job over his head?

"You need to get someone else to do this fucking job,

Bert. I've had enough." He didn't mince his words. There was no point. He and Bert had been on the outs from the minute Mav had set foot in the company Bert owned, but Mav made it worse by making Bert look bad at an event two years ago.

Hence the reason he ended up babysitting Douglas fucking Sutcliffe. Oh, His Royal Highness, Douglas fucking Sutcliffe.

"Maverick? What the hell are you doing calling me at two in the morning?"

"Because this assignment has gone on long enough, and you know it."

"If you want to work for this company, Maverick, you'll do as I say. You're finished there when I say you're finished. Now, get back to work."

The silence from the other end of the phone indicated Bert had hung up, and Mav clenched his hand around it and breathed deeply until the urge to throw the offending object had passed. Instead, he rested it on the table next to the tablet and dropped onto the sofa, staring at the chandelier—a small one, but a chandelier, nonetheless.

He shook his head at the extravagance, but he could hardly complain when he was currently in a historic castle. Closing his eyes, he sighed, wishing there was a way out of this job, except for him to quit, which he refused to do because, despite the inconveniences and long hours, he enjoyed what he did, and he refused to mess up his dad's job. Was it too much to ask for Douglas to calm the fuck down? Mav could do with a holiday.

Dragging himself to the bathroom once he'd finished with his nightly pity party, he switched on the shower and undressed, wanting nothing more than to fall into bed but knowing he had several hours of work ahead of him.

As the water pounded his muscles, leeching the tension from them, he pressed his hands against the cold tiles and lowered his head. A headache pinched at the base of his skull. The king had made his job ten times harder with the punishment he'd given Douglas. By stopping him from socialising anywhere but the club, he'd inadvertently set Douglas on a collision course with defiance once again.

The way Douglas pushed back sometimes came out of the blue, but mostly, Mav could intervene early enough for it not to cause more problems. Luckily for Mav, being at the club meant Douglas was confined to certain areas, and after working for the sovereigns as long as he had, Mav knew the trouble he could get into.

The extra workload Mav would take on until the king lifted the punishment was enough to keep him busy and away from the wrong men he always seemed to pick. Earlier that night, he'd been on a date with a guy when he'd received the call to return to Windsor. In some ways, Mav was ecstatic to have escaped from the painfully dull date. He could've done with the release, though.

After washing and drying, he padded into the room, grabbing a set of spare clothes he kept there for this reason. Once he was comfortable in joggers and a T-shirt, he sat at the table, booting up his laptop and pulling the tablet closer.

Caught with His Pants Down!

Prince Douglas, the second in line to the throne, was letting off steam in an alley tonight. His unnamed companion was unable to give a statement, as he was otherwise occupied. Who wouldn't be with Prince Douglas standing half-naked in front of them?

Mav snorted at the article that had started the whole debacle. There were many more now, and it was his job to spin the story and come up with something beneficial to the throne. Unfortunately, the phrase "pictures are worth a thousand words" was apt in this case. Douglas had his back to the camera, but there was no denying his trousers were loose around his waist, and his shirt had ridden high enough to show the skin of his lower back and the start of his ass.

He tore his gaze away from the dimples on either side of Douglas's spine and focused on the article again. The guy didn't think about anyone but himself. At thirty-six, he was two years younger than Mav but acted like he was in his early twenties without a care in the world.

He spent the next three hours trying to play up Douglas's charity work, showing the world what he had achieved through tenacity and determination. Although the royal family supported many charities, Douglas's focus was on different charities that he believed were important. Mav couldn't help being impressed by his perseverance.

At five-thirty, he dropped onto the bed, unable to keep his eyes open any longer.

At eight o'clock, the call Mav had been expecting interrupted his deep sleep. The children's charity had postponed Douglas's appointment. Douglas would be pissed, but it could be the push he needed to think before he acted.

Mav snorted. Not a chance in hell.

He sighed and rubbed his face, trying to wake himself further. When it didn't work, he jumped into the shower again. Short of using matchsticks to keep his eyes open, he would spend the day filling up on caffeine and subduing his headache with paracetamol.

The first coffee of the day had already gone, and he made

another in his travel cup before retracing his steps from earlier that morning and knocking on Douglas's door.

"Come in!"

Mav swallowed hard, entering with his head held high and his heart pounding. "Good morning. We have some changes to your schedule today." He stood several steps inside the door with it firmly closed behind him. No need to advertise what had happened to the rest of the household.

Douglas clenched his jaw, the play of the muscles not as clear under his stubble, but Mav knew and sat on a chair. "The children's charity." A statement, not a question.

Mav felt sorry for him for a moment before firming his resolve—it was Douglas's own fault. "Yes. They would like to reschedule for a month's time."

"A month! Jesus." Douglas dropped his head into his hands and threaded his fingers through his short dark hair, leaving it dishevelled.

"Your father has requested you attend a couple of events this week." Mav focused on his tablet. "A luncheon meeting with Erica Price regarding the new hospital wing opening in three months, and he wants you in attendance at the opening ceremony for the college in Cambridge."

"Tell me this…how much time do I have for myself?"

Mav swallowed the retort he wanted to say. "Several hours. At the moment."

He met Douglas's gaze. The startlingly blue orbs fixed on him held no humour. "Any ideas how long this will last?"

Mav licked his lips and tore his gaze away. "If past experience is anything to go by, expect at least two weeks of a heavy schedule. As for the media, a similar timeframe."

Douglas stood, pacing from one side of the room to the other with his hands on his hips. Mav let him walk it off; it was his way of calming down, he'd found. He worked quietly on his tablet, reducing the brightness of the screen until Douglas stopped in front of him.

"Is there any way to encourage a phone or video call with the children's charity before the meeting?"

Mav raised his eyebrows. "I can have the conversation."

"Please do. I'd like to get my ideas across as soon as possible. If they are agreeable, we could start progress before the meeting."

Mav nodded. "I'll ask." He noted it down on his list.

"Are my other appointments today going ahead?"

Douglas wandered over to his dresser, and before Mav could figure his intent, he'd stripped his shirt off and thrown it on the bed. There was nothing casual about the body of this man. He knew of other royal members who refused to take care of themselves, but he could not accuse Douglas of that.

His skin tanned easily, especially with how much he went without a shirt in the gardens, and the warm hues showcased the body of a man who took care of his appearance. Mav knew the club needed the Monitors to have a certain strength in case of security issues, but this was above and beyond the requirement for that role.

Mav could attest to the hours Douglas spent working out. Douglas had taken to adding it into his schedule to ensure he always had time to do it.

Clearing his throat, Mav refocused on the tablet. "Yes. The Secretary of State at one o'clock, dinner with your family at seven o'clock, and the club at ten o'clock."

"Are you ever going to visit the club?"

Douglas spun around to face Mav, pulling a grey T-shirt over his head and hiding away the feast.

Mav tried to recall the question. "Um, no. Not planning to. I've told you before, it's not my thing."

"How do you know unless you've tried it?" Douglas stalked closer.

"Do you have everything you require for your first appointment?" Mav ignored Douglas's words.

Douglas's mouth curled at one side. "One of these days, you'll surprise me and agree to visit, even if it's to assuage your curiosity." He stepped back. "Yes, I have the paperwork I need."

"Good. If you need anything else, please let me know. I will be in my room." Getting some sleep if he could.

"Thank you, Maverick."

"You're welcome, Your Highness."

Mav strode to the door, pausing with his hand on the handle when Douglas called his name.

"If you came to the club, I'm sure someone would help you lose some of your tightly woven control."

Mav lowered his head, then exited the room. He'd never willingly let go of his control. He'd worked too hard to become a solid, dependable force of nature for more reasons than Douglas could imagine. Mav refused to lose control.

He concentrated on the steps that took him back to his room, breathing slowly and deeply until he was behind closed doors. Resting his head back against the wood, his eyelids fluttered shut. The headache had turned into spikes, hammering into his brain. He needed paracetamol and sleep because a migraine was on its way, if the aura spinning in his eyes was anything to go by.

Stumbling to his bed, he took the tablets, signed off to ensure no one disturbed him for a few hours, then climbed into bed fully clothed. Pulling the cover over his head to block out any light, he sighed as the pain eased partially.

The trill of his phone woke him, and he fumbled for the device, knocking it to the floor. He cursed and shuffled closer to the edge of the bed, reaching for it. When it was in his hand, it rang again, and he shoved it under the covers to answer.

"Maverick, the king would like an update on the incident from yesterday—or this morning."

Mav cleared his throat. "What time is it?"

His friend and the king's personal assistant, Randall, chuckled. "It's three o'clock."

"Oh, shit!" He threw the covers off and trudged to the bathroom. "Give me half an hour."

"You got it." Randall paused. "Are you okay?"

"Yeah, I was catching up on some sleep after the late night. I forgot to set my alarm." Nobody needed to know about his headaches.

"All right. Let me know if you need anything."

"Will do."

Mav cancelled the call and jumped into the shower, washing away some of his sleepiness. It appeared he spent most of his time working, sleeping or showering. His migraine, however, had dulled but had not disappeared. Because of that, he knew it would return later that day, if not sooner.

Within twenty minutes, he dashed through the hallways to the king's chambers, his footsteps loud and fast. He stopped at the door, smoothing his clothes and allowing his heart rate to decrease enough to talk without sounding breathless.

He knocked and entered when told, bowing his head. "Good afternoon, Your Majesties."

"Ah, thank you for coming, Maverick. Please take a seat." Louisa Sutcliffe, the queen consort, waved her hand in the direction of the sofa. "I trust Douglas is behaving."

Mav perched on the edge of the sofa. "Douglas should be finishing up his appointment with the Secretary of State if he hasn't already. I've advised him of the additions to his schedule."

"What is the media saying?" The king rested his head on his hand, his elbow leaning on the arm of the chair in which he sat.

Mav had checked the sites before rushing to this meeting. "Most are rehashing what happened the last time and comparing it to this time. Some are debating what he will do next. It's the same as usual."

"Any suggestions to encourage Douglas to stop acting out?"

The door opened behind him, and he glanced over his shoulder, watching Douglas's face colour and his jaw firm. His eyebrows lowered, and Mav knew they'd upset him.

"Yeah, Maverick, any ideas on how to get me to toe the line?"

Mav didn't want to answer.

3

DOUGLAS

*D*ouglas couldn't believe his parents were asking for advice on how to handle him. How old did they think he was? Granted, he didn't make the best decisions sometimes, but why did he need to be *handled*?

He stood facing the occupants of the room and closed the door behind him. The fewer people who heard this conversation, the better. His preference would be for Maverick not to hear it either, but as they had involved the other man, there was nothing for it.

"Douglas, you have to admit you are not behaving as a royal should." His mother crossed her legs and tilted her head at him.

"And what about how I want to live?" Douglas had this conversation many times over the years with his mother.

He saw her mouth twitch. "Within the privacy of your home or ours, you can behave however you wish. Unfortunately, our status within the country, as you know, differs from many other people. We do not have the luxury to do whatever we want to. The people look up to us. What the media publishes reflects on our family as a whole, not just you."

Douglas's gaze flicked to Maverick, then to the floor. His cheeks heated, and he clenched his fingers together in front of him. "I'm sorry, Mother, Father. I will try better." It wasn't what he wanted to say, but what more could he offer? His actions showed more than his words did, even when the media misinterpreted his actions.

"We will revisit this conversation in two weeks." His father stood. "I do not want to hear any more stories about what trouble you have managed to get into. If I do, you will not like the consequences." His father kissed his mother on her cheek, whispered something to her and strode to the door. "Maverick, keep me abreast of the situation."

Maverick glanced at Douglas. "Yes, sir."

Douglas clenched his jaw again, trying hard to contain what he thought of his *situation.* When the door closed behind his father, Douglas relaxed his stance and approached his mother, kneeling by her feet.

"I'm sorry, Mother. I really am. I don't know..." He didn't finish his sentence, peering at Maverick, not wanting to expose his feelings further.

Maverick stood. "If that is all, Your Majesty?"

Louisa nodded her head. "Thank you, Maverick."

Maverick glanced at Douglas and bowed to them before retreating. Douglas dropped his head forward, waiting for the inevitable reprimand. A hand rested against his head, the fingers running through his hair.

"Oh, Douglas. Whatever am I going to do with you?"

He lifted his head, his forehead creasing at her words. "Mother?"

"You have always been the mischievous one of the family."

She smiled. "Of all the cousins, you were the one who I expected to get into trouble for your antics when you were younger. Why are you still doing it now?" She sighed. "Things are difficult for us, Douglas. You need to start taking your role seriously." She held up her hand to stop his interruption. "I know you don't mean for it to happen, but it always does."

"I know, and I'm sorry. There are things…" He stopped, unwilling to explain his real actions when he knew he'd be told to stop, which he refused to do.

Louisa pursed her lips. To anyone else, it would seem like she was angry, but he knew she was thinking. "You need to work with Maverick. Properly, I mean. I know he oversees your schedule for your appearances, but you should get him involved with the charities as well. By working together, you could create something amazing."

Douglas's heart skipped a beat. He wasn't sure he could deal with Maverick any more than he already was. "Isn't he doing enough work already?" Douglas glanced over his shoulder as if he could see the man. "He seemed tired."

Louisa chuckled. "Are you surprised? If I know Maverick as well as I think I do, you kept him up half the night with your antics. He would've been working to put a good spin on things after you went to bed, no doubt."

Douglas hadn't thought about that.

"While I remember, we have postponed tonight's dinner until tomorrow. Your father has an unexpected guest arriving for the evening."

Douglas frowned. "Does he need me to be there?"

Louisa shook her head. "No. You're free for the evening."

He huffed a laugh and stood. "Not quite. I have to pay my dues, remember?"

His mother snorted, the sound inelegant from her lips. "Yes, it's such a hardship to be doing something you enjoy."

"It's the fact that I'm being made to do it that makes it less appealing." He smiled.

"It wouldn't be a punishment if you wanted to do it too much. Think of it as honing your skills."

"Yes, Mother."

"Be gone with you, you insolent child." His mother grinned at him, and Douglas bent low to kiss her cheek, inhaling her scent. She seemed so fragile next to him.

"Have a good day, Mother."

He wandered to his rooms, focusing on the polished tiled floors and the sound of his footsteps reverberating around the large space instead of the noise inside his head. By the time he had closed the sitting room door behind him, he was calmer. Inhaling, he grabbed a cup of tea from the continually ready pot. He chose a seat near the window overlooking the rear gardens and pondered his mother's words. Could he work with Maverick as she suggested? Maverick's opinion of him was low, and Douglas wasn't sure whether he could deal with the constant arguments they seemed to have.

As the shadows of the plants and trees changed shape and size, Douglas went through every memory he could remember. He refilled his cup several times before his need for the bathroom outweighed his tumultuous thoughts. Something needed to change, and working at the club would be a good option for him. Though his father had deemed it punishment, his mother had made him view it as a time to work through everything that had happened.

After showering, he dressed in a conservative shirt and trouser combination for the journey to the club. As he would be working, he chose to drive and climbed into his Bentley

Continental GT V8. His choice of car had not come as a surprise to anyone who knew him. It was sporty and fast, though he never exceeded the speed limit; he'd seen the result of accidents too many times for him not to be cautious. Plus, he didn't want his bodyguard, Eric, to lose him. As rash as he could sometimes be, he refused to mess with Eric's job.

He allowed the hum and vibration of the engine to soothe him and, after being waved through the gates, parked in the underground car park with a sense of calm. As the lift took him to the reception area of Club Royal, he sniggered and shook his head. Whoever had thought of the name hadn't been original in their ideas. He was sure the public who knew about the place also knew who frequented it, but because of the non-disclosure agreements every member signed, no one would ever confirm the details.

The club had begun as a hidden kink by one of his ancestors, who had made a room he solely used for his own pleasures. When his son became out of control, the king had introduced his son to it, hoping to curb his wild ways. From there, it had branched out throughout the years, introducing more and more family members into it as a way to bring the family closer and teach them the control and humility needed to be a royal public figure. In recent years, they had created the club to allow a safer place for them to play out of the prying eyes of the media. Despite the rumours, no one could ever confirm anything, and therefore, no one knew for sure, except for the people who frequented the club.

The lift doors opened to an earthy-coloured room with dark wooden floors and furniture, emerald-green walls and different shades of cream as accent colours. He wandered across the expanse to the receptionist.

"Good evening, Your Highness." She bowed her head.

He had told her several times to stop, but she refused to ignore the royal protocols despite his assurances she wouldn't be reprimanded for it. Once he stepped inside the club itself, they would address him as Master or Sir.

"Good evening, Clarice. How is everything going tonight?"

"Very well, sir. There have been no altercations at all. Everyone seems to be on their best behaviour."

"Good to hear. Who are the Monitors tonight? I forgot to check before I came." He pressed his finger to the electronic pad on the reception desk. Everyone who entered the club had to first be a member but also "clock in" with their fingerprint to show they were present. Everyone had to book their time at the club so they could adhere to the maximum number of people for the building regulations, and so it would be possible to know who was present on any given day should anything happen. It made it easy to speak to those who were there instead of having to go through the whole club member list.

"Princess Lottie, Princex Alice and Princes Christian, Patrick and Henry."

Douglas rolled his lips inwards, hiding his mirth at the use of their titles. "Thank you." Clarice handed him a phone for use within the club walls. It enabled him to call whoever he needed for assistance, but he could use it as a loudspeaker if he needed to be heard above conversation level.

"Have a good evening, Your Highness."

Douglas smiled and stepped towards the wooden door for the changing rooms. Once he was inside, he veered to the right towards the Monitors' rooms. The changing rooms themselves were gender-neutral, but the Monitors had their own room, unlocked using their fingerprint due to their royal status.

He entered the room, aiming for his locker, his shoulders loosening further when his leathers came into view. He had no idea what it was about the leather, but he always felt more real when he wore them. More so than the suits and uniforms he had to wear for royal events.

He sat in a comfortable leather armchair as he removed his shoes, allowing the routine of getting ready to centre him more than anything else. Once he secured the final strap across his chest, he shut his locker. Stopping in front of a full-length mirror, he checked his appearance. His several days' worth of stubble gave him a harder edge, which was exacerbated by the supple black leather vest and trousers encasing his body. Straps held the vest closed and wrapped around his thighs in decoration. He completed the outfit with lightweight leather boots.

Satisfied he looked the part, he exited through reception to the double doors and into the main club. The first room is what Douglas called the "conversation room." It was the hub where people could sit, have a chat and a drink before or after their play. He wandered towards the bar to grab a bottle of water to take with him. The bartender had been with them for many years and knew everything about everything and everyone relating to the club, though he would never break confidentiality unless necessary.

"Good evening, Oliver. Water, please. How is your evening so far?" Douglas rested his folded arms on the counter.

"Very good, thank you, sir."

Oliver's tanned skin and muscular physique were high-lighted when he wore the bartending uniform: a white waistcoat with nothing underneath, accompanied by black suit trousers and white cuffs attached to nothing else. He also wore a black studded collar, which advertised his "taken" status to every member.

"I'm glad to hear it. Anything I need to know about?" Douglas made a point of asking staff members for their take on the happenings at the club; he found it helped them relax around him, which meant they were more likely to approach him with problems. It also helped since he didn't have eyes in the back of his head.

"No, sir. All's quiet."

"Good." He lifted the bottle Oliver had passed him in a toast. "Have a good evening. Give my best to Griffin."

"You may find my husband in there." Oliver indicated the play area with his head. "I gave him free rein tonight." The twinkle in his eye showed his hunger for his husband. Douglas knew their relationship was open to anything except intercourse with anyone other than each other. Neither minded if the other had any kind of play, as long as someone other than their spouse did not penetrate them. Toys were fine, according to both of them.

"I'll keep an eye out."

Douglas uncapped his water and sipped the chilled liquid as he approached the heavy wooden entrance to the play area. Some members deemed it the play zone, but Douglas had trouble calling it that when it reminded him of a kid's soft play area. He had no clue why he could differentiate between play *area* and kids, but he could, and he would not complain about the distinction in his head.

He rested his finger on the scanner and pushed the door open when it clicked. The low playing music and gentle hum of lowered conversation was the first thing to reach his ears, then the moans and groans accompanied by slaps and smacks of skin on skin and implements hitting skin. His mouth curled. He didn't need to witness the scenes to imagine the expression of pure bliss on the recipients' faces.

Douglas glanced around the area, trying to see any of his cousins. A server passed, and he caught their attention. "Could you tell me where to find the Dungeon Monitors, please?"

"Mistress Lottie is in the pet play area, Master Christian is in the bondage area, Master Patrick is in the medical area, and Masters Alice and Henry are taking the floor, sir."

"Thank you."

The server, wearing a similar outfit to what Oliver had been wearing, except shorts instead of trousers, continued on their way, and Douglas watched as they exited the area back to the main room. The only drink available in the play area was water, but the servers meant the members could stay within the play area without having to fetch their own drinks.

Douglas wandered around, the light dimmer in this area than in the main room. He saw several couples in the throes of scenes with members surrounding them. This primary area was for those who enjoy being watched and watching. He found Henry standing with his back to the wall, arms crossed and what Douglas called his serious face—the thin, stern line of their mouth brooked no argument.

"Evening, Master Henry." He climbed the two steps to stand beside him.

"Master Douglas."

"I'm assuming I have the sensation area tonight?" His gaze surveyed the room from his higher perspective.

Henry quirked a smile. "You got it. You snooze, you lose."

Douglas snorted. "You know I don't mind."

"Exactly, which is why you ended up with it. I don't understand why there isn't one area you're more interested in over another. Obviously, it's not a problem; I'm just curious."

"I want to be a Jack of all trades." Douglas grinned.

"You already are. Does nothing take your fancy?" Henry tilted his head at him.

Douglas shrugged. "I like them all. Why limit myself?"

Henry's mouth turned down for a second, and he raised an eyebrow. "True."

"Anything happened tonight?"

"Nope. All is well. Although I may have jinxed us."

Douglas chuckled. "I'll take my chances. See you later."

He stepped down and strode towards one of the back hallways. There were two hallways on either side of where Henry was standing, each leading to different rooms. The hallway on the right led to private rooms, and the hallway on the left, which was where he was, led to themed rooms and areas.

As soon as he entered the hallway, he opened the door to his right. This was where the sensation play area was based and decorated in the same dark wood furniture with emerald-green walls and cream fabrics as the rest of the club. In the centre on the farthest wall rested a comfortable bed covered with silk sheets. To his left was a hospital-style bed, which had restraints attached to the sides. To his right stood a set of shelves and a wooden trunk containing several unique items.

Douglas had been telling the truth when he'd told Henry he didn't want to limit himself. He loved all aspects of BDSM, but there was something about sensation play that called to him. The idea of making someone feel such intensity from something so soft and innocent was powerful. When he had to do his teaching, he enjoyed talking and explaining the uses of sensation play within all areas of the BDSM lifestyle. Many thought it was limited to temperature play, but there were many ways it could be used to overwhelm someone in a good way.

Douglas stepped further into the room, leaving the door ajar—this was to let members know there was no scene, but someone could request one. Next to the door he came through was a large window. Although the door would be closed when the scene was in progress, it didn't stop members from being able to watch what happened. A cover was available if the recipient didn't want to be observed.

A knock sounded, and Douglas glanced over his shoulder to see a red-haired, slender man standing in the doorway. He was wearing nothing except a pair of black briefs.

"Good evening. How can I help?" Douglas faced the newcomer, offering his complete attention.

"Good evening, Master Douglas. I wondered if I could request to play tonight, sir?"

"Such manners. You're welcome. Please, come in." He waited until the submissive had entered and closed the door behind him, head lowered. "Would you like to be watched?"

A flush entered the man's cheeks and flowed down his neck to his bare chest. "Yes, please, sir." His voice was shaky, though not with fear. With excitement.

Douglas's mouth twitched. "Very good. Please lay down on the bed."

This was going to be fun.

4

MAVERICK

$\mathcal{M}$av hated bloody migraines. He'd suffered with them since he was a teen, though, at that time of his life, they hadn't been as incapacitating as they were these days. He suffered from daily headaches, but the migraines happened once a week or so. It was more than he wanted to have them but better than daily.

At that moment, his head felt like it would explode if he didn't do something about it. Unfortunately, nothing except a dark room and sleep would help, and he didn't have time to do it now. He was working his ass off to make certain the alley-job—as the media had nicknamed the event—was being thwarted by good news reviews instead. It wasn't always possible, but soon a new story would show up.

Mav held a hand over his mouth and breathed through his nose to ease the nausea accompanying the pickaxe in his head. The aura from his migraine had lasted around twenty minutes, and it had left him with a hammering behind his eyes and at the base of his neck. At least he could see again, which was beneficial, as he was on his way to meet with Douglas.

As far as Mav could tell, Douglas had behaved himself for the past forty-eight hours. Mav couldn't ask for more, in all honesty, and at eight o'clock in the morning, he was glad.

He knocked on Douglas's door, waiting for the command to enter, then stepped inside, closing the door behind him.

"Good morning, Your Highness."

"Are you ever going to call me Douglas?"

"No, Your Highness."

Douglas tilted his head from where he was sitting at the window. "I could order you to call me it."

"You could." Mav knew he was walking a fine line and let out a soft sigh when Douglas laughed. He had no problem thinking of the man as Douglas, but he couldn't say it.

"What duties do I have spread across my hours today?" Douglas stood and crossed the room to where his tea was, always filled and hot.

Mav hadn't realised how much tea Douglas drank until a few months into his job and they had spent several hours together. Douglas must have drunk ten cups in those few hours. Mav preferred decaf coffee.

He cleared his throat and brought the tablet higher. "At eleven o'clock, you have a visit to a library to meet some children and parents who are trying to get funding to keep the library open. You have a lunch meeting here at two o'clock. Then you have a meeting with Prince Frederick at five and the club at eight."

Douglas sighed, stirring the liquid in his cup. "I keep telling myself it's two weeks, but it's tedious."

"If I may say, Your Highness?" He paused until Douglas nodded. "If you request some additional teaching assignments, you may receive fewer...appointments you don't enjoy."

Mav didn't mind fitting appointments and events into Douglas's schedule, but the teaching was something Douglas enjoyed, and Mav had already come to terms with the idea he hated Douglas being unhappy, even if he didn't show it.

Douglas drifted to stand in front of him, and Mav lifted his head to keep their gazes locked. His heart rate increased, and he swallowed hard. Despite not saying a word, Douglas had a presence that blocked everything else out. His crystal blue eyes shone in the lighting, and Mav was transfixed.

"Thank you. I never thought to do that."

The words were soft and barely reached Mav's ears.

"Though, if you took more care with your public appearances, this wouldn't have happened."

And just like that, he broke the spell when Douglas's jaw firmed, and he stalked away as Mav had wanted him to. Mav took a shaky breath now that he was free from the spell Douglas cast over him. Getting Douglas angry was the best way to keep his distance, though he hated every minute.

No, he didn't. It was necessary.

The nausea came back with a vengeance, and Mav rubbed at his temple with his fingers and thumb, closing his eyes at the brightness in the room. How he wished he could've retreated to bed and pulled the covers over his head for the next two days.

"What's wrong?"

Douglas's voice was closer than Mav expected it to be, and he startled, nearly dropping the tablet.

"A headache. I'm fine." Mav tried for a smile.

Douglas's eyes narrowed. "Have you taken anything for it?"

Mav's cheeks heated. "Yes, although I have to let it run its course. It won't stop me from doing my job."

Douglas's forehead creased. "I never thought it would, but you also shouldn't be working if it's bad. Why don't you take the rest of the day off?"

"I'm fine, Your Highness."

"I insist. In fact, let me help you. I have experience with head massages. It will help to alleviate some of the pain if you'll allow me."

Mav didn't think he could manage with Douglas touching him. "Honestly, Your Highness, I'm—"

"If you say fine, I won't be pleased because I know you're lying."

Mav closed his eyes and inhaled through his nose to stop from saying something he'd regret. And to stop a shiver running down his spine from becoming visible. That voice. "It will go away on its own."

Douglas worked his jaw from side to side. "It's a migraine, isn't it?"

Mav sighed and gave a dismissive wave of his hand. "Yes, which is why it will go away in time. I'm used to it, Your Highness."

"How often do you get them?"

Mav didn't want any information to get out that would stop him from doing his job, so he remained silent. Douglas narrowed his eyes again.

"Right, come on. Back to your room, and I will give you a head massage. You can sleep for a few hours afterwards."

"Your Highness, please. I promise I'm fine."

"It's not up for debate, Maverick. Lead the way."

The tone brooked no argument, and with a heavy sigh, Mav pivoted so he didn't lose his balance and aimed for his room. He'd never had the prince in his room before; it was kind of surreal. Another bout of nausea hit, and he breathed.

A hand touched his elbow. "Are you all right?"

Mav didn't answer for a few seconds. "Yes. The nausea comes and goes." More information he hadn't meant to give Douglas. With all the issues Mav was exposing, Douglas would have all the evidence he needed to get him fired.

His nerves grew as they approached his door, and he tried again to dissuade Douglas, but it was no good. Mav opened his door and indicated for Douglas to enter.

Douglas glanced around the room, then pointed to a burgundy chaise lounge. "If you sit there with a cushion behind your lower back and rest your head on the cushioned side, I will be able to reach easily."

Mav hesitated but placed the tablet on the table and took the seat, pausing again before moving a cushion as Douglas asked. He had no idea what he was doing, but he couldn't stop. He told himself it was because he wanted the headache to go.

He clenched his jaw and breathed heavily as another roll of sickness washed over him. Laying back, he rested his head on the side of the chaise lounge. Mav stared at the ceiling and waited for further instructions, running his thumbs over the soft fabric beneath him. When none came, he moved his head to watch what Douglas was doing. The prince was returning from the bathroom with a washcloth, and Mav frowned. As Douglas came closer, Mav had trouble breathing.

Douglas picked up a chair and carried it to behind where Mav lay, and Mav returned his head to stare at the ceiling.

"I'm going to place this warm flannel over your eyes. The

heat should help, as will the darkness. Then I will massage certain points on your head and your hands."

"This is too much."

"After everything you have put up with from me, this is the least I can do."

That shut Mav up. He'd never expected Douglas to care about how much work he was causing Mav. He lay the flannel over his eyes, leaving his nose and mouth free. Immediately, the heat seeped into his skin, and he felt a loosening in the tension of his body.

"That's it. Relax for me."

Douglas's voice rolled over him, and Mav sighed. He doubted this would work, but if Douglas wanted to try, Mav would let him.

Soft fingers threaded through his hair, pressing mildly into his scalp. He lost track of how long this carried on for before Douglas moved to press against a point in the centre of Mav's forehead. The pressure lasted for several minutes, moving to the corners of his eyebrows, at the top of his nose, on either side. After, Douglas moved to his ears, pressing against different areas.

With every action, Mav relaxed further until he was limp as a noodle, and Douglas was back to massaging his scalp. He didn't know if it was because he couldn't see, but every time Douglas moved his hand, Mav tingled everywhere, and goosebumps skated over his skin.

Douglas removed his hands, and Mav might've whimpered, though he would forever deny it. He heard a soft sound, then a warmth encased his right hand, and he realised it was Douglas's hand. Douglas turned Mav's hand palm up and put pressure between his thumb and forefinger. It continued for several moments, and Mav wouldn't have been able to move if he tried.

His muscles jerked when something began tracing the fingers and palm of his hand. It tickled, but also...didn't. It was as if a small current was trickling along his skin, leaving behind more tingles.

Several minutes later, Douglas replaced his hand on his lap, and his left hand was lifted and subjected to the same ministrations.

When Douglas spoke, he sounded far away, "Let's get you into bed."

Mav felt hands sliding under his body, and he tried to argue, but he was too tired. He could scarcely hold his own head up. The sheets were cool through his clothes, the pillows chilled beneath his head, and he absently noticed Douglas removing his shoes. The flannel was still over his eyes, though it, too, had cooled.

Douglas pulled a cover over him as he sank closer to slumber. He tried to wake up enough to speak to Douglas, but his body was too far gone.

"Sleep. Rest. Relax."

And it was the last thing he remembered.

Mav woke gradually, opening his eyes and allowing them to close repeatedly until he broke the surface of sleep. He rolled to his side and slid a hand under the pillow, trying to get comfortable again. His clothes were all twisted up, and he tried to pull at them when he found he was still in his shirt and trousers.

He frowned, then his eyes widened as the events from

earlier flew through his mind. Covering his eyes, he pulled the cover over his head and groaned as his cheeks flushed. He'd let the prince tuck him into bed like a child. What would Douglas think about him now?

Mav took stock of his body. His migraine had gone, as had his nausea, and his mind was clear. He didn't know whether it was what Douglas had done or the sleep he'd received, but either way, he was glad to be feeling normal.

He gingerly sat upright, swinging his legs over the edge of the bed and paused, waiting to see if his body argued, but it didn't. He stood and hesitated. Nothing. Taking a chance, he wandered to the bathroom to do his business, washed his hands and stared at his reflection, which appeared more relaxed and less pinched than it had that morning.

What time was it?

He shuffled back to the bedroom, wondering where he'd put his phone. It had been in his pocket. It was waiting for him on his bedside table, and he checked for messages. There were several from unimportant people and nothing from anyone he might be in trouble with, save Douglas. He opened the message.

DOUGLAS: When you wake up, make sure you drink the juice and the water on your bedside table. Drink BOTH! If you're awake in time, I would like to see you before the meeting with Frederick. If not, afterwards. I hope you're feeling better.

Maverick raised his eyebrows. Why would he need to see him? He checked the time. Douglas would be finishing up his lunch meeting; therefore, Mav had time for a shower and a change of clothes before going to see what he needed.

As he showered—after drinking both cups—he recalled

the sensations that had flowed through him when Douglas was massaging him. He'd felt nothing like it before. Mav loved the feel of different fabrics and was a tactile person, but this was on another level.

His cock rose at the memory, and he reached for his loofah, which he didn't use for exfoliating. He bit his lip, arousal smouldering in his nerve endings. Standing with his back to the spray, Mav held the green circle of fabric to his chest and lightly brushed it over his skin, which pebbled in response. When he reached his groin, he circled around to his balls; the gentle scratch on his sensitive skin had him harder than ever. After playing around there for a few minutes, he ran it up the underside of his cock, hissing in pleasure.

He moved it in circles as he rose, unable to tell when the uneven fabric would catch on his skin. The underside of the head of his shaft was so sensitive, Mav lessened the pressure and flicked gently back and forth, his breath catching each time it hit the right spot. Precum pearled on his tip, and his eyes flickered as he continued his ministrations in the same area until fluid dripped from his slit.

Moving the loofah around the head changed the sensation again, and Mav gasped for a breath and reached his free hand to the side to rest on the cool tiles.

"Fuck!" He gritted his teeth, refusing to allow anything else to escape his lips where anyone could hear him.

Lowering his head, he closed his eyes and let it all bombard him. The memories of Douglas's hands on him, the gentle scratch of the loofah on his cock, the warm water pounding his back, the coolness of the tiles—it was too much, yet not enough. He returned the loofah to the sensitive underside and, within seconds, released with the strongest climax he'd felt in years.

When he came back to himself, he was kneeling in the shower, hands braced on the floor, loofah discarded, panting. He hoped he hadn't yelled or screamed as his orgasm had claimed him. It was more terrifying than he could imagine, thinking the whole of Windsor heard him.

Climbing to his feet, he washed off, glad the water never lowered in temperature, no matter how long it ran for. The perks of being in the royal household, he assumed. He dressed in a royal blue silk shirt, black cotton trousers and a black silk waistcoat. He added a black tie to the outfit and checked his appearance in the mirror. The fabrics felt comfortable against his skin, and he smiled. Nothing like feeling your best when you're heading to meet someone who antagonises you regularly. His clothes were like his armour.

Snorting at the thought, he exited his room and wandered down the excessively long, decorated hallways to the prince's room. On the way, Prince Frederick stopped him.

"Maverick, I'm glad I saw you. I wanted to have a quick word about Douglas, if I may?"

"Of course, Your Highness. How can I help?"

"We both know Douglas is chafing at the restrictions placed on him, not just this week, but in normal daily life as well. I wondered whether you had any ideas to make this easier on him? I know it's not your job, but you're a smart man from what Douglas has told me, and you work closely with him."

Mav was speechless. "Um…I can certainly have a think. I don't know what use my ideas will be, but I can see what I can come up with."

Frederick held out his hands, palm uppermost. "It's all I can ask. Thank you, Maverick. Anything you can think of would help. I want Douglas to be happy, not chomping to get away from us all the time. I hardly see him as it is."

Mav was an only child, but he understood the sentiment. "I will do my best."

"Thank you. I won't keep you any longer." Frederick squeezed his shoulder and departed, his footsteps heavy and certain.

Mav stared at the floor. Where had *that* come from? Why would Frederick be asking him for help? They all knew Douglas better than Mav did. Or was that why he'd asked him? They were too close to the situation to think clearly and needed an outsider's perception.

Well, he'd keep his promise and try to think of something to help Douglas be more content with his life. The teaching idea from earlier had been a good idea, but there might be something else he'd not considered.

"I want Douglas to be happy..."

Yeah, so did Mav.

5

DOUGLAS

It had taken every restraint Douglas possessed to not climb into bed with Maverick. He had been so responsive to what Douglas had done. Despite what Maverick said, Douglas believed he would do well in the club, especially the sensation play, and what he wouldn't give to see it.

The tiny movements of Maverick's body towards Douglas's touches advertised a need for more. When he had skimmed his fingers along Maverick's hand, unable to stop himself, the hitches in his breath had been barely audible but were there all the same. Douglas was angry with himself for taking liberties while Maverick had been on a high. It wasn't decent of him, and it was the reason he'd stopped and tucked him into bed with the drinks he'd need when he woke.

He hoped Maverick would forgive him and meet with him, as Douglas had requested. He wasn't sure if he would, and he wouldn't blame him if he didn't.

"I'm such an idiot!"

He slammed through to his sitting room and ground to a halt.

"What have you done now, and how much work do I have ahead of me?"

The words startled a laugh from him, and his heart raced at the vision Maverick made in black and blue. The fabrics were soft, he could tell, and Douglas understood more about what made Maverick tick. He stared at him, thoughts swirling around but unable to be caught. But one thing was certain, his attraction to Maverick was increasing, and he needed it to stop.

"Well?"

Douglas had to think about what Maverick had asked. "Oh, nothing. I've not done anything. Promise." He smiled and stepped forward. "How are you feeling?"

A gentle flush coloured Maverick's cheek, and he ducked his head, fiddling with his tablet. "Much better. Thank you for what you did."

Douglas shoved his hands in his pockets to stop from reaching out and tracing the blush disappearing into the collar of Maverick's shirt. "You're welcome. Any time."

Maverick glanced up at him, his eyebrows drawing together, then smoothing out again. "What did you need to see me about?"

"I wanted to check on you, that's all. You should rest up for a few days. I promise I'll behave." Maverick raised one eyebrow, and Douglas raised his hands. "I promise. I'll do my best."

"Hmm." Maverick diverted his gaze, his fingers continuing to flick the case of the tablet, belying his nerves.

"I want some crisps." Douglas's words flew out of him, making Maverick jump. He didn't know where the thought came from, but as soon as he said it, it was all he could think about. He needed his fix. Pulling his phone out, he called the kitchen and asked for his usual, checking if Maverick wanted anything. Maverick declined, but Douglas narrowed his gaze, smiling when Maverick amended his words and ordered some fruit and a yoghurt.

While they waited, they sat on the sofa opposite each other.

"I've been thinking—"

"That's dangerous." Douglas smirked at Maverick's glare.

"I know you don't like the different events you have to go to. What if we found some you wouldn't mind attending and approach your parents with it?"

"Like what?" Douglas rested his ankle on his opposite knee and linked his fingers over his stomach, getting comfortable.

Maverick appeared to gather his thoughts, and Douglas was pleased to see his usual self emerging from the unsure person he had been when Douglas first entered his rooms. "Well, I know you're interested in the children's charities, so that's a given, but what about the historical society or some other aspect within the historical area? I know you enjoy history. What else do you like?"

Douglas gaped at him. He'd never expected this. "Um…I enjoy researching things. Like the BDSM stuff from the past and how they did it." He bit his lip. "I also like teaching."

Maverick tilted his head. "Teaching in what way?"

Douglas's neck warmed, and he slid a finger between his shirt and his neck, trying to ease the tightness. "Yeah. You know I do it at the club…" He waited for Maverick to nod. "I enjoy helping people to understand. Finding a new way to explain something if someone doesn't understand."

When Maverick said nothing, Douglas shifted uncomfortably.

"I can see you doing it." Maverick cleared his throat. "All right. I'll research a few things, and we can discuss them another time."

"You will not research today. You'll go home and get some rest for the next two days—at the least."

"I can't take two days off."

"Yes, you can. I'll speak to Frederick if you're worried and get him to keep an eye on me." And despite how much it rankled, he would do it if it meant Maverick would rest easier.

Maverick's jaw clenched, and Douglas knew he would decline. Maverick's shoulders fell, and he ran a hand through his hair. "Okay. Thank you."

"Seriously?" The incredulity in his voice was clear. He had not expected Maverick to agree.

Maverick nodded. "I'm tired, and I know I won't do as good a job for you if I don't get some more sleep. It makes sense, however much I hate doing it."

Douglas leaned forward to comment when a knock sounded. "Come in!" A member of the household staff entered, carrying a tray with several items on it. "Thank you, Aubrey."

"You're welcome, Your Highness." She curtsied and left, closing the door behind her.

"Eat up, and you can go home to relax."

"You realise I will only be able to relax if you behave, don't you?"

Douglas frowned. "What do you mean?"

"If you get into trouble, I'll receive a call to sort it out. You need to keep your end of the bargain."

Douglas's mouth twitched as he studied Maverick. "You're right. I will be on my best behaviour."

Maverick placed the tablet to the side and reached for the bowl of fruit. Spearing a strawberry with a fork, he lifted it to his mouth, and Douglas watched as his teeth settled around the succulent fruit. Douglas swallowed hard as Maverick chewed and hummed, his eyes fluttering closed for a few seconds before meeting Douglas's gaze.

Immediately, Maverick's gaze dropped, and he sniffed and fidgeted on the sofa while finishing his mouthful. Douglas had figured out Maverick sniffed when he was uncomfortable with a situation. Douglas grabbed his cheesy crisps and sour cream and chive dip—his favourite snack of all time. He lifted one crisp, dipped it, then crunched it, groaning as the flavours burst onto his tongue. It was nowhere near orgasm level, but it was damn good, nonetheless.

"Eat up," he repeated his earlier words when he found Maverick staring at him, not moving. "You need the energy."

Maverick stared at him for a second longer and dutifully devoured the fruit. Once he'd started on the yoghurt, Douglas settled in and ate more crisps. They were bad for him, but he exercised enough he could eat them whenever he wanted.

There was something about sitting alongside someone else in near silence. Something...companionable. He wasn't used to it. Most people he interacted with liked the sound of their own voices and couldn't wait to ask for what they wanted, regardless of what Douglas thought or said. It was the reason he hated formal events so much. At them, he was forever being asked if he could give more visibility, more money, more...anything. He understood the need, but sometimes, he would've liked for someone to speak to him as a person first and a benefactor second.

Maverick didn't appear to be like that, although Douglas's instincts had steered him wrong before. Many past relationships, if he could call them a relationship, had ended on a sour note when they sold the story to the highest bidder. It had happened more times than he could count, and Douglas had thought all of those guys were different.

No, nothing could happen between him and Maverick, but he could introduce him to the club. He was sure Maverick would benefit from being there. The problem was getting him there.

"Thank you for the food. I'm going to leave you to your meeting with Prince Frederick."

Maverick stood, and although it had been Douglas's idea to get some rest, he found himself reluctant to part ways.

"Get some sleep, and I'll see you in a couple of days."

"Yes, Your Highness."

"If your migraine returns, come see me." His tone brooked no argument, and he received an imperceptible nod from the man.

He watched as Maverick collected the tablet and strode to the door. Maverick hesitated with his hand on the door handle. "Thank you for earlier. It was…eye-opening."

With those cryptic words, Maverick exited. What did he mean by them? Eye-opening in what way?

Douglas groaned and laid his head on the back of the sofa, staring at the ceiling. He needed to forget about Maverick because the guy worked for him, or rather, his father. It would cause many problems.

He placed the plate on the coffee table and stood, brushing off any crumbs that may have found their way onto his clothes. Sighing, he made his way down the corridor to Freddie's rooms. He had no knowledge of what the meeting was about because Freddie had requested it, but it couldn't be anything too formal; otherwise, they would be in one of the offices or meeting rooms.

"Hi. What's all this about? You rarely need to arrange a meeting to speak with me." Douglas sat across from his brother and feigned relaxation when, in fact, he was as tense as a sub expecting a spanking.

"Glad you could make it. This meeting has two aims. One is to get more than five minutes of your time to talk to you. I know you've been busy, and it brings me onto number two. To give you a bit of spare time to get away from all the different meetings you've had." Freddie grinned.

Douglas shook his head and laughed. "And Mother thinks *I'm* the one who needs watching."

"There's nothing wrong with what we're doing. If anyone asks, we're talking about the charities you'd like to be involved in."

"And will we be discussing them?" Douglas reached for the mug of tea on the coffee table after Freddie had pointed to it.

Freddie sipped his own brew. "We will, but it can wait for the moment."

Douglas crossed his ankle over his knee and rested his cup on his leg. "I sent Maverick home."

Eyebrows lowered, Freddie sat forward. "Why?"

"He had a migraine earlier, and he's been working too hard." Douglas cleared his throat and diverted his gaze to his cup, which he moved in circles to swirl the contents around. "I gave him a head massage to help ease the headache." He wasn't sure why he'd admitted it, but Freddie might help him encourage Maverick to try the club.

"I thought for a minute he'd done something wrong." Freddie sat back again, studying Douglas like he would the reactions of his sub. "That was nice of you." He paused, tilting his head. "What's troubling you?"

Douglas stood, pacing over to the window, and leaned his shoulder against the frame. "I think he would benefit from visiting the club, but he doesn't seem interested."

"You can't force someone to go if they don't want to."

"I know!"

Freddie was quiet for a beat. "Why do you think it would be good for him?"

Douglas winced and faced his brother, readying himself to be berated for his actions. "When I was massaging the pressure points in his head, he was extremely responsive. As I moved to his hand, I couldn't help but trace my fingers along his palm. His reactions were…" *perfect,* "significant."

"Have you asked him?"

"He's made it clear he didn't think the club was his 'kind of thing.' I don't want to go on about it."

"I mean, have you asked him since then?"

Douglas threw a hand in the air. "How can I? What would I say? 'Sorry I touched you while you weren't aware, but I think you'd do well in the sensation area at the club?' Do you honestly think it would do me any favours?"

Freddie's mouth quirked up. "Well, I wouldn't start with those words, no." He rubbed his forefinger across his lips, which he did when he was thinking. "Instead of taking him to the club, why not bring the club to him?"

His mind churned a mile a minute when Freddie finished speaking. Could he do it? He'd have to get Maverick's permission, but they could start with something slow, hands or arms possibly. Getting Maverick to agree would be the issue. Douglas said as much to his brother.

"That I can't help you with. You know him much better than I do. If he agrees, treat it as you would if you were at the club. Same rules apply, and if you need me there for any reason, let me know."

Douglas sat opposite him again. "Thanks. I'll try to figure it out."

They spoke about the club for a few minutes, and Freddie turned the conversation to Douglas's calendar.

"If you could do or be anything, what would it be?"

The question surprised Douglas, and he gave it some thought. He'd always had a rote reply for questions such as these, but that was for the media, not his brother. "Something to do with archaeology or history. You know I loved it when I did it at Oxford. It was always going to be put on the back burner, wasn't it?"

Freddie nodded. "What if we could find something to benefit *you* as well as stay within the role you need to play?"

Douglas leaned forward, resting his arms on his knees. "What do you mean?"

"Something you enjoy doing so it won't seem like a chore."

Douglas narrowed his gaze. "Have you been talking to Maverick because he said a similar thing earlier?"

"I might've asked him to investigate some things, yes."

"Then, yes. If we could find something more interesting for me to do, I'd be all in."

"Good. I'm going to hold you to it."

Douglas chuckled. "You always do."

"Who's checking your schedule since you sent Maverick home for two days?"

Douglas's eyes widened. "Shit! I have no idea!"

Freddie laughed and shook his head. "You need to think before you act."

Douglas threw a cushion at him.

Douglas sat on his bed with his laptop open in front of him and a paper and pen to his right. As snobby as it could sound, it had been a long time since he'd done any kind of research—since his time at Oxford, in all honesty. He refused to allow Maverick to do all the work for him when he had the time to do it himself; therefore, he pulled up the internet and set to work finding charities and anything else he might be interested in helping that he could get his parents to agree on.

There were a surprising number of charities who worked within archaeology: campaigns to help protect the rural areas of the country, helping to open archaeology to everyone, helping small historical towns, conservation and much more.

Hours passed as Douglas researched each charity and what they did and had done over the past few years, and it was well past midnight by the time he rubbed his blurry eyes and called it a night. Closing the laptop, he yawned and piled his notes on top, resting everything on his bedside table.

Before he knew it, his phone was beeping at him, and he groaned. There was no way he'd slept enough. Surely it wasn't morning yet. But the sunlight streaming through the windows told otherwise.

Douglas rolled to his back and threw the covers off. He

stared at the ceiling, trying and failing to get his eyes to remain open for longer than a second until he swung his legs over the bed and stood. Necessity demanded his eyes open so that he didn't fall, and although he yawned continuously, he made it into the shower without incident.

Washing took most of his energy, but his mind buzzed with the ideas from the previous night's work. He needed to do more before he could approach his parents, but if he could collate everything together, he could ask Maverick to help him make it sound better. Once he was back from his break, anyway.

When his thoughts turned to Maverick, his cock hardened. He hadn't finished berating himself for taking advantage of Maverick, so Douglas refused to do anything about it. It would go down—eventually.

After he was presentable, he grabbed his laptop and papers and moved to his desk in the sitting room. He called down for breakfast to be delivered to his room, and when it arrived, his eyebrows rose at the printed schedule provided with it. The staff member told him Maverick had requested it sent to him that morning.

Douglas leaned back in his chair and pulled out his phone.

DOUGLAS: Good morning. I hope this doesn't wake you. How are you feeling today? Thank you for the schedule. I must admit, I wasn't sure who I needed to approach about asking for it. I've been leaning on you too much, and for that, I'm sorry. Have a relaxing break, and I'll see you in a day or two.

Douglas's eyebrows lowered as he put his phone down. Despite being a Dominant, he was dropping the ball on real-life things, especially when he should handle them instead of palming them off on someone else. It needed to stop. As Freddie had told him several times, he needed to grow up. He thought he had been, but at thirty-six, he obviously had a lot more to do.

Starting today, it would change.

6

MAVERICK

The first thing Mav did when he arrived home was to grab some dinner. He threw a packet of pasta and sauce into a saucepan and cooked it, standing and eating it straight from the pan when it was ready. Once his stomach was full, he filled the pan with water and left it in the sink to soak for when he washed up later. He didn't have a dishwasher; there was no point when there was only him there.

Double-checking he'd locked the front door, he strode down the hallway to his bedroom, undressed and climbed into bed. Despite the early hour—it was seven o'clock in the evening—and the sleep he'd managed that afternoon, exhaustion consumed him, and he was asleep as soon as his head hit the pillow.

When he woke, he checked the clock to see it was six in the morning. He lay staring at the ceiling. What was he going to do with an entire day off? Two days off? He'd taken no extended breaks for months—it wasn't anyone's fault but his own because he should've requested someone to take over from him on his days off. The idea of someone else doing what he considered his job was inconceivable, and he never requested a substitute. Instead, he sometimes worked seven days a week to complete the job.

It meant he had less free time to do the things he enjoyed doing. Now, he had two long days of free hours, and he wasn't sure what to do first.

Climbing out of bed, he jumped into the shower, cleaned and dried off, then dressed in a silk shirt and a pair of cotton trousers. He loved the combination, and the fabrics felt delightful on his skin. Silk was a bugger to clean, but he couldn't resist, though his dry-clean bill had increased with the more shirts he bought.

Mav switched the radio on as he wandered past it, aiming for the kitchen for breakfast. He never minded getting up early, but no matter what time it was, there was always the hustle and bustle of traffic outside. Sitting at the small dining table to scrambled eggs on toast and a cup of coffee, he stared out of the window as London continued to wake up. He rose once to refill his cup and reclaimed his seat, watching the world go by. It was nice to not have to rush anywhere.

His phone beeped distantly. Patting his pockets, he couldn't find it and retraced his steps to the kitchen and bedroom until he found it on his bedside table. There wasn't much charge left, so he plugged it into the living room socket and settled on the sofa. The message was from Douglas, and Mav's heart raced. He rubbed his forehead and told himself to stop being stupid. Nothing could happen between him and Douglas because of the BDSM thing. Douglas was a Dom, and Mav wasn't in the lifestyle. He needed to stop the fanciful thoughts.

He read the message, a small smile playing on his lips.

He'd purposefully written up the schedule for the next couple of days so Douglas wouldn't have to ask anyone, which Mav knew Douglas hated doing. As for leaning on him, wasn't that what Mav's job was? He was not only Douglas's social media manager but in charge of his schedule, too.

It was nice of Douglas to check on him. Mav hadn't expected him to—out of sight, out of mind sort of thing. He tapped his fingers against his lips, remembering the way Douglas had helped him the day before. His hands tingled, and he stared at his palm. Did the sensations Mav felt happen because it was Douglas doing it, or would it have happened with anyone?

He lifted his other hand, his fingertips caressing his skin, sending little sparks of electricity through his hand. Pausing, he clenched his fist to remove the feeling, then opened it wide again. Using his forefinger, he started at the tip of a finger and softly skimmed it over his skin, following the path up and down his fingers and around his palm. Tingles raced after his movement until his hand was one ball of sensation, and his eyelids fluttered. It wasn't the same as when Douglas had done it, but it still felt amazing. When he stopped, he could feel the ghost of the tickle.

He licked his dry lips when his cock made its presence known. It was hard beneath his trousers, but not in an urgent way. Mav would leave dealing with it until later; he enjoyed waiting occasionally.

He'd set his guitar strap over his head when another message came through.

ZARA: Are we going to have time to video call at some point soon, TG?

Mav laughed. He'd not seen Zara in person for about a year, but they always called or messaged. They'd met in university, both doing media studies, and Zara had moved to Edinburgh with her girlfriend, Tex, as soon as they had finished the course. She and Tex had built an amazing event planning business with Zara taking on the social media side of things and Tex the actual planning.

He dialled her number. It rang a few times before Zara's face filled the screen, accompanied by a squeal.

"Oh my god! I dropped my phone when you rang because I couldn't believe you were actually ringing! He lives! Praise be! He lives!"

Mav snorted. "Stop being a bloody drama queen. You know I live because I've been answering your random messages all hours of the day and night."

Zara's full lips spread into a smile, her teeth showing brightly. "But it's different to see your face." She frowned. "You're tired, TG. What's going on?"

'TG' had become Zara's nickname for him as soon as he had told her his name was Maverick. She had shortened the film *Top Gun* to TG and forever called him it.

"Nothing a couple of days off won't cure."

"You have two days off?" Zara's mouth dropped open. "Now I know you're ill. What happened?"

Mav rolled his eyes. "I had a migraine. They offered me a couple of days to get over it. That's all."

"Hmm." Zara narrowed her eyes. "Not sure I believe it's everything, but whatever. You're as stubborn as a mule with explaining stuff. Ooh, were you playing?" She gestured towards the phone, and Mav assumed she meant the guitar.

"I was about to when you messaged."

"Please! Play me something. I've not heard you for ages!"

She pouted and clasped her hands together, her phone obviously on a stand on her desk from what Mav could see in the background.

"All right. What do you want to hear? Bear in mind, I've not practised for a while."

"You don't need to ask, do you?"

Mav shook his head. "Give me a sec." He reached for his stand and rested his phone on it on the coffee table. She wouldn't be able to see all of him, but she could hear. He hoped he could do it justice since he'd not played it for months.

As the first bars of *California Dreamin'* shakily floated through the air, he lost himself to the music. The song took him back to his university days when they would sit on the grass in the sunshine, and he would play the guitar, and Zara would sing, along with anyone else who wanted to join in. It was a regular event many people looked forward to, he was told later.

The last note ended, and he opened his eyes, focusing on the phone where Zara was sitting with tears in her eyes.

"I love the way you play that song."

Mav chuckled and ducked his head, uncomfortable with the words. "What are you doing today?" He changed the subject, removing the guitar strap and resting the instrument against the sofa. Picking up the phone, he drifted to the kitchen for more coffee while Zara told him about the events they had booked in. Their business was growing so fast, they'd needed to hire two employees to keep up with the workload.

He discussed several ideas with her for their business while he made a snack—cheese and crackers and a bowl of mixed fruit—and sat with his feet up on the coffee table. He'd taken a bite when Zara's words made him choke.

After he'd cleared his throat, he drank some water, then asked her to repeat what she'd said.

She chuckled. "Someone booked us to provide a BDSM-themed wedding."

"Isn't it…Won't they…Why?" Mav couldn't get his mouth to work.

Zara's eyes twinkled. "Why not? If it's what they want, and they don't want to hide, why not?"

Mav frowned, staring out of the window into the cloudless sky. Why would someone want such an intimate part of their relationship spread out before their family and friends? He could hardly talk about what his relationships were like, and he certainly couldn't let them view it.

"You're thinking awfully hard over there."

Mav glanced back to Zara, who had her head propped on her palm. "I don't understand how someone could be so…" He paused, unable to find the right word.

"Upfront? Outgoing? Exposed? Free?"

"Yeah, any of them."

Zara sighed. "The world is changing, Mav. People are not as shy about their relationships now. They choose happiness instead of hiding."

He understood the underlying meaning of her words, though he knew she wouldn't say anything to him. Opening up to people was his downfall, as several previous relationships had taught him. Or as his exes had said when they explained why they had cheated on him.

He bit his lip, chewing on the side of it. He didn't see his life changing soon, especially with the high-profile job he had now. It wasn't only the royal family scrutinised in the media; staff members were, too. Including him.

"How is *your* Highness?"

Mav pursed his lips and tried not to laugh. "He isn't *my* anything. And he's a thorn in my side, most of the time." The words hurt to say because Douglas had been so kind the last couple of times they'd met. The animosity they usually displayed had disappeared for some reason.

"Bet you'd like his thorn somewhere else." Zara waggled her eyebrows and shoulders.

This time he did laugh. "Grow up, Z."

"That's better. I prefer the smile on your face instead of a frown."

They talked for a few more minutes until Tex called for her in the background.

"I have to go, but don't be a stranger, yeah? Call me."

"Promise. Now, buzz off."

Zara blew him a kiss and ended the call. Mav stayed where he was, transferring his focus to the window once more. He had always thought BDSM was something you didn't advertise to people, but the royal family had an entire club where people knew about it. Was it different if people from the same background knew about it than people with a...vanilla—he had no idea if it was the right word—lifestyle? He didn't know much about BDSM, but he knew he wasn't into pain or punishment.

But Douglas had been careful with him when he'd given him the massage. What did it mean?

The thoughts circled through his mind once more before he brushed them aside. They were getting him nowhere, anyway. Despite telling Douglas he would take two days off, he grabbed his tablet and phone and did a cursory check of the media sites. Nothing jumped out at him as important or hinting at Douglas having done something; therefore, he appeared to be keeping his word.

Relaxing further, Mav picked up his guitar once more and played a few songs, his fingers remembering the placements they needed to be in. Out of practice, he had to stop after a few songs because his fingers hurt, but he planned to make it a regular thing. He might take it back to Windsor with him if he had to stay there for a while again.

He made homemade cheesy chips and a cheeseburger for dinner and settled in front of the TV. It was strange to be home and not working on something relating to the royal family. Nice, but strange.

A knock on his door woke him from where he'd fallen asleep on the sofa, and he blinked to clear his vision. When it didn't work, he rubbed at his eyes and yawned. The knock sounded again, and he scrambled to his feet, frowning. He never had any visitors. Who would be here? He checked the peephole, and his mouth dropped open.

"What?" He wrenched the door open and yanked Douglas inside, closing the door again. "What are you doing here? This isn't a place for a prince to be roaming around." He put his hands on his hips and glared at him. "Please tell me someone knows where you are?"

"You didn't answer my messages. I was...worried." Douglas straightened and turned to the TV. "And yes, Eric is outside."

Mav couldn't see his expression. "Worried? Why?"

Douglas cleared his throat and faced him again. "You

weren't feeling well yesterday, and then you didn't reply to my messages. I thought something had happened."

Mav dropped his head forward and massaged the back of his neck. "Sorry. After I got your message, I received another one from a friend, and I got sidetracked."

"Do you still have a headache?" Douglas took a step closer.

Mav shook his head. "No, why?"

"You've been rubbing the back of your neck."

He slid his hands into his pockets. "Oh. No, I'm feeling much better now. I slept eleven hours last night." He lifted one shoulder.

"You definitely needed a break." Douglas raised his eyebrows. "I'm glad you're feeling better." He hesitated. "I'll leave you."

Douglas stepped past him, brushing against Mav. Mav shivered. "Wait." He hadn't realised he was going to speak before the words whispered in the air. His heart pounded, his breathing increased, and he focused on a spot on the floor, too scared to move. He didn't know what he was asking for.

Heat bled through his silk shirt, and he knew Douglas had closed the space between them, though they didn't touch. The hair on Mav's body lifted as he noticed the slightest movement from behind him.

"What do you want, Maverick?"

The warmth from Douglas's whisper coasted across his ear, and Mav tilted his head, his eyelids flickering closed. His nails dug into his thighs, from where they were resting in his pockets. He could hear nothing except the soft exhales of the man behind him and his own ragged breathing. His legs trembled, and he swallowed hard, unable to say a word when he didn't know what he wanted. Except he knew what he wanted—he wanted Douglas, but he couldn't have him when he came complete with a BDSM lifestyle.

As if cold water doused him, he stepped away and cleared his throat. "Sorry. Thank you for checking up on me." He knew his cheeks were red from arousal, but he faced the prince anyway, ignoring the obvious signs.

Douglas narrowed his eyes and firmed his lips, then nodded. "I'll see you the day after tomorrow. Enjoy your break."

He let himself out of the apartment and clicked the door closed behind him. Mav exhaled a long breath, pressing a hand against his cock. What the hell had that been about? If he wanted to keep his job, and therefore, remain in Bert's good graces, he needed to keep his lust in check around the prince because there was nothing there for him except pain. And he wasn't talking about the BDSM kind.

He locked the front door and returned to the TV, staring at the screen but not seeing anything.

7

DOUGLAS

ouglas's gaze took in the number of people within the main area of the club. No one was disobeying the rules, and everyone seemed to be enjoying themselves. He watched a couple on the swing, who had gathered a bit of an audience. The slap of skin on skin, along with the smack of a paddle on skin, merged with groans and moans floating from all directions. He could push most of it to the back of his mind when he was working.

A threesome was using the stage in the back corner where the fucking bench was situated. One woman was pegging another woman from behind while the man was fucking her mouth. Douglas's mouth curled. He loved how inclusive the club was. He'd asked his father once why it was —not that he didn't want it to be, but it had surprised him— and his father had told him what people did was their own business, and it was part of the rules that if anyone objected, then they were free to exit, although the non-disclosure agreements stay in place indefinitely.

A sub approached him and bowed his head. "Master

Douglas, would you be able to help me find someone who could introduce me to the suspension bar, please?"

"Of course. Do you have a preference for gender?"

"No, sir."

"Wait with me for a moment." Douglas lifted his head, scanning the room to see who was free. His gaze snagged on his younger brother. "Come with me."

He strode over to George, clapping him on the back. "I wasn't expecting to see you here tonight."

George grinned. "I'm in the mood to play."

"Glad to hear it. I have someone who needs your expertise if you're willing?" Douglas indicated the sub, who was waiting patiently beside them. "They would like an introduction to the suspension bar." Douglas raised his eyebrows.

"Sounds good." George approached the sub. "Would you allow me the honour of showing you the joy you can receive from it?"

"Yes, please, sir."

Douglas leaned forward and lowered his voice. "I believe they're new."

George nodded his head in acknowledgement. "Shall we?"

Douglas watched as George led the way to the other side of the room, where a suspension bar was situated. Returning to his perch at the back of the main area, he resumed his scrutiny of the occupants until angry words met his ears.

"Don't you 'red' me! You deserve this after what you've done to me!" A smack and a cry. "You'll take what I give you after that performance." Smack and sobbing.

Douglas's gaze turned to his left, trying to find the people those words belonged to. His heart raced when he couldn't find them until a whimper drew him to the doorway leading to the private rooms. He glanced over to the doors he could see and saw one ajar. No doors were left open because they booked each private room in advance. If a room was empty, the door was closed.

Douglas stepped down and over to the door, swinging it open without preamble. "What's happening here?"

He took in the scene before anyone had a chance to react to his words. A sub was bent over a table, gripping the edges with white knuckles, and a Dom was leaning over his back, paddle in hand, raised to lay another blow. The Dom turned a furious face towards him, but Douglas was pleased to see the blood drain from his face at who had interrupted him. The paddle dropped to the floor with a thunk, making the sub flinch.

"I was disciplining my sub, Master Douglas. There's nothing wrong with it."

Douglas spared a glance at the sub's body, their ass and thighs red and raw with blood weeping from the cuts. He clenched his jaw to keep his anger in check; he refused to scare the sub further. He depressed a button on the phone attached to his belt, which summoned help.

"Step away from the sub." His voice brooked no argument, though the Dom tried.

"Master Douglas—"

"Step. Away."

Talon's jaw tightened, but he stepped back to the wall, his hands fisting.

"I'm here." His cousin Christian appeared behind him.

"Ensure Talon stays where he is." Douglas purposefully dropped the 'Master' title, so both men knew Talon was in serious trouble.

Douglas wandered over to the sub, making sure to always

keep in the sub's vision, and therefore, being able to see Talon, too. He crouched in front of the sub, lifting his hand slowly to wipe the tears from their face.

"Are you okay?" The sub shook their head. "Okay. Let's get you settled on the bed. Can you bear with us a few more minutes, then I will personally ensure you are safe and cared for?" The sub nodded, more tears overflowing. "You are so brave. Thank you." Douglas helped him to stand upright, and with effort, the sub shuffled to the bed, climbing on with several winces and painful cries. When they were lying on their stomach with their face to the side to see him, Douglas covered them with a light sheet.

"What happened?" His other cousin Patrick appeared in the room.

Douglas stood and transferred his focus to Talon. "*Talon* became a little too heavy-handed with a sub who said 'red.'"

"He didn't—"

Douglas held up a finger. "Talon's exact words were, 'Don't you red me! You deserve this after what you've done to me! You'll take what I give you after that performance.'" Douglas inhaled, calming his anger. "I'm assuming you're not happy with something that happened tonight?"

Talon waved a hand towards the sub. "He humiliated me in front of the entire room. Despite me giving him what he asked for, he didn't come and pretended I was hurting him."

Douglas glanced at his cousins, observing the fury on their faces, which undoubtedly mirrored his own. The sub sobbed beside him, and Douglas, telegraphing his movements, rested his hand on the sub's head, stroking through his hair.

"Take him to the office. Get Frederick here."

"No! I am within my rights to—"

"You have no rights here anymore!" Douglas's words whipped across the room, stunning Talon. "Anyone who could do this because he refused to listen to his sub is not welcome in this club." He focused on Patrick and Christian. "Take him. Do not leave him alone. I will be out of commission while I tend to the aftercare of this sub."

Both nodded and escorted Talon out of the room, closing the door after them, and Douglas refocused on the sub. "What's your name?"

"Eddie." A hiccup accompanied the words.

"Okay, Eddie. I'm going to tend to the wounds on your body."

"Yes, sir."

"I'm going to grab the things I need. Everything is in this room. I won't be leaving you alone."

He fetched the first aid kit from the cupboard in the corner of the room—the same as what was present in all the rooms—grabbed a bowl, and filled it with warm water, taking it all back to the bed. Douglas sat next to Eddie's hip and met his gaze.

"This is going to sting, sorry."

Eddie nodded and pinched his lips. Douglas wet a gauze swab and dabbed it tenderly over the wounds, cleaning it repeatedly to ensure it was free from potential infection. The antiseptic cream he used made Eddie hiss and flinch, but Douglas couldn't do anything about it.

"Despite what happened and how, the marks look good on your skin." He skimmed his hand along the sub's spine in circles, soothing Eddie with his words and his hands. "I am so proud of you for speaking up and using your safe word. Never feel you can't do that, okay? Don't let his ignorance stop you from believing in the power of your safe word."

He could see Eddie's tears seeping into the pillow, and he changed position, sliding onto the bed next to him. Douglas rested his head on the pillow, facing each other, and stroked Eddie's head and back. He pressed a kiss to his forehead and settled in to stay with him. He didn't want to cover the wounds yet; they needed to breathe a little first, but he pulled the cover over Eddie's back and another over his lower legs and feet.

They lay in that position for several long minutes. Douglas tried not to think about Talon because he knew his tension would bleed into his aftercare, but it was difficult. Instead, his thoughts moved to Maverick. Frederick's words circled his head. Could he somehow bring what he'd learned in the club into his and Maverick's interactions? What would be suitable and sneaky enough to slip by unnoticed? Douglas didn't want to do something without Maverick's knowledge, but he wanted to prove Maverick would be interested in it.

Before anything could happen, he needed a conversation with him. For some reason, Maverick's body language whenever the club came up showed what he thought was fear. Douglas would talk about the side of BDSM some new people didn't realise—it wasn't all about pain and hurt.

Douglas kept Eddie safely in the cocoon, chatting about inconsequential things until it was time for him to head home. It would be an uncomfortable ride, and he would be on bed rest for a few days to ensure his wounds healed properly. The club would ensure they properly recompensed Eddie for any wages lost during the time he couldn't work.

"Okay, little one. I'm going to bandage your wounds for the journey home. When you get there, I want you to take them off to air them and rest up for the next few days. If you need someone to come to your house and help with anything, let me know, and I will sort it for you."

"Thank you, Master Douglas."

"You're welcome."

He pressed another kiss to Eddie's forehead and stood, making quick work of the gauze and bandage, and helped Eddie to get dressed in the clothes brought from the changing room for him. If it wouldn't have hurt Eddie more, Douglas would've carried him to the entrance, but he knew it would. Instead, he helped support him whilst shuffling carefully.

A member of staff waited in the reception area to escort Eddie home, and after a few more words of encouragement and praise, Douglas transferred him to the other person's care. Douglas stood, hands on hips, moving his jaw back and forth while he tried to calm the heat invading his body. He glanced at Clarice.

"Is Frederick here?"

"Yes, Your Highness. He's waiting for you in the main office. I've also called in Princes Albert and Arthur to cover."

Douglas nodded, and although he knew the way, Clarice pointed toward the offices, and Douglas strode towards it. He knocked and entered the darkly decorated room. All the furnishings were in the same dark wood, but the walls were of a dark port colour, making it appear smaller than it was.

"Douglas. I hear it's been a tricky night." Freddie rounded the desk he'd been sitting behind and clapped Douglas on the shoulder.

"Have you spoken to anyone else yet?"

Freddie shook his head. "No, I wanted to hear from you first. And besides, I've not long been here. Tell me what happened." He pointed to the seats, and they both sat.

Douglas explained what he'd seen and heard, finishing with what he'd done to care for Eddie.

"You've done well. I know you don't need me to tell you, but you've done everything you could. And no doubt, you will contact Eddie to check on him over the next few days as well." Douglas didn't need to answer because Freddie knew him well. "Let's see what Talon has to say."

Freddie exited with Douglas close behind, and they strode towards the office used for discussions about behaviours if needed, which wasn't often, but often enough that they dedicated a room to it. The room comprised a large desk with two chairs in front and three behind it. Talon and Christian were sitting on the chairs in front, and Patrick was standing to the side, leaning on the wall with his arm crossed.

All straightened and stood as they entered. Freddie and Douglas rounded the desk, each taking a seat in a chair.

"I assume because you have no one to help represent you, you do not want anyone?" Freddie directed his question to Talon.

"I don't need anyone to fight my corner, Your Highness. I did nothing wrong."

Freddie leaned back in his chair and waved his hand in Talon's direction before linking his fingers over his stomach. "By all means, explain away."

Douglas could tell by the tone of Freddie's voice he was less than pleased with Talon's show of cockiness. As Douglas expected, Talon described a scene where Eddie had been on a fuck bench, enjoying himself when he'd begun pushing back against Talon. Talon had assumed—wrongly—Eddie was eager and wanted more, and he'd given it.

"He was pretending to cry and humiliated me in front of the people watching." Talon's jaw and hands clenched.

Silence reigned for a short time, then Freddie sat forward. "This is not the first time you've hurt a sub, although they recorded it as accidental the last time. Unfortunately, your actions after the scene ended have proved to me you are a liability here." Talon spluttered, but Freddie held up a hand. "You appear unable to take criticism, even when it comes from a sub who said their safe word. Just because they safe word doesn't mean there is an unresolvable issue."

Douglas inhaled. "What you did after was unnecessary and cruel. Every person within these walls and outside of them deserves to be treated with respect and not penalised for having different views than you. If you had an issue with a sub, you should have involved a Dungeon Monitor."

"He is my sub to punish as I see—"

"There was no need for punishment." Freddie's voice whipped across the distance, and Talon reared back. "You hurt him because you were angry. No other reason. With that in mind, we revoke your membership. Please remember the non-disclosure agreement still stands, and we will prosecute you should it come to light you released information about this club."

"You can't—"

"We can. Master Christian, Master Patrick, please see Talon to the changing rooms to gather his belongings. After that, escort him to his car until he leaves the premises."

"Yes, Master Frederick." Both men flanked Talon and manhandled him to the door.

"This isn't fair! Subs need to be punished when they

misbehave! Why am I the one being punished?" Talon's voice disappeared as the office door closed.

Douglas scratched his chin. "We need to monitor Eddie. Talon may blame him for losing his membership."

"Undoubtedly. I'll arrange for protection." Freddie rubbed a hand over his head. "I hate this part of the job, but I'm happier he's not making trouble inside the club. We'll have to watch his movements as well. I have a feeling this won't be the last time we'll hear from him."

"I agree." Douglas gave a small smile, finding it amusing how much Freddie's accent changed when he was talking to family to when he spoke to the public. He affected a posher tone for public speaking and events.

"Why don't you head home. I'll deal with the rest of this. Remember to get your statement down on paper and bring it back for the file. We need this as clean as possible to stop Talon from causing us undue issues if he decides to take this further."

Douglas rubbed his forehead. "I will take you up on that. I know I'm supposed to be here for several more hours, but this has wiped me out."

Freddie rested his hand on the back of Douglas's neck and squeezed gently. "I knew it would. Go. If there are any repercussions from Father, I'll deal with it."

"Thanks." Douglas stood. "Let me know if you need anything else."

"Will do. Get some sleep."

They said goodbye in the usual manner, and Douglas drifted to the changing rooms, his body heavy but tight as if he'd been holding onto tension for hours without respite. Which, in a way, he had been. As he changed into his street clothes, he hoped Eddie would come out of this encounter unscathed, and Talon would stay the fuck away.

He checked his phone before leaving, surprised to see a message from Maverick.

75

MAVERICK: I have a proposition for you.

8

PATRICK

Patrick grabbed hold of one of Talon's arms while Christian took his other and wrestled him through the office door and towards the changing room. He didn't care who saw them because Talon would be disgraced after this. It was nothing less than he deserved.

"Get your hands off me!"

Talon fought the restraints, but neither relinquished their hold. They shared a smirk, though.

Christian opened the door to the changing rooms and pushed Talon inside. Patrick added a little extra momentum, and he ended up sprawled on the floor.

"What the hell?" Talon rolled to his knees and stood, whirling around to face them. "You need to watch your step."

Patrick pressed against the finger that was pointed at his chest as he stepped closer. He lowered his voice. "No, you do. This is the best outcome for you. I think Frederick and Douglas have been lenient with you. If I had the choice, I would've castrated you. You make me sick. The power of a Dominant is sacred, and you should not be allowed to take part ever again. Unfortunately, I can't stop you, but I can make damn sure you don't set foot in this club again."

Talon had paled as Patrick spoke, but he still lifted his chin. "I understand."

"Glad we had this chat." Patrick crossed his arms over his chest. "Get your belongings."

Talon strode over to a locker and pressed his thumb against the sensor. The lock clicked, and Patrick watched every item that Talon removed and placed in a bag. It wasn't much. Talon slammed the locker shut and turned to face them, shouldering his bag.

Christian thumbed over his shoulder. "Let's take a trip to Clarice."

If anything, Talon paled further. They marched him from the changing rooms to the reception desk.

"Clarice, can you please wipe Talon's prints from the system and ensure he's barred from access to the premises from now on," Christian said.

"Yes, Your Highness."

Clarice pressed several buttons before declaring it done.

"Can we double-check, please?" Patrick said. "I'm not saying you haven't done your job, Clarice, but I'd like to be certain."

"Of course, Your Highness. Please press your thumb to the sensor," she asked Talon as she swung the computer screen towards them.

Talon did so, and the white words highlighted in red declared him a non-member.

"Thank you, Clarice."

"You're very welcome, Your Highnesses." She glared at Talon.

"This way." Patrick shoved at Talon's shoulder and

received a withering stare in response.

They entered the lift and back out again at the garage level. After following Talon to his car, Talon put up his middle finger and climbed in, throwing his bag onto the passenger seat.

"I'm not moving until he's out of the garage," Patrick stated to Christian.

"Me neither. I'm glad he's out of here. He's always given me the creeps, and I hated it whenever a sub agreed to do a scene with him. There wasn't any one thing that I could put my finger on, but there was just something about him." Christian shook his head.

"I know what you mean. I hope to god he never does it again, but I know that's a wish that will never get granted," Patrick said.

"I wondered if it was better the devil you know. If he's under our roof, we can keep an eye on him. If he's out there, he has no restraints."

"Hmm. I guess we have to hope he's learnt his lesson." Patrick sighed. Talon reversed out of the space and spun his wheels as he raced for the exit. Luckily for Talon, he slowed down and didn't break through the gates; otherwise, he would've had a whole heap of trouble land on his doorstep. Which, if Patrick was honest, he wished he had.

When Talon gunned out of the car park, Patrick clapped Christian on the shoulder. "Come on. Let's get back. I wonder what other trouble has happened while we've been dealing with this shit."

Christian chuckled. "I dread to think."

They entered the lift. "I don't understand some people's

way of thinking," Patrick said when he'd depressed the button for the foyer. "How can anyone think it's okay to hurt someone without their consent? It's different when it's consensual, as you know. My brain can't understand when it's done to emotionally hurt someone as well as physically."

"I'm right there with you. It doesn't make sense."

When they entered the foyer, Douglas met them.

"Are you heading out?"

Douglas nodded. "Yeah, after that, I need to decompress. I'll catch you later."

Patrick touched Douglas's chin, as did Christian, then let him go. He watched after him until he got into the lift, then turned back to his other cousin.

"Something is going on with him. He seems more down than usual."

Christian frowned. "I've not noticed. Do you think it has something to do with the photos from the paper?"

"It might. It's not like that's unusual, though."

"True." Christian squeezed his shoulder. "We'll monitor him, as we do everyone in the Scandalous Six." He grinned.

Patrick groaned as he aimed for the doors to the conversation room—Douglas's name for it was fast becoming the name they used. "Don't you start with that name, too. George has a lot to answer for."

Christian laughed and pressed his finger against Patrick's chin as they split up to get back to work. Patrick exhaled and followed the route to the pet play area. In some ways, he was glad to be in that area now. The playful banter of the pets always brought a smile to his face. He would need it tonight.

By the time he got home that night, exhaustion had claimed him, but he couldn't sleep, his nightmares too close to the surface. Instead, he lost himself in the monotony of his favourite TV show and tried to distract himself from the pain he'd sworn he'd seen in Douglas's eyes when he'd left. Sooner or later, the man would explain what was going on.

9

MAVERICK

What had Mav been thinking when he'd sent the message to Douglas? For several hours after Douglas had left his apartment, he'd been trying to figure out where he stood on the BDSM front. He knew pain was not his kink, in no way, shape or form. He'd spent another half an hour checking out internet sites, researching what he could. There were so many of them, and they were confusing, although Mav had found that not all BDSM was pain-related. When he'd seen those words, he'd tried searching for more but couldn't.

In the end, he'd decided to ask Douglas about it but wanted to ensure they were on even footing. Propositioning Douglas for information into the BDSM lifestyle was not his best move. He planned to provide Douglas with ways to encourage good behaviour—though he would word it better —and hopefully ease some of the tension between him and his father.

As he drove towards the castle on his first day back, he recalled the message he'd received from Douglas.

DOUGLAS: We'll talk about it when you return. I'll book you in for a meeting.

Mav hadn't been sure if Douglas was joking and hadn't replied. Clenching the steering wheel gave him no relief from the butterflies taking flight in his stomach or the increase in his breathing. Why had he sent the message? He should've continued to research.

Showing his badge to the castle guard, he entered the car park and parked in his designated spot. He turned off the engine and stared out through the windscreen. What the hell was he doing?

A knock next to him made him jump, but he lowered the window when he saw a guard.

"Is everything okay, sir? You seem a little out of sorts."

Mav wanted to laugh but nodded instead. "Yes, sorry. I'm a little in my head this morning."

"No problem, sir. I was just checking. Have a good day."

"You too. Thank you."

He knew the guard would be watching him closer—they were never too careful when someone started acting strange —but Mav didn't want to have to explain the reason for his behaviour. He could imagine the scenario. Grabbing his bag and jacket, he climbed out of the car, locked it and aimed for the main house. His hands felt clammy, but he continued until he entered his room and took a deep breath to settle himself.

"What the fuck am I doing?" His words were a whisper.

Ignoring the proposition for the moment, Mav strode to his desk, slid the jacket on the back of the chair and booted up the laptop. While it started, he unpacked his bag. Once he had his bottle of water by his side, he sat, bringing up the schedule. His eyes widened. Douglas had added Mav to the schedule…three hours before dinner. His heart raced, and he was tempted to cancel it, but since he'd come this far, he might as well continue.

He pushed the appointment to the back of his mind and concentrated on what was happening that day. Douglas had an appointment to visit a military school that morning and would stay for lunch. Mav had arranged for a photographer to be there to capture some photos to help mend Douglas's tarnished reputation. He needed to meet with Douglas before he left to go through some things, but he didn't want to.

Rolling his eyes at himself, he stood, grabbing the tablet, which was linked to the laptop, and strode for the door. He reached for the handle as a knock sounded, and he hesitated for a second, then opened it.

"You are here! Fantastic." Douglas slid past Mav into his room, and Mav stared at him. He didn't remember Douglas having visited him there before—except when he'd helped with his migraine—and it was disconcerting.

"Yes, Your Highness. How can I help?"

"I'm going to the Royal School of Military Engineering in an hour, but I wanted to check in with you if there was anything I needed to know that I didn't already."

Mav rolled his lips inwards, trying not to laugh at his words. How would he know what Douglas knew and what he didn't? He cleared his throat. "I can certainly explain the basics of the school if that's what you need?"

"Yes! I don't want to go in and sound like an idiot. I checked out the website and the document I'd received, but I know this is a big deal. Why Father wants me to do this visit, I have no idea." Douglas paced across Mav's room, sliding his hand over his head and down his face several times. It was unusual to see Douglas so…apprehensive.

Mav inhaled and sat on the sofa. "Your Highness, please, have a seat." He waited until Douglas sat opposite him. "I'm sure your father believes in your abilities. He's giving you a chance to show what you're capable of. I'll go through what I can with you, but we only have an hour."

"Brilliant. Give me the most important details." Douglas leaned forward on his knees, staring at Mav with enough focus Mav shivered.

He brought his tablet up, pressing a few buttons and trying to regain his equilibrium before showing Douglas as much as he could. Partway through their conversation, Douglas moved to sit beside him, stating it was easier to see the tablet, but Mav wasn't sure he believed him, as they were hardly using it. Ignoring their proximity, Mav continued until Douglas needed to leave.

The prince stood, and Mav followed suit, not wanting to be at too much of a disadvantage, height-wise. He smoothed a hand down the front of his clothes and glanced up, startled to find Douglas close.

Douglas clasped his hand. "Thank you. I appreciate you going through it with me. I don't trust anyone else not to tell me incorrect information to make me look a fool."

They stared at one another for a second longer than appropriate, then Douglas smiled and bid goodbye. Mav didn't move as he exited the room and silence descended. What the hell?

Mav exhaled and slumped. What he wouldn't give for coffee, but he'd have to make do with tea. For him, unless it was decaf, coffee gave him migraines, so he avoided it where possible. He'd never requested decaf while he'd been at Windsor and had chosen tea instead.

Once his beverage was ready, he sat at his laptop and dug into the reams of emails and correspondence he needed to catch up on. Also, he had to analyse how Douglas's reputation was faring in the media and figure out how to do more to help him recover. It would mean spending most of the morning updating Douglas's social media platforms and scheduling some more posts to go live at relevant times. When today's photographer provided the images, he could add more posts, too.

Despite the long hours—and troublesome charges—Mav enjoyed his job. Researching and analysing performance and creating engaging activities were what he did best.

His phone rang, and Mav sighed when he saw who it was. "Hello?"

"Mav, status update."

His boss's voice had Mav resting his forehead in his palm. "As per usual, I'm updating the analysis now. I will give the results to you in a couple of hours."

"You should have updated them yesterday."

Mav's eyes flicked to the calendar, and he winced. "Yesterday was busy. They will be with you shortly."

"Don't take that tone with me, Maverick. You know the result of talking back to me. I'm sure your father would love to know what you've been up to. He'd be so disappointed."

Mav gritted his teeth and clenched his jaw. "I understand. You will have the analysis shortly." There was nothing else he could do except get it done as soon as possible. Bert was within his rights to demand the results because you should have submitted them yesterday. Mav had, unfortunately, forgotten the date. Otherwise, he would've returned the previous day.

"If they are not in my inbox within the hour...well, you know what will happen." He hung up.

Mav dropped the phone on the desk. If only he'd minded his manners two years earlier.

Mav entered the ballroom, where everyone was mingling. It was his first event, though he'd been working with Bert for the last six years. Mav's father had requested Mav see first-hand what it was like to schmooze with other professionals. Bert hadn't been happy, but he'd agreed, as usual, when it came to Mav's father. For some reason, Bert did a lot of things his father asked, including hiring Mav when the previous company he'd worked for had gone bankrupt.

Mav had been entertaining the idea of going freelance, but he knew he needed some money behind him before he could attempt it. Working for Bert was a stop-gap until he could run his own business. The suit fit Mav to perfection. His father had spared no expense to ensure he had a properly fitted suit for one of the most prestigious events in the annual social media calendar.

His gaze found Bert straight away, laughing with his head thrown back. He was older than Mav's father, but he appeared younger sometimes. Bert was a nice enough guy, but Mav wished he would give him a bit more responsibility. He felt like a trainee at times.

A server wandered towards him, and he took the proffered glass, though he didn't drink. He would keep up appearances, but alcohol played havoc with his migraines. He steered clear as he sauntered towards where Bert held court.

"Ah, here he is. Everyone, this is Ronald's son, Maverick." Bert

clapped him on the shoulder and gave a small smile. "Been with us a while now but is showing promise."

Mav smiled through gritted teeth at the description of his work, but he refused to say anything to antagonise his boss. He knew Bert had a hair-trigger temper.

"Nice to meet you."

Mav's words were sincere. He wasn't introduced to any of them by name, but he knew many from his research. He listened to the conversation, noting who seemed to be invested in Bert's words and who seemed to placate him. Many appeared to be the latter, which might work to Mav's advantage in the future.

As the hours wore on, Mav mingled with a few other groups, being called back to Bert's side regularly, as if Bert didn't want him to make connections of his own.

"Personally, I think Instagram won't last much longer. I don't think we should concentrate on that area of the market when there are more up-and-coming platforms that will take the world by storm."

Mav frowned. "If that's the case, then why are there over one billion active users every month?"

The minute he spoke, he knew he'd made a grave error. Bert's face reddened, and his eyes narrowed, and there was a collective inhale of the group.

Bert laughed, the sound a little forced. "This is why you're still learning, and I'm paid the big bucks." He turned away, continuing the conversation and pushing Mav's opinion aside. He caught the eye of several of the group, a couple who winced, another who nodded his head. Bert was obviously right; Mav needed to learn to play the game better.

Once the evening drew to a close, Bert offered Mav a ride home, and although he wanted to decline, he knew he couldn't. As soon as they were on the road, Bert laid into him.

"At what point do you believe you have any right to argue against my opinions to those in the business? Those people rely on my information to be correct. If they have other people contradicting me, then how will they know what to do? You think you're so smart and have it all worked out. You don't! Stick to where I put you, and you might learn something."

"I just don't understand—"

"You don't need to understand anything apart from what I'm telling you."

They spent the rest of the journey with Bert berating everything Mav had ever done in his career until Mav felt two feet tall. Bert said nothing as Mav climbed out of the car.

It was only when Mav entered their office building the following Monday that he realised the words he'd spoken at the event had paved the way for a new life for him. One spent in the clutches of a misbehaving royal who nobody wanted to deal with. When Mav argued, Bert threatened not only Mav's job but his father's job, too. Unfortunately, it was a threat that he could carry out because Mav's father worked for Bert's brother.

Mav gritted his teeth and acknowledged his new position. As soon as he had enough money saved up, he was going out on his own. He would no longer be under anyone's thumb.

Mav knocked on Douglas's door with a trembling hand, licking his dry lips. Butterflies had taken up residence in his stomach, and nausea followed their path. He didn't know what Douglas needed a whole three hours to talk about with him. Douglas called him in, and Mav inhaled before entering.

"Good afternoon, Your Highness." Mav was proud his voice was only slightly shaky.

Douglas grinned at him from the sofa on which he sat. "I think we can refrain from titles while we chat, don't you think?"

Mav didn't know what to say, but he took a seat opposite the prince, resting the tablet on his lap. They sat in silence for a few minutes until Douglas called his name.

"Talk to me about your proposition. I won't bite."

Mav sniffed, his fingers running along the edge of the tablet case. "It's nothing. It doesn't matter now." He couldn't do it, not with Douglas staring as he was.

Douglas tilted his head. "If it didn't matter, you would've cancelled the meeting." His voice was soft yet confident.

And right. Damn him.

"I don't...I..." Mav shook his head, cursing silently. He had never been so unsure.

"Take your time. There's no rush. Would you like a cup of tea?" Douglas rose, making quick work of two drinks before holding a mug out to Mav. "The meeting today went well. I was surprised by the number of courses available and the enthusiasm from not only the staff but the students, too."

Douglas carried on talking while Mav calmed, and after a few seconds, Mav interrupted, wanting to say something before he lost his nerve.

"In return for what I ask, I will help you find a life you are happy to live, and by that, I mean finding charities and events to support that mean something to you, giving you something to get excited about in your royal role instead of hating every minute." He took a deep breath. "I want you to explain to me about BDSM. The pain-free stuff." He stared at the tablet on his lap, unable to meet Douglas's eyes. "Please."

When Douglas said nothing, Mav chanced a glance at him, seeing a blank expression on his face, but his eyes...his eyes had dilated, and heat rose in Mav's body in response. He locked onto the gaze, unable to tear himself away until Douglas blinked. Mav's heart pounded, and he panted as if he'd run a race.

Douglas cleared his throat. "What are you interested in?"

Mav's cheeks heated. "I don't know." He tried to find the words to explain. "I researched some things, and I found a lot about the pain and punishment side of things, but not much showed any painless elements, though some hinted at it. I wasn't sure who else to ask." He whispered the last sentence and felt foolish. He was a grown man, older than Douglas even, but inside he was back to being a teenager who had no clue what they were doing.

"I'm glad you came to me. It's better to get the information from someone in the lifestyle than to research and receive misleading information. The key thing you need to realise is everyone within a BDSM lifestyle differs from the next person. Wants and needs vary from person to person. There is no right or wrong way to go about it." Douglas sipped his drink, and Mav watched the movement of his Adam's apple as it bobbed with the motion. "Despite the BDSM definition, the moniker has become known as the umbrella term for everything relating to the lifestyle, although it covers a whole other area that has nothing to do with sadism or masochism. With someone new to BDSM, it's about discovery, exploring and finding what best fits the person."

"And it can include pain-free elements?" Mav wanted to make sure he wasn't going down a road he couldn't turn back on.

"Yes, but it can also be pain-free at all times. It's why

discussions with a Dominant are important before anything else happens. All parties need to be on the same wavelength."

Mav sniffed and fidgeted, unsure about asking his next question. "Does it need to happen at the club?"

Douglas exhaled. "No. I would recommend whoever you choose as the Dominant checks out and other people are aware of the situation in case anything happens. But generally, BDSM can happen anywhere."

Mav's shoulders dropped. He didn't want to go to the club until he knew whether it was something he'd like. Being exposed to all those people while he was new and unsure sounded like hell.

"I could recommend someone to guide you through it if you want?" Mav glanced up at him, noticing a small crease between his eyebrows. His heart hammered at Douglas's next words. "Or I can teach you myself."

10

DOUGLAS

*D*ouglas wanted nothing more than to teach Maverick everything he could about everything he knew, but it was more important Maverick felt comfortable with the person who would be his Dominant. Because of their working relationship, Maverick might say it was not right, but Douglas hoped he'd agree.

It also brought to light the reminder Douglas needed to come clean about the massage the other day.

"Actually, before you answer, I need to talk to you about something. It would be better if you knew about it before you decide."

"What?" Maverick's fingers fiddled with the case of the tablet.

Douglas uncrossed his legs and placed his cup on the table between them, then leaned his arms on his knees. As a man, he wanted to shy away from the potential animosity from Maverick, but as a Dominant, he knew he needed to face this head-on. He lifted his gaze to Maverick's.

"When I gave you the head massage the other day, I

should've asked you before I touched your hand for more than what the massage required." Maverick frowned at him. "Do you remember me pressing against the base of your thumb?" He showed the action on his own hand and waited for Maverick to nod. He swallowed hard. "That was all I should've done, but I couldn't resist touching your palm, and I should have." He shook his head and glanced down, cursing himself silently again.

"I don't understand."

Douglas sighed. "You gave me permission to touch you for a massage for your migraine. The touches to your palm were because I couldn't resist how sensitive you were to being touched. It was wrong of me to do it without your consent. It's a big part of my training and my lifestyle. I should've asked you first, and I didn't. I'm sorry."

Douglas watched Maverick run his knuckles over his mouth, gaze on the floor. He didn't want to plead his case any longer because he couldn't sway Maverick's mind. Maverick needed to make the choice himself, to decide whether he trusted Douglas anymore.

Abruptly, Maverick stood, striding to the window, and stared out into the sunlit garden. He crossed his arms over his chest, but Douglas could see he was trembling. Was he scared or angry? Several minutes passed. Douglas allowed him time to go through all the information he'd given him, including the incriminating evidence about Douglas. He hoped he'd get the opportunity to show Maverick what he was missing out on, but if he needed Douglas to find him someone else, he would find someone worthy of him.

Maverick faced him, and Douglas held his breath. The other man stepped closer, the distance between them narrowing, then Maverick did something Douglas never expected. He dropped to his knees by Douglas's feet and rested his hands, palm upwards, on Douglas's knees.

"Teach me," Maverick whispered, eyes lowered.

Douglas inhaled shakily, overwhelmed by the trust Maverick was showing in him. Lifting his hands, he skimmed his middle fingers of each along Maverick's skin from wrist to the end of his finger, receiving a tremble in return.

"It will be my pleasure."

Reining in his libido because he knew what needed to be done first, he cupped Maverick's chin with his forefinger and lifted his face to his. "Maverick, we have things to discuss before this can go any further."

"Mav."

Maverick's eyes were heavy-lidded, and it took everything in Douglas to keep from closing the gap. Douglas blinked a few times and frowned. "Sorry?"

"Please, call me Mav."

Douglas licked his lips and pulled back, releasing Mav. "Okay. Mav, take a seat. We have things to talk about."

"Yes, Your Highness."

Maverick—Mav—stumbled over to the sofa opposite, which was much farther than Douglas wanted him to be, but a suitable distance to allow Douglas to think properly. When Mav sat, Douglas took a breath.

"Before we go any further, we need to decide what it is you want from this relationship. What do you like? What don't you like? And safe words are a few questions." Mav cleared his throat, but Douglas held up a hand. "Let me ask you one at a time, and you need to think before you answer. I will take whatever you say as truthful unless your body language says otherwise." Mav nodded. "I think I have an idea, but tell me, what *don't* you want?"

Mav gripped his own hands, rubbing the thumb of one over the back of the other as he contemplated Douglas's question. "I don't want to be hurt. Pain for me is just that, pain. I don't have a high pain threshold, I don't think."

"I beg to differ." When Mav raised his eyebrows in silent question, Douglas continued, "You manage to continue working when you have a migraine. Now, I've never suffered from them before, but I know they can be debilitating. If you have the strength to work through those, then your pain threshold is higher than you think."

Mav tilted his head, and Douglas could see his brain whirling. "Regardless, though, I don't like pain. I don't find it sexy. I don't find it arousing. I find it painful. It's why I've shied away from BDSM in the past. I thought it was all about pain."

Douglas narrowed his eyes. "What made you decide to research?"

Mav's cheeks darkened until red stained his cheeks and neck. "After thinking about the massage and what you did, I was curious." Douglas wasn't sure if Mav was aware he was skimming his fingers across his own palms as he spoke, but the action heated Douglas's blood. "I know I'm a tactile person. I like the feel of things."

"Do you know what a safe word is?"

"Something a sub can say if what's happening is too much for them."

"Good. You will need to decide on a safe word, or we can use the traffic light system, which is green to keep going, yellow to slow down and red to stop."

"The traffic lights are fine."

"Okay. What about penetrative sex? Is it something you want to be part of the relationship?" Mav chewed his bottom lip. "Be honest. Either way is fine with me." It might kill him to hold back, but he would.

Douglas watched him swallow. "It's not off the table."

"We can work up to it and decide at that moment, then there's no pressure for you. How does it sound?" Mav nodded. "I need words, Mav. One thing I will be strict about is you must use your words unless I've told you otherwise."

"Yes. That's fine, Your Highness."

"And call me Master or Sir. Your Highness is a bit of a mouthful." Douglas stood, pushing the coffee table to the right, out of his way. Stepping closer to Mav, he dropped to his knees in front of him, eliciting a gasp from Mav.

"Let's try something simple. See if you like it. Close your eyes and rest your head against the back of the sofa."

He waited while Mav examined his face, the slight tightening of his features expressing his nerves, and he didn't think Mav would do it, but after a small nod, which Douglas ignored this time, Mav did as he had asked him. The trust Mav was showing in him floored Douglas.

"Now, all you need to do is feel. If you want to say something, say it. There are no restrictions on anything this time. Talk, make noise, move, whatever you need. Feel what your body is showing you."

Douglas rested his hands on Mav's knees, which jerked in reaction. He rubbed his palms against Mav's legs, getting him used to being touched, moving higher up his thighs. As he returned to Mav's knees, he lightened his touch bit by bit until he was skimming his nails across the fabric of Mav's trousers. Although the touch was light and through fabric,

Mav should feel it and, hopefully, it would send tingles along his nerve endings.

Bypassing Mav's groin, which was showing the effects of Mav being touched, Douglas continued further up, tickling his fingers across the silk fabric of Mav's shirt. Mav's hands fisted against the sofa cushions, and his chest lifted and fell faster. Douglas made a circuit from Mav's abs, around his pecs and down the centre of his chest and back to his abs again, each time circling closer to his nipples but not touching.

The first time he skimmed over the stiff nubs, Mav exhaled a breath and arched his back. Douglas left one hand continuing its movements, and the other reached to the coffee table, where he silently picked up a teaspoon. Flipping it so that he was holding the spoon part, he rested the handle below Mav's earlobe, dragging the chilly edge down the column of his neck. Mav gasped and tilted his head to the side, giving Douglas better access.

Douglas followed the edge of Mav's shirt, around to his throat, then over to the other side and up to his ear. By this point, Mav was trembling and panting.

Removing the spoon, he tossed it aside and stood, always keeping one hand on Mav. Douglas rested one hand against the back of the sofa and leaned down, gliding his nose above Mav's five o'clock shadow, his heated breath blowing against his skin. The scent of Mav enveloped him, and his eyes fluttered shut as fire shot through his veins. Mav whimpered, turning into him.

With regret, Douglas pulled a short distance away before their lips could meet.

"Open your eyes." Though whispered, his tone brooked

no argument, and he rewarded him with the pupil-blown, steel blue gaze he hoped he'd see regularly. "Colour?"

Mav blinked several times. "Green. Please?"

Douglas smoothed his fingers up Mav's throat to cup the back of his neck. "Do you want a kiss?"

"Please."

Douglas lowered his head, brushing his lips against his forehead, on his nose, across each eyelid, each cheek before finally descending on his mouth. Mav gasped at the contact, and Douglas sipped at his top lip, his bottom lip, and swiped his tongue into Mav's mouth. He kept the kiss light, exploring and discovering Mav's unique taste while his hand slipped across his body, taking the intensity down by using firmer and more insistent strokes.

When he finally pulled away, they were breathing heavily, but Mav's eyes had cleared. Douglas's hand lifted off Mav's body and mirrored his other on the back of the sofa, caging Mav in.

"Colour?"

"Green." Mav licked his lips, and it took everything in Douglas to hold back.

Douglas sank into the seat beside Mav and wrapped his arm around Mav's shoulder, pulling him into his embrace. He pressed his lips to Mav's forehead. Mav was tense for a moment before sinking into Douglas's body, sliding his arm around Douglas's waist and resting his head on his shoulder.

Douglas allowed him the silence to think through what had happened for a minute or two. He rubbed a hand up and down Mav's arm. "Are you okay?"

"Mmm."

Douglas's mouth twitched. "Words, Mav."

"Yes. I'm good."

Douglas reached for his phone and called down to the kitchen. "Could I have two glasses of orange juice brought to my room, please? Thank you." Mav tried to get up. "Where are you going?"

"We shouldn't be seen like this when staff is around."

Douglas pulled him back into his arms. "They will be a few minutes and won't enter until I let them. We're fine. You, however, need to drink and eat."

Mav sank back into Douglas, nuzzling his head into the prince's neck. "I'm going to feel like a fool when I finally sit by myself again, but for now…" He held Douglas tighter, inhaling, and Douglas returned the embrace, closing his eyes in contentment.

When the knock came, Mav groaned quietly.

"Wait, please."

Douglas cupped Mav's jaw, lifting his face, and once their gazes locked, he lowered his mouth, leaving a gentle kiss on Mav's lips. The hardest thing he'd ever had to do was pull away and go to the door. He took the tray from the surprised staff member and closed the door again. He placed it on the coffee table, sliding the table back to its original place, and returned to his seat next to Mav. He passed a glass of orange juice to Mav.

"Make sure you drink all of it. It will help regulate your sugars."

"You left me this after the massage, too."

Douglas nodded. "It helps to regulate your body's response to the elevated endorphins it went through. It's called sub-drop. Helping take care of you after we've played is an important part of our relationship. It's up to me to ensure you are well taken care of and don't suffer any ill effects." He put his drink back on the table once he'd taken a sip. "At the beginning, we don't know how you will react to what we're doing. Some subs have no sub-drop, while others have a crash period, anything from crying, emotional outbursts, depression, anxiety. Everyone reacts differently. Until we know how you will react, I will try to mitigate it by giving you sugar, care, attention and whatever else I think might help to keep your body and mind on an even keel."

Mav tunnelled his fingers through his hair, then sipped his orange juice. "But we didn't do much."

"It may not seem like it, but you went through a lot. You must remember, this is your first foray into this. Your body is not familiar with what we're doing, and it will take some time to learn your body's reaction and your mind's reaction."

Mav finished his drink in silence, and Douglas changed the subject, giving him time to collect his thoughts.

"I've been checking out some charities I might be interested in supporting. Would you be able to go through them with me and see whether we'd be a good fit?"

Mav raised his eyebrows. "Of course. I had it on my task list, anyway. What made you do it?"

"I had a conversation with Freddie, and it made me think about what I wanted. What I want, I can't have. I need to find a different way to live." Douglas swallowed, deciding to lay everything on the line. It was the least he could do when Mav had trusted Douglas so fully. He sat forward, resting his arms on his knees, staring at the glass in his hand. "A lot of the media photos and articles get taken out of context, but it's a context I can't explain to them."

Mav mirrored his position but faced him, resting a hand on his arm. "Despite who I work for, you can tell me anything. It won't go any further."

"Most of the photos showing me leaving a guy's house early in the morning are welfare checks."

Mav frowned. "Welfare checks? What do you mean?"

Douglas twisted to face Mav, taking his hands. "No one knows I do this." He took a breath. "I check on subs to make sure they are happy with their roles, that they aren't being forced into anything they don't want to do. There's only so much we can do at the club, but for some reason, as soon as members step off club property, the club no longer cares, except to ensure they keep up the non-disclosure agreement. I hate it. So much of a sub's life is outside of the club's walls. We only get to see a small part of it."

Mav slid his hand along Douglas's jaw. "You're a hero, and nobody fucking knows it." He surprised Douglas by leaning forward and pressing their lips together. "Thank you for telling me."

Douglas held up a finger. "Hold on. The latest photo? The guy on his knees? He was a sub from the club. I'd seen him in the bar I was in, and he was going from one guy to another with his so-called friend who was offering the guy's services. He seemed worse for wear. I was trying to take him home when he dropped to his knees in the alley and yanked at my jeans. They took the pictures as he caught me off guard and before I could pull them back up." He shrugged. "You might not believe me, but that's how it was."

"Why are you letting everyone think...? You can't tell anyone."

Douglas nodded at Mav's realisation. "I can't let the club know I'm doing it because it's not part of the membership, but I can't sit by and do nothing if someone is unhappy or hurting. I also don't want the Dominants to find out in case it causes problems for the subs."

Mav stared at him, forehead creased. "I'm so sorry."

Douglas frowned. "Why?"

Mav rubbed his hands over his face. "I thought the same thing as everyone else. You were sleeping around and causing mayhem wherever you went. I'm sorry."

"You don't need to be sorry. You saw what I wanted people to see. There's nothing wrong with it. It just gets tiring after a while."

Douglas tipped Mav's head up and stole his breath in a kiss that made his head spin. No longer could he be soft and gentle. He needed Mav, but if all he could have was this kiss for now, then he'd make it last.

When they were both gasping for air, he rested their foreheads together. "Thank you for listening."

"I'm always here. Now, when my brain is functioning as it should, we can go through those charities."

Mav rested his head back on the sofa and panted, eyes closed, and Douglas wanted to cover him and do it all over again.

He pressed against his hard cock, willing it to go down. He'd have Mav when the other man was ready, but in the meantime, he thought of everything he could show him.

It didn't help his cock go down.

11

MAVERICK

"What the hell did you do?"

The words pierced the silence of Maverick's apartment, and he winced. "Hello to you, too, Zara."

"Don't hello me. Talk."

Mav shook his head. "I have done nothing. What are you on about?"

"Either the cat got the canary, or Bert got his comeuppance."

"If it was the latter, I'd be dancing around the room, not sitting here." Mav rolled his eyes and sighed.

Zara jiggled her shoulders on the video call. "Ooh, that means the cat got the canary! Tell all!"

"Why am I friends with you again?"

"Because I'm the best!" She turned away from the camera, smiling at someone offscreen. "Tex says hi."

"Hey, Tex. Please remind me why we put up with her!" Mav laughed when Tex entered the picture, placing her hands on Zara's shoulders and leaning down.

"Because it's better to keep her where we can see her." Tex

laughed when Zara swatted at her, then pressed a kiss to her lips and danced away.

Their relationship was easy, seamless. It was what Mav had always aimed for with his relationships but laying himself bare to someone he didn't know well was difficult. Except with Douglas. Of course, there was embarrassment when he first started explaining what he wanted from the prince, but some things came tumbling out of his mouth before he realised he was saying them.

"That! That's what I mean! What's the smile for?"

Mav returned his attention to Zara and tried to temper his smile, but he couldn't. "I have no idea what you're talking about."

"Don't lie to me, boy. You got laid!"

"No, I didn't." Though he had been swept away as if he had.

Zara narrowed her eyes. "Something happened." She pouted. "Why won't you tell me?"

Mav sniffed, dropping his gaze. He couldn't tell her everything, but he could allude to a few things. "I'm testing the waters of a new BDSM...relationship."

Zara's squeal hurt his eardrums, and he pinched the bridge of his nose. "Fantastic! Tell me everything!"

"I can't."

"Why?" Mav rolled his eyes again. She whined like a child.

He rubbed his face. "I signed NDAs. I can't tell you everything." He held up his hand when she went to interrupt. "But I can tell you some things." She clapped her hands. "It appears my liking of textures and touch is a thing in the BDSM lifestyle. When I first heard about BDSM, I thought it was about pain and punishment, but I've seen it doesn't have to be about that—if it had been, I wouldn't be doing it."

"I wondered. You've never expressly said you weren't into BDSM, but it showed from your reactions to certain things. I'm glad you've found something to fit you. Who's the lucky guy?"

Mav licked his lips. He spoke to Douglas about what he could and couldn't say to Zara, and Douglas had agreed Mav could tell Zara about him because he trusted Mav's taste in friends, but now that it came down to it, he was worried.

"It's Prince Douglas, isn't it?"

Mav couldn't hide his reaction, and if Zara's laughter was any indication, he looked a fool. "What...? How...?"

"It wasn't hard to figure out. Everyone knows he's a playboy." Her expression tightened. "Be careful, Mav, okay? I know you work closely with him and know him better than I do, but I don't want you to get hurt."

"He's not...how he seems in the media, Zara. There's more to him that people don't see."

Zara nodded. "I believe you, but be careful. He has a whole royal family behind him. Don't let him take advantage."

Mav bit his lip to stop him from saying more, but he acknowledged her words. "I will be careful. When aren't I?"

Zara grinned. "Are you going to play for me tonight?"

Mav sighed as if he was fed up but smiled. "Sure." He grabbed his guitar, which had been next to him because he knew she would ask, and began warming up. He loved that she didn't push for more information than he was willing to give. Hoping he wasn't making a huge mistake with Douglas, he slid into a song.

Mav wrenched away from Douglas's lips with effort, placing a palm on his chest and pushing. "We need to finish work first." Sandwiched between the door and Douglas, he had never felt better while his blue silk shirt rubbed deliciously against his skin. It took him a moment to get his bearings again. "Your Highness, please!"

Douglas growled but released him and stepped back. "As you wish." The heat in his eyes was unmistakable. "Work, then play."

Mav inhaled shakily, running a hand through his hair and smoothing down his shirt, hissing when it slid against his overheated skin. Glancing at Douglas, Mav pursed his lips when Douglas quirked his mouth.

Clearing his throat, he sat opposite the prince. "You have a busy day today. At ten o'clock, you meet with the Secretary of State again. At one o'clock, you have lunch with Frederick. At three-thirty, a meeting with the Council for British Archaeology about becoming involved with them. At six, you have dinner scheduled with your parents—they would like an update about your…situation. After, you have a teaching spot at eight o'clock and the club at ten-thirty."

Douglas grumbled, put his hands over his face, and dropped to his side on the opposite sofa. "I thought you were helping me, not filling my day with appointments." His voice was faint, hidden behind his hands as it was.

Mav smiled. "I am." At Douglas's glare through his fingers, he added, "Except for dinner with your parents— which I have no control over—which of those appointments aren't you happy about?"

Douglas was silent, then sat upright once more, his forehead furrowed. "You're right. I should stop complaining, shouldn't I?"

"Life would be easier for me if you did," Mav said the words whilst he was focusing on his tablet and didn't think about the repercussions of his answer.

Douglas yanked the tablet from his hands, and his gaze flew to him, whose eyes flashed at him, accompanied by a half-smile. "Playtime."

"We've not finished discussin—"

Douglas cut his words short by fusing their mouths. Douglas cupped the sides of Mav's face, holding him still as he ravaged him before pulling back as fast as he'd taken him. "The next time we do this, we're going to my apartment." Douglas licked inside Mav's mouth, his tongue exploring every inch of him and leaving behind a tingle Mav eased with his own tongue. "For now, we have a short time for me to show you something else."

Douglas eased off him and pulled him to standing. Holding his hands, he tugged him across the floor to the window. The weak, early morning sunlight shone through the intermittent clouds, and he glanced at the enormous expanse of the garden beyond the window. Douglas turned Mav to face the view and lifted Mav's hands to press his palms against the cool glass. Mav glanced over his shoulder, an eyebrow quirked. Douglas pushed Mav's chin back to face the window. Where he was standing, he could not see what Douglas was doing.

His shirt lifted from where it was tucked into his trousers, and his breath hitched. He didn't know what to expect, but wasn't that the point?

When warm hands smoothed up his back, Mav's eyes fluttered, but one word from Douglas had them widening. As the view came back into focus, Douglas's hands continued to move across his pebbled skin. When they reached his shoulders, bunching the shirt up, the hands curled, and nails dragged gently down his spine. Mav's breathing sped up, and he bit his lower lip.

The hands and fingers reached his waistband, and nails turned back into the pads of fingers, following the path of his trousers until they met across his stomach. Here, they repeated the process that had played out on his back.

Mav's fingers clenched on the windowpane while Douglas avoided the one area that tightened, readying for a touch that never came. Instead, Douglas's mouth attached to Mav's earlobe, biting down lightly and sending another spear of pleasure down his spine.

Douglas's fingers circled Mav's nipples but never touched. The fingers stroked up his stomach around his pecs and back down, repeating the path in ever-narrowing circles while Douglas's mouth kissed down the column of his neck, encouraging Mav to tilt his head.

Mav's breath shuddered out of him, his body twitching with every touch, every lick, every kiss, his gaze on the view, but his focus on his body. His cock was hard, and his hips thrust and bucked involuntarily.

Douglas's nose dragged along Mav's stubble, then his mouth was at his ear. "Can you come for me like this, I wonder? Can you come hands-free, just from the touch of my hands to your skin, my voice in your ear, detailing every…little…thing I want to do to you?"

Mav dropped his head back, resting it against Douglas's shoulder when he could no longer hold it up. His eyes closed as his nipples sparked an ember when Douglas skimmed over the tip.

"Can you come for me, Mav? Will you give me what we

both know you want? Will you allow me to catch you when you fall?"

Douglas's fingers were more insistent now, though the soft touches alternated with the scratch of nails. Mav concentrated on the touches and the whispers drifting into his ear, pushing everything else aside.

"I can feel your arousal heightening. Your body is readying for release, Mav. Will you give it to me?" Douglas continued his ministrations, plucking and circling his nipples, bringing his climax nearer.

He whimpered, pushing his ass against Douglas, wanting more, needing more.

"You can do it. Your Master is ordering you now." Douglas's voice firmed. "Come for me. Come for your Master." Douglas bit into a sensitive part behind Mav's ear and flicked his nubs, and Mav detonated. His vision whitened as if a sunbeam had shone directly into his eyes, and everything drifted away.

He came back around to find himself cradled in Douglas's lap, his head on Douglas's chest, tucked beneath his chin with Douglas's arms wrapped tightly around him. He inhaled and nuzzled his cheek against Douglas, earning a chuckle from him.

"How are you feeling?" Douglas's voice rumbled through his chest, and Mav sighed, resting his hand over Douglas's heart.

He took stock of his body and mind and found himself relaxed and boneless, if a little sticky. He grimaced at the mess in his trousers. "Fine, except for the mess."

Douglas lifted Mav's face with a finger under his chin until they faced each other. "I can imagine."

"What time is it?"

Douglas checked his watch. "Just after nine."

Mav closed his eyes again, wrapping his arm around Douglas's neck and holding tight. "Thank you."

"I could lend you some trousers if you want to clean up before you leave."

Mav sighed. "As much as it would be the most comfortable option, if I leave here wearing your clothes, gossip mills will run riot." Mav exhaled. "I'll hold my tablet over the front of me." Mav lifted his head, staring at the prince.

Douglas pressed a kiss to his lips. "This is why the next time will be at my apartment. Let's schedule an appointment now." He stood, Mav scrambling to hold on to his neck as he carried Mav with him and sat on the sofa. "Here's your tablet." He passed it over, and Mav laughed, shaking his head.

"Yes, Your Highness. When would you like the appointment for?"

"Tomorrow. Block out from dinner to when I need to be at the club."

Mav raised his eyebrows but did as asked. "What do you want me to tag it as?"

Douglas frowned. "Frederick. He won't mind being used as a screen."

Mav typed the note and saved it. "All set."

Douglas kissed him chastely. "Good. I want to take my time with you."

They rested in silence before Mav deemed himself too uncomfortable to stay as he was, then he said goodbye, receiving a long, tantalising kiss before he exited. Mav kept his head down, holding the tablet in front of him to hide the remains of his now cold release. Every step had him grimacing.

"Good morning, Maverick. How are things going with my son?"

Mav bowed his head to the king, his heart pounding at the implications of his words, which he immediately quashed with reason. "Your Majesty, things are going well. Prince Douglas is becoming more involved in charities to show his compassionate and fore-thinking self. We have arranged for some new charities to be included on his schedule that he may be more inclined to attend. He will have more information for you this evening."

"Glad to hear it. You have been a boon to the team, Maverick. Thank you for your tireless work ethic. I will ensure your boss hears about it."

Maverick felt the heat invade his cheeks at the thought of what work he'd finished doing with Douglas that morning. "Thank you, Your Majesty. I'm glad you're happy with my work."

King Andrew squeezed his shoulder and moved on, his entourage following, and Mav watched them leave, slumping against the wall. Of all the people he hadn't wanted to see while his come was still staining his trousers, the king was the first. He was sure he would lose his job if his and Douglas's relationship was to be exposed.

Sighing, he rushed through the remaining corridors to his room, thankful when he locked his door behind him. Placing the tablet on the table, he aimed for his bathroom. The shower was calling, plus a new set of clothes.

He couldn't find it in himself to care about the repercussions of their illicit lessons when he remembered how Douglas had felt surrounding him, teasing him, caring for him.

He wanted more.

With the rest of the day clear unless anything went wrong at Douglas's appointments—and they would contact him should anything happen—Mav drove across the city to his father's house.

Ronald Houghton was sixty years old and a part-time accountant for Calverdere Associates—Bert's brother, Jeffrey's business. He had been working with Jeffrey for over twenty years and had grown up with them both. Unfortunately for Maverick, it meant Bert had him between a rock and a hard place when it came to making sure Mav did as he was told. His father was two years away from retirement, and Mav wouldn't do anything to stop it from happening if he could help it.

As he parked in his father's driveway, he shook his head at the picture of his dad halfway up a ladder, cleaning the gutters of the house. Mav had told him repeatedly not to do it when there was no one there with him because if he fell, he'd be in trouble, but did his father listen? No.

"Dad, what have I told you?" Mav strode to the ladder, holding the base steady while his father worked.

"Ah, I'm good. It's a few leaves and moss. Anyway, the neighbour's kid usually does it, but they're away on holiday this week, and with the forecasted rain, I didn't want to take the chance."

Ron climbed down, carrying the bucket full of rubbish, and Mav stepped back when he reached the bottom. "You should've called me."

His dad chuckled, the weathered lines on his face deepening with his mirth, though his eyes lightened. "You've got enough to do without dropping everything to help me plod around the house, Maverick. Come on, the kettle's not long been on."

Following his father into his childhood home immediately took Mav back to simpler times when Mav didn't have as many worries on his shoulders. The photographs on the walls were an album of his life, hung with methodical precision for every milestone he reached.

"Tea? Although you probably drink some fancy coffee at the castle, don't you?" His dad cackled.

Mav rolled his eyes, following the voice to the kitchen. "They do have fancy coffee, but they drink as much tea as we do." He sat at the worn dining table, fingering the gaps in the wood as he listened to his father pottering around the room. If he closed his eyes, he could imagine it being twenty years ago. Nothing much had changed, and he loved it.

"Here you go." Ron settled a mug of steaming tea in front of him, then slid into a seat beside him, his arms trembling. The white in his hair and beard made Ron appear older than his sixty years. "What's bothering you?"

"What do you mean?"

"It's not that I dislike your visits, Maverick, but when you turn up unannounced, it's usually because something's wrong." His father tilted his head, narrowing his eyes.

Mav frowned. "Do I?" At his dad's nod, he sighed. "I'm sorry."

"Don't be sorry, son. I don't mind you visiting at all, but I can try to help if something's troubling you."

There was no way Mav could get into all the different aspects of his life that were causing him to be unsettled, but he could use a sounding board, for one thing.

"How do you let someone in when you know it could end badly?"

Ron rolled his shoulders, staring at his mug. "If you cared about them enough, it shouldn't matter. Letting someone see who you are shouldn't be a choice. If they mean that much to you, it just happens. You can't *not* give them everything. If the relationship has a time limit…" He shrugged. "You still have no choice, Maverick. Allowing yourself to feel is second nature. Love, lust, attraction all compete with hate, loss and disappointment. It's natural to feel all those things, and if you try to stop yourself, you're not living…you're existing. There's an enormous difference, and I wouldn't want the latter for you."

Mav understood what his father was trying to tell him, and it gave him a lot to think about. He changed the subject, and they chatted for a while, Mav staying for lunch before going home to get some more work done. He wouldn't see Douglas until tomorrow now, but he wanted nothing else. If he went to the club, he would see him, but Mav wasn't ready. Douglas had told him he could teach him everything he needed to from outside of it, and Mav was happy with that.

It's a shame his brain teased him with images of Douglas with others in the same way he was with him. He brushed aside the thought several times as he worked, but it didn't want to disappear.

Mav could give Douglas his body, but could he give him his trust?

12

DOUGLAS

*D*ouglas could not get the image of Mav climaxing hands-free out of his head. He'd seen subs do it before, but Mav differed from the rest of them. Mav appeared in control, but as soon as Douglas's hands touched him, he was as meek as a kitten, and it suited him well.

He couldn't wait for Mav to arrive at his apartment that evening. He hoped everything would go to plan, and Mav could get into the building without being seen. Once he was in there, no one would bat an eyelid at him being there, but Mav had never needed to meet with him outside of Windsor before. If Douglas wanted to ensure Mav was safe from scrutiny, then, although he wanted him there with him, he needed to consider other factors.

The meetings that day had finished, and he was excited about the unity between him and the Council for British Archaeology. Being able to open archaeology to all people, not just those who could afford it, was something Douglas liked the sound of. Encouraging young children especially was something he wanted to explore. Imagine the fun they'd have digging for fossils and learning where they came from.

He pulled his tie off, deciding not to wear one to dinner with his parents. They wouldn't mind. Although they always dressed up despite it being with their children, the siblings didn't have to. Douglas usually appeared well-dressed, mainly because he wanted his father to see he was taking his role seriously, but tonight, he wanted to let loose a little.

Checking his watch, he sighed and left his rooms, his footsteps advertising his presence ahead of him. He pushed into the family dining room, smiling when he saw George already seated but checking his phone. His brother would hide it as soon as their parents arrived because they refused to allow phones at the dinner table. Douglas could imagine the controversy should they ignore their parents and answer messages instead.

"Hey." He slapped George on the back. "How're things?" Douglas took his seat, which was always next to his mother's, and relaxed back.

"Good, good. Everything is going as well as expected. How's the media circus going for you?" George crossed his arms and leaned on the table—another thing that wouldn't be allowed soon.

Douglas held back what he wanted to say and instead explained the new plan of focusing on charities and events *he* wanted to support.

"Obviously, I'll take part in the ones Father and Mother say are necessary for me to be involved in, but I want to focus more on those close to my heart. I didn't study archae-ology for nothing." He lifted his filled water glass, sipping to stop his flow of words.

George held up his hands. "I know you didn't. You don't

need to plead your case to me. Whatever you've been doing has worked wonders on your mood, if nothing else." George winked.

"Shut up!" Douglas shook his head, his mouth unable to stop from curling.

"What's he done now?" Freddie entered the room, looking every inch the prince he was, and Douglas was, once more, happy he didn't have the weight of the crown on his shoulders. He knew Frederick was the best person for the job, although there were other members of their extended family who would like to see someone else as the heir apparent. Douglas should be more grateful for small mercies in that respect.

"He's being his usual cocky self." Douglas grinned.

"There's a word to describe our entire family." Freddie laughed and took his seat to Father's right, reaching for his glass. "Don't forget to put your phone on silent this time, George."

"Shit, yeah." George fumbled with his phone and shrugged as he replaced it in his pocket. "I don't know why I always forget. It's not like the rule has ever changed since we were first given them."

"It's because you have so many things cluttering up that brain of yours." Freddie's eyes gleamed, but he hid his grin behind his glass.

"Well, that's what happens when you have a brain," George shot back, straightening his spine and rolling his lips inwards, and Douglas knew he was trying to stop his smile.

"Who has a brain, and what are they using it for?"

His father's voice was loud in the small area but filled with humour, much to Douglas's relief. He hoped it meant

Father was in a good mood himself, and therefore, Douglas might escape unscathed.

His father helped his mother into her chair as he did for every meal they had together, then sat, staring around the table at his family. "I'm glad you could all make it."

"Oh, hush, dear. Stop sounding so strict. You know they always make time for family dinners." His mother smiled at his father and tapped his hand as if reprimanding him.

"Quite right too. Family is important. Being a unit is important. Facing everything as one is important. It's what I want to point out today. You are individuals, yes, but you also have a duty to your family."

Douglas transferred his gaze to his glass and swallowed hard. He didn't need the reminder, but he assumed it was for his benefit.

"Don't forget…your family is also there for *you*." Douglas glanced back at his father at those words to find his father's gaze already on him. "I'm harsh on you all. I know that, and it sometimes takes your mother to remind me you are also adults in your own right. Your decisions affect us all, but our decisions affect you, too. Hopefully, we can all remember that."

"Amen to that."

George's not-so-whispered words made his father's mouth twitch, and Douglas couldn't hide his smile.

"Let's eat."

As soon as his father said the words, the staff brought plates of food to them. The delicious smelling beef bourguignon was melt in your mouth good, and the conversation around the table was lively and relaxing. Surprisingly, nobody said anything about Douglas's antics, which was good as far as he was concerned. Although he wouldn't hold his breath until after he'd left the room.

"How was the meeting with the Secretary?"

Douglas finished what was in his mouth and followed it with a sip of water. "It went well. She's outlined how the benefits system works currently and how she would like it to work, but I think there needs to be some improvement." He peered at Freddie. "Freddie, do you think you could go over the details with me tomorrow night before my club session?"

Freddie hid his smile in his glass and nodded. "Sure. You'll have to bring me up to speed on what the objective is, but I can certainly be a sounding board if nothing else."

"Great, thanks."

Douglas thanked his lucky stars he'd already spoken to Freddie at lunch about his plans for tomorrow evening, and Freddie had agreed to cover for him. He would need to remember to pass some details onto him about the benefits project in case their father checked in with him about it.

His mother rested her hand on his forearm. "I can also help a little should you need it, sweetheart. I've been through the situation many times and know the things they've tried previously. After you've spoken with Freddie and done some more thinking on it, come see me, and we can go through your ideas."

"Thank you, Mother."

She patted his arm and removed it, leaving a warmth behind. Despite their occasional disagreements, he loved his family dearly and would never wish for anything to hurt them. His own actions, though justified, would need to stop or change because they were hurting his family. He hadn't seen how much before now.

The dinner passed by with conversation and laughter, with their mother bemoaning ever having grandchildren to fuss over. It wasn't something Douglas had never thought about, except when his mother brought it up, but the idea of sharing that with someone else was a better picture than doing it alone.

His father called him as he rose to leave, and he sat again. "I spoke to Maverick earlier. He said you have taken on some more charities you're interested in?"

"Yes, Father."

"Have you spoken to any of them yet to ensure they fit what we need?"

"I'm meeting with them before I decide on which I will add to my itinerary. I had my first meeting with the Council of British Archaeology today, and it went well. I would be interested in adding them to my responsibilities if you agree."

His father stood, buttoning the jacket he'd opened before dinner began. "I don't see why it would be a problem as long as it doesn't interfere with your duties and stops you from attracting these silly media articles."

Douglas bit his lip to stop himself from arguing. He'd managed to keep his visits secret for many years, and he refused to blow his chances now. "It won't interfere with anything important. I promise."

"You'd do well to listen to Maverick, Douglas. He knows what he's talking about."

Douglas didn't think his father would appreciate what type of listening he did to Mav. "He's doing a great job, Father. He's helped me out a lot."

King Andrew tilted his head and narrowed his gaze on Douglas. "As long as his helping does not lead to other things."

Douglas's heart raced, and he swallowed several times before he could answer. "Of course not, Father. He's helping me get my media presence as pristine as it can be. That's all."

"Glad to hear it. Make sure you speak to him about the club again. I'd like to see him take an interest in it."

Frowning, Douglas rose. "Why?"

"Because he'd understand us better if he did."

"I think he understands us enough, Father. It's not part of his interests."

His father's eyes bored into him. "Hmm. I don't like it but never mind. Have a good evening, Douglas."

His father left the room, and Douglas blew out his cheeks. He hoped he hadn't been too forceful with his words because it would be the first thing his father would pick up on. He needed to make sure none of this touched Mav.

Draining his water glass, he exited and strode to his rooms, having a shower before dressing for his teaching lesson. Each lesson was an hour long and based at the club, but as soon as he finished, he'd be back to monitoring the crowd instead. He enjoyed the teaching aspect of it more than being a Dungeon Monitor, and as far as he was concerned, he would've preferred to be teaching every day instead of monitoring. He supposed that was why it was a punishment and not something he loved.

With a few days left of his penance, he could manage. It wasn't like it varied in his usual life, after all. He wished he had more time with Mav, but as soon as his punishment was over, he would be with him as much as he could.

He let himself into the teaching room after signing himself in at reception and checked to ensure the items he needed were present. Tonight's lesson was about caning. The couple who had requested the lesson wanted to try something different and asked for help. That was one of the best things about the club. It didn't matter what someone wanted to be taught; they could find someone who would advise them.

When the couple arrived, Douglas went through the first aspects of caning: discussing the different canes and the maintenance and care of them. Once completed, Douglas explained how to use a cane and the areas of the body that were low risk compared to the higher risk areas. He also troubleshot a few issues they might come across and high-lighted what to check for in body language. When the instructional part of the lesson was complete, he demon-strated on a sub who entered the room for that specific reason.

Once the demonstration finished, the couple left the room, and Douglas took care of the sub. He spent several minutes holding her after he wrapped her in a blanket once he'd ensured she had taken some paracetamol and he'd applied some lotion. When the aftercare was complete, the couple returned to the room, and Douglas witnessed their first caning experience. Finishing with a few tips, Douglas left the couple to their aftercare routine and returned to the changing room, sitting with a cup of tea and some food.

Pulling out his phone, he opened a message thread to Mav.

DOUGLAS: Don't work too hard tonight. You need your rest for tomorrow.

Smiling, he finished his food, locked his phone away and stepped back into the fray. He had plenty of hours to decide what he was going to show Mav tomorrow.

"You need to stay away from my sub, Master Douglas."

Douglas turned to face his cousin Charles, whose expression was less than kind, as usual. Charles was Albert's brother and the son of Aunt Charlotte, Douglas's father's sister. Aunt Charlotte was a vicious woman who believed LGBTQ+ people were less than she was and had no place in the royal line. She had never quieted her opinions, even when faced with her brother, the king.

Douglas had never understood how Albert had become such a pleasant person with Aunt Charlotte as a mother, whereas he could tell who Charles took after.

"I don't know what you mean."

"I saw the video of you speaking with Juliet. There is no need for you to speak with her when I'm not present."

Douglas raised his eyebrows. "What video? And anyway, she's my cousin. Why wouldn't I talk to her? If I remember rightly, we were discussing your birthday."

Charles sneered, stepping closer. "I doubt it very much. She is not your concern. She is my wife and sub, not yours. Stay out of it."

"I wasn't getting into anything, Charles. We crossed paths, and I mentioned your birthday coming up. She said you weren't planning a party this year. Why not?" He tried to divert the subject, knowing he couldn't give Charles an inch because he'd run with it, and he'd expose Douglas's secret.

Charles narrowed his grey eyes, then straightened. "I didn't see the point. It would be the same people who turn up each time. I'd prefer to spend the time with my family instead."

Douglas smiled. "How are Alex, Lizzie and Charlie?" He purposefully called them by the names the children preferred instead of the full names, knowing it would annoy Charles.

His children were eight, six and three, respectively, and were named after their great-grandparents, Alexander and Elizabeth, and their grandmother, Charlotte. No wonder they wanted nicknames.

Charles's body language softened somewhat, but he glared at Douglas. "They're doing well. Charlotte starts preschool next week."

"That's splendid news. I'm sure she'll love it."

Douglas glanced over Charles's shoulder, seeing a server several steps behind him. "I'm sorry, Charles, I have to go. I'm monitoring tonight. Have a good evening and say hello to the kids."

He stepped past the man, expecting him to grab hold and whirl him around, but when nothing came, he let out a breath and approached the server.

"Is everything okay?"

The server dipped their head. "Yes, Master Douglas." They wrung their hands together, not meeting his gaze. "I'm sorry to step over a line, but it appeared as though your conversation was…upsetting?"

The slight inflection in their tone made Douglas smile. "Thank you, little one. I appreciate it more than you know."

"You're welcome, Master Douglas. I'll return to my duties now."

"Thank you once again."

The server lowered their head and rushed away while Douglas watched their retreat, perplexed. He'd never had anyone step in when he and his family were talking, but he understood the ramifications if emotions heightened too much. While it was confusing, he let it go. He'd mention it to Clarice before he left, ensuring he didn't mention any names.

Entering the play area, he checked in with Mistress Elizabeth and Master Albert, then weaved his way to the themed area he was overseeing that night. This side of the club had individually themed voyeur rooms and open-plan themed areas for anyone who wanted to be there. He stopped at each voyeur room, watching the play inside and ensuring all was fine before moving onto the areas.

The sounds and scents of sexual activity hardly registered with him any longer, but the sounds of barking and miaowing always brought a smile to his face. It wasn't an area that interested him sexually but seeing the joyful rough and tumble of the pets was something no one could frown at.

He wandered through the area, speaking with a few members who asked questions or greeted him, and edged towards the medical area. This room was different from the open plan of the pet play area. It had two separate rooms, which had identical instruments in each. The windows to the rooms enabled the occupants to change it to see-through for all to view the play, to one-way if the occupants wanted the audience to watch but not see them watching, and blacked out for privacy. At that point of his walk-through, one window was blacked out and occupied; the other was empty and visible.

He made another circuit, ensuring he stopped for conversation with some members—he didn't believe in being so stiff and proper as to not talk to anyone despite his job description.

As the night continued, his thoughts veered to Mav more often than he'd expected. What would he think of Douglas's plans?

13

HENRY

"*Stay out of it.*"

Henry kept to the side of the room, away from the hustle and bustle in the centre. He'd heard every word Charles had said to Douglas, and it made him sick to his stomach. Charles knew Douglas was gay, as did every member of the family, but Charles had a huge dislike for the LGBTQ+ community as did his mother. Henry knew it on a different scale than others' hatred. Their dislike was a lot worse than what the word hinted at.

He shuddered and rested back against the wall, sipping his water to calm his nerves. Taking a break as soon as Douglas returned had seemed like a good idea, but he wished he hadn't heard the threat in Charles's tone.

"Everything okay, sir?"

Henry opened his eyes, which he hadn't realised he'd closed, and smiled at the server. "Yes, thank you. Just taking a breather."

"Okay, sir."

He watched the server return to her duties and refocused on his drink. The condensation cooled his fingers, and the pounding of his heart could almost drown out the music of the room. He swapped hands and pressed his cooled hand to his forehead, ignoring the trembling. He wished there was something they could do about Charles, but with his mother's backing, they were far stronger than Henry wanted them to be. Nausea swam over him, and he hoped Charles and Aunt Charlotte would leave them all alone.

Shaking his head, he finished his drink and threw his bottle into the recycling, then strode for the doors to the main club. The noise bombarded him as soon as he entered, but he smiled. The energy of the club made things easier to bear, and mostly, the members were amazing. They excluded no one, despite what the few undesirables thought and wished for.

"Master Henry, could you help me with the stocks, please?"

Henry pivoted to see a woman with a full-length catsuit minus the hood, which showed off her long blonde hair trapped in a ponytail. With his thoughts in the past as they were, the idea of locking someone in stocks made goosebumps rise on his arms.

"I'm sorry, little one. I can't right now, but bear with me a moment." He grabbed the radio by his side and depressed a button. "All Monitors. Do we have someone to spare for a stocks experience, please?" His heart pounded in a harsh staccato rhythm while he waited for an answer through his earpiece.

"Yes, Master Henry. Send the guest to the stocks, and Mistress Elizabeth will be with them shortly."

"Thank you, Master Frederick," Henry said. He smiled at

the woman. "Mistress Elizabeth will be at the stocks shortly. Please wait for her there."

The woman lowered her head. "Thank you, Master Henry." She whirled around and disappeared into the crowd.

Henry inhaled through his nose and exhaled through his mouth several times while the images of what happened to the man in the stocks all those years ago ran through his mind. He sometimes wondered if he had PTSD and needed therapy to help him, but how would he explain his situation to someone without getting into the details about it. It was next to impossible. He needed to focus on the here and now and forget about the past as much as he could.

He pressed the button again. "Master Frederick, please advise where I am situated tonight. My brain is on hiatus."

"Master Henry, your brain is probably asleep in your bed. Maybe you should remember to wake it up and bring it with you next time." Henry chuckled at Frederick's tone. "You are working in the medical area tonight."

Of course, he was. He shook his head when he remembered the questions from several viewing members earlier that evening. It was a short distance to the medical area, and when he saw one room with blacked-out windows and the other with several viewers in front of it, he settled in to monitor the goings-on. At least this was one area of BDSM that they hadn't ruined for him.

That was until he caught Charles's eyes from across the corridor. Charles wasn't a monitor, but he was a member of Club Royal, so he could come and go as he pleased. Most of the time, Henry could avoid him, but there was the odd occasion he couldn't. Like then. Charles didn't come any closer, but he stared at Henry as if he were something on the end of his shoe. No idea how long they stared at each other; it was only when someone bumped into him that he dislodged his gaze. After apologising, he glanced back, and Charles tapped the side of his nose and pointed at Henry, then disappeared.

Henry crossed his arms over his chest, hiding his trembling hands under his armpits and focused on the scene through the window. Real-life could take a leap as far as he was concerned. He'd received enough reminders that night.

14

MAVERICK

av tapped his fingers against the steering wheel, staring through his windscreen, his whole body trembling. Whether it was fear or excitement, he wasn't sure. Douglas had told him to use the underground parking and had given him a key to the lift that took him straight to the penthouse. Apart from the cameras in the car park, no one would see him, and no one would think anything of him visiting Douglas anyway—at least, he hoped they wouldn't.

He needed to get out of the car; otherwise, the security team would likely see him as suspicious. Problem was, he couldn't move.

Closing his eyes, he took a deep breath and blew it out fast, repeating the action a few times before opening his car door and climbing out. He grabbed a bag from the passenger seat and locked his car, heading for the lift. There was no music in it as he expected there to be—it was one of the most prestigious apartment buildings in London, after all.

When the doors opened, Mav stepped off, then stopped

and stared. The entrance hall was about the size of his apartment and extremely white. Concerned he would track dirt into the pristine area, he toed off his shoes and placed them to the side. On socked feet, he trailed to where he could hear humming, gripping his bag tighter with every step.

"I won't bite, you know."

The words were loud in the silence, and they startled Mav. He paused, then carried on, rounding a corner until he stopped and raised his eyebrows. Douglas stood on one side of a kitchen counter, chopping vegetables—a sight Mav never expected to see, which was stereotypical of him.

Douglas's mouth twitched. "Don't be too shocked. I know how to cook, although I don't do it often. And besides, my chef made the main course. I was allowed to make the accompanying vegetables." He grinned and put a piece of carrot in his mouth and chomped down on it, the crunch loud.

Mav's body settled the longer Douglas spoke, and he was grateful for the normality. "I'm surprised he allowed you to hold a knife." He rested his bag on the floor by the wall, shuffling over to the counter on the opposite side and stealing a carrot piece.

"It took some persuading, I'll tell you. His ego allowed me to convince him he could add private cooking lessons for royalty on his resume." Douglas added the vegetables to a pan.

Mav chuckled. "I can't imagine him arguing with you about it."

Douglas held up a finger. "They purposefully gave Chef Matthieu to me because of his nature. Mother believed my attitude wouldn't sway him. After several years of head-butting, we've come to an agreement that works for us both." Douglas grinned again.

Mav's blood heated the more he watched Douglas's sure movements, the play of the muscles in his arms and back visible in his white T-shirt. He cleared his throat, resting his elbows on the counter. "I wasn't expecting dinner."

"I know. I thought we could use the energy." Douglas winked and pivoted to the oven to check on the vegetables.

Mav breathed through his nose, trying to cool his body, but he ached to kiss Douglas, to feel their tongues tangling, to taste him.

As if Douglas had the same thought, he cursed, rounded the counter and took Mav's face into his hands before slamming their mouths together. Mav could do nothing except grip Douglas's wrists to stop himself from falling off the stool and take everything. His eyelids fluttered closed, and he sank into the kiss. Douglas's tongue licked along Mav's bottom lip and dived in when Mav opened his mouth. Douglas moved his head to the side for a deeper kiss, and Mav lost himself in the heat.

After several minutes—or days, Mav wasn't sure—Douglas pulled back, leaning their foreheads together while holding his face. Their breaths mingled, and Mav opened his eyes, wanting to see Douglas's face, though going cross-eyed with how close he was. Douglas's lips were red, puffy and wet, and Mav wanted to take them again, but Douglas pulled back.

"I need to check on the food." He pressed a chaste kiss to Mav's mouth and stepped away, Mav's hands sliding from his wrists.

He couldn't think after and watched Douglas move around the kitchen before placing a steaming plate of lasagne in front of him. Mav's stomach growled, and Douglas threw his head back and laughed.

Mav's cheeks heated. "I was too nervous to eat before I came."

Douglas slid onto the stool next to him and cupped his nape, squeezing lightly. "I didn't think you would, hence the food. Enjoy." He released Mav and grabbed his cutlery, slicing into the wedge of cooked meat and pasta.

Mav continued to watch for several minutes before Douglas reminded him to eat. He groaned at the taste and vowed to poach the chef, to which Douglas chuckled and agreed he could. Once the plates were empty, Douglas took them to the sink and rinsed them off, waving away Mav's offer of help.

As Douglas stacked them in the dishwasher, Mav's heart pounded. He knew they would try something new tonight, and he had no sense of what it might be. Douglas had told him the not knowing would be an additional level to tonight. Despite his nervousness, he couldn't take his eyes off Douglas and knew when he stepped closer with intent in his expression.

"Time for bed." The words were low and quiet, but Mav felt every one of them deep inside.

Mav didn't move. Douglas came closer, holding his hands and pulling him to standing.

"Do you remember your safe words?"

Mav nodded and, when Douglas raised an eyebrow, whispered, "Yes, sir. Red for stop, yellow for slow down and green for keep going."

Douglas smiled, entwining their fingers and walking backwards, dragging Mav with him. Mav was unaware of their surroundings, entranced by the heat swirling in

Douglas's eyes until they entered the bedroom. Once he crossed the threshold, he studied his surroundings. The black and white theme from the main area disappeared, and in its place was an ocean blue and white landscape. Front and centre stood a beech wood, four-poster bed with white voile curtains tied at the corners.

A squeeze of his hands returned his attention to Douglas, who had a small smile on his face. "Do you like it?"

Mav nodded. "It's amazing. Makes me feel like I'm by the ocean."

"That was the intention. Let's get more comfortable."

Douglas let go of Mav's hand and yanked his own T-shirt over his head, throwing it to the floor near the door. Mav's breathing increased, but he lifted his trembling fingers to the buttons of his shirt. He fumbled the first few buttons, too engrossed in the tanned skin before him. Soon, his shirt followed Douglas's shirt's path. Douglas stepped closer, his hands following the meagre dips and valleys Mav's body provided. Mav's breath hitched as Douglas's palms skimmed his nipples.

Mav dropped his head back, air escaping his lungs in a rush. When Douglas's hands slid around his back, Mav stroked his fingers along the defined muscles of Douglas's chest and shoulders until he was gripping his own wrist behind Douglas's neck.

"I need to kiss you." Douglas nipped at Mav's lips.

"Please."

Douglas lowered his head until their mouths sealed together. Once more, it depleted Mav of oxygen as their lips, tongues and teeth took over. After several long seconds, Douglas pulled back, much to Mav's disagreement. He wanted more, no, needed more.

"Hush. Let's get comfortable. I have something I think you'll like." Douglas guided Mav over to the bed, nuzzling against him to encourage him to lie down. "Scoot your head to the pillows." Mav did what he asked.

Douglas left him, and he watched as the prince opened the top drawer of the chest on the opposite side of the room. He couldn't see what Douglas retrieved because he held it behind his back as he approached the bed.

"Now, we've spoken about this, but I would like to try you with a blindfold on tonight. Are you happy to try?"

Mav swallowed hard. "Yes, Sir. Green, Sir."

"Well done. Would you like to see it first?"

Mav nodded. "Yes, please, Sir."

Douglas pulled his hand from behind his back, showcasing a shiny black blindfold with an elasticated strap. "It's soft and silky against your skin." Douglas lowered the blindfold to Mav's stomach, gently caressing the skin with the fabric. "Once it's on, you won't be able to see anything." Mav's breath hitched again. "Are you ready?"

"Yes, Sir."

Douglas kneeled beside Mav, dropping a kiss to his lips before resting the fabric over Mav's eyes and tucking the strap behind his head. Douglas was right. There was not a sliver of light, although he couldn't open his eyes properly to know for sure. He lifted his hands, then hesitated.

"Can I touch it, Sir?"

"Yes, you may, but don't take it off, and only this once."

Mav followed the edge of the blindfold with his fingers, the silkiness of it heaven against his fingertips. His breath stuttered when his hands were tugged away and replaced by his side.

"As we discussed before, I won't be telling you what I'm

going to do to you, but you have the security of your safe words. If you say either yellow or red, we will stop and discuss it. This should be a pleasurable experience. No harm will come to you, I promise."

The honey-coated tone lifted goosebumps along Mav's skin, and he licked his dry lips. He strained to hear anything aside from his own ragged breathing. He heard a clink and turned his head in its direction. There was a rustle of fabric alongside more jingling, then silence once more. He gripped the covers below him.

The bed dipped, his body moving to the right. He held his breath, waiting. A soft pressure began at his wrist, along with a tickle. It was strange, and he couldn't figure out what it was.

When it reached his inner elbow, he squirmed as the tickle became intense, and his entire body twitched. It continued up his biceps to the top of his shoulder, where it played around as Mav tensed and shuddered beneath it. He had never realised his shoulder to neck area was so sensitive.

His mouth was dry, and he swallowed hard, his breath catching while the sensation rose up the column of his neck to his ear and along his jaw. Mav rolled his head to give more access, and the prickling feeling followed along in the item's aftermath. Not uncomfortable, though. The touch moved down the front of his neck, over his Adam's apple and down the centre of his chest before diverting to his pecs.

Mav tensed, knowing what was coming but not knowing what to expect. The featherlight touch to his nipple was disheartening—he could barely feel anything, and he knew he wouldn't get a high from it.

Until the touch became firmer and circled around his nipple at a fast rate. Arrows of arousal spiked towards his groin, and he arched his head back, biting his lip to contain his moan for more. The touch moved away, and it left Mav panting. It skimmed across his stomach and sides, where Mav twisted away as the sensation heightened once more until it disappeared.

Silence reigned, and Mav relaxed back into the covers.

"Colour?"

The words didn't make him jump, soft as they were.

"Green, Sir."

"Well done. I'm going to remove your trousers now."

Mav hadn't realised he still wore them. "Yes, Sir." Mav didn't move his hands from their clenched position in the covers as Douglas opened and pulled his trousers and socks off, leaving him in his briefs. He rearranged his legs and spread them a little wider, and Douglas sat between them. Mav could tell because of the dip of the mattress and the heat from Douglas's body.

Something slid along his shin, and he jerked. It was a little scratchier than the first item but smoothed across his skin and up his legs. It was like tassels of some sort, and his first thought was it was a flogger. When it lifted off his legs, he breathed deeply, expecting to be swatted with it, but nothing came. He relaxed a little, knowing Douglas said he wouldn't hurt him.

The sensation returned, starting at the side of his stomach and dragging across to the other side and back again. He squirmed as it rose, closer and closer to his nipples again before retreating instead of touching them. Despite his uncertainty of what was happening, his cock was hard, straining against his briefs.

Mav wanted to reach for Douglas and pull him closer, to rut against him and make himself come, but he hadn't been given permission. Douglas shifted, and the sensation disappeared. Mav's head followed the sound and movement of the bed, but it was a shock when something skimmed across his dick. He couldn't decide whether he wanted to thrust up into the sensation or back away from it.

"Ah." He let out the sound on a long exhale.

The flogger, or whatever it was, went back and forth above his cock, catching either side of it alternately. His fingers stretched out, then clenched the sheets tighter as he writhed beneath the onslaught. He arched his head into the pillow, reaching for something for more. The brushing noise of the flogger catching on his dick was like a clock ticking in a silent room, louder than you realised, and once he noticed it, it was difficult to stop listening for it.

Soft fingers caressed his thighs, which bunched and relaxed with his fidgeting. Mav gasped as everything overwhelmed him; it was too much, yet not enough all at the same time.

"Colour?"

Mav licked his lips, trying to speak. "Gr-Green. I'm good."

Douglas's chuckle was dark and foreboding. "Yes, you are."

All touches left, and Mav whimpered. The mattress dipped again, and fingers tugged at his briefs, lifting them over his leaking cock and tucking them under his balls. Before Mav could comprehend, wet heat surrounded his shaft, and he bucked.

"Fuck!"

Douglas's mouth pulled off, licking the head before swallowing him down again. Mav was helpless against the tide dragging him under. Douglas rose, keeping the head of his cock in his mouth, but stopped sucking or moving. Mav arched, and Douglas smoothed his hands across Mav's abs, sides and chest, everywhere he could reach. Mav tried not to move too much, wanting to be good for Douglas, but he felt like he needed something more.

Douglas's fingers became his fingernails, lightly rasping across his skin. Mav's cock twitched, and Douglas swiped his tongue across the tip, all while keeping the head in his mouth. Mav's climax was out of reach by a millimetre, and he didn't know what to do. He was green as to his safe words, but…

"Ah!" Douglas flicked a fingernail over Mav's nipples, and he exploded.

Pure, unadulterated pleasure suffused his body with every wave of his orgasm, and his mind blanked of everything but the decadence flowing through him.

When he came to, the blindfold had gone, and Douglas had him wrapped in a warm blanket, draped across Douglas's lap and nestled under his chin. One of Douglas's hands rubbed up and down Mav's back, the other against his leg. The scent of Douglas overwhelmed him, and he felt tears trickling down his face, though he didn't know why.

He closed his eyes and replayed what they'd done. Everything was perfect and so much more than Mav had ever experienced before. Why was he crying?

"It's a natural reaction for some people after a scene like this. There is nothing wrong with you." Mav sniffed and wiped at his face with his hand. "This is part of the sub-drop I was talking about before. Here, have a drink."

A small glass appeared in front of him, and he drank, slowly at first, until he realised how thirsty he was. Once he'd drained the drink, he passed it back to Douglas. "Thank you."

The two words couldn't encompass everything Mav wanted to tell Douglas, but he didn't know how else to do it. What he'd experienced was everything he'd always wanted and not realised he needed. How Douglas had seen what he hadn't was anyone's guess.

"How are you feeling?"

Mav took stock of his body. "Tingly, boneless, tired."

Douglas pressed a kiss to his head. "All usual effects. What did you think of it?"

Mav slid a hand out of the blanket and rested it against Douglas's neck, feeling his heartbeat and allowing it to centre him. "It was...I..." He yawned. "Amazing."

Douglas chuckled, the sound vibrating through the blanket to Mav's body. His eyelids drooped, and he snuggled closer, sighing when Douglas tightened his hold around him.

"Sleep. I'll be here."

Mav was helpless to argue.

15

DOUGLAS

*D*ouglas had so much control over himself on a daily basis, but one taste of Mav and his body had released hands-free as if he was a teenager. He had not done that *since* he was a teenager. In some ways, it annoyed him he'd lost control, but in other ways, he'd enjoyed Mav's reactions so much, he wasn't surprised. He wouldn't be advertising the fact—he'd never hear the end of it from his brothers if he did.

He rested his head back against the headboard, holding Mav while he slept. His instincts had been correct because Mav had enjoyed the sensations Douglas had used. Not wanting to push Mav too far, Douglas had chosen some "lighter" sensations: a makeup brush and some feathers on the end of tassels, and of course, his fingers and hands.

Despite the tears Mav had shed, he hoped Mav wanted to try more. Douglas believed he would benefit from a visit to the club, but he wouldn't push him too fast. It would be the worst thing to do because Mav might pull back, and it would ruin everything. Douglas was happy to keep things here for now, though he would love to show Mav what he was like at the club. He grinned to the ceiling. It might shock him.

Straining his neck, he checked the clock and stroked Mav's hair and face when he realised he needed to get ready for the club. Mav snuffled and rubbed his face against Douglas's chest.

"Wake up for me, sweetheart." He tried not to think too much about how the endearments rolled off his tongue for Mav.

"Hmm?" Mav lifted his head until his face was against Douglas's neck and inhaled. "You smell good," he mumbled.

Douglas snorted. "I need a shower."

Mav slid his arm around Douglas's neck and tightened his hold, keeping him in place. "No, you don't."

"We both do. Come on. Time to get up."

When Mav didn't move, Douglas shook his head and scooted to the edge of the bed, holding him. He lifted Mav bridal-style and stepped towards the bathroom when his name was called from the front of the apartment.

"Shit. Who's that?" Mav wriggled, and Douglas put him down before he dropped him.

"Douglas!"

"It's my father." Mav's eyes widened, and they stared at each other for a long second. "Stay here. I'll see what he wants."

Mav nodded, tightening the blanket around him. Douglas dropped a kiss on his lips, hoping to reassure him, but he couldn't do much else. What was his father doing there?

He dragged on his trousers, going commando, and grabbed his T-shirt before slipping out of the room and closing the door behind him. His father was every inch the king as he stood in the centre of Douglas's apartment with his hands on his hips, his gaze taking in every minor detail he and Mav had left behind. He pulled his T-shirt over his head.

"I was hoping to speak to both you and Frederick, but I'm assuming by your state of undress, your brother is not in the bedroom with you."

"How can I help you, Father?"

"I wanted to inform you your punishment has ended. You can return to your original shift pattern at the club."

Douglas's heart soared. "Thank you, Father."

King Andrew pointed out Mav's bag sitting by the kitchen. "I'll allow your…play with him but ensure it does not become public knowledge. With his job and background, it shouldn't be too hard. A little fun on the side is fine, but there will be no relationship with him. Understood?"

Douglas had to wonder how his father knew who was there, but he'd never figured out from where the king received his information. "It's my business who—"

"No, it's not. The royal family must uphold their family values. Messing around with staff is not part of the picture. Therefore, everything you do is my business. I know I said at dinner before I was being hard on you, but it's because I know what you're capable of, Douglas. You have so much potential."

Douglas ground his teeth, holding back what he wanted to say because he knew there was no way his father would listen. He felt like he was a kid again, instead of a thirty-six-year-old man.

"If the media gets wind of this, this latest punishment will seem like fun." His father turned to leave, throwing a comment over his shoulder, "You should keep this out of the club. Ensure people don't see you together, other than for royal business."

Douglas shook his head, listening to his father leave the penthouse. The door opened behind him, and he whirled around. Mav was dressed and silently moved to his bag, lifting it and disappearing around the corner to the exit.

"Wait!" He rushed to the entrance. "Where are you going?"

Mav raised his eyebrows. "Where do you think I'm going? I'm going where the 'staff' should be." He slid on one shoe.

Douglas stepped closer. "No. He wasn't saying we couldn't do this."

Mav laughed. "We're disillusioning ourselves, *Your Highness*. Thank you for sharing this with me, but this won't work." He pulled the other shoe on.

Douglas gripped his upper arms, holding him close. "Yes, it will. I can teach you what I was planning to. We don't need to do anything else if you don't want to, but I'd love to show you what your body is capable of."

He waited while Mav stared at him, his breath coasting across Douglas's chin with how close they were standing.

"We shouldn't—"

"I know you're worried about this getting out, but I'm happy to do whatever you think we should do to make sure this stays between us. Father knows, and so does Freddie, but we can keep it quiet."

"It's a bit of a cliché, isn't it? A prince and his help?" Mav frowned.

Douglas cupped Mav's jaw. "We can do this, Mav. Please." For some reason, he needed Mav to agree. He needed Mav to stay longer. He wanted Mav in his life and knew if this got out, Mav would leave.

Mav sniffed and lowered his eyes, and Douglas waited him out. "Okay."

Douglas smiled and pressed his lips to Mav's for a quick kiss. "Come on. We need our shower." He grabbed Mav's hands and tugged him towards the bedroom where his en-suite waited.

"Wait! My shoes! They'll mess up your carpet." Mav hopped and kicked his shoes off, then continued with Douglas.

Douglas didn't want Mav to think too hard about their situation at that moment. He wanted him to feel, to taste, to learn as he'd told him. It was also partially selfish reasons. Douglas needed to feel Mav in his arms and wrapped around his cock. There was no guarantee Mav would want it. They'd discussed it, but Douglas wanted everything Mav could give him. It was a good thing patience had been drummed into him as a royal and a Dom.

Letting go of Mav for a second to switch on the shower, he returned immediately, resting his hands on Mav's hips. Locking gazes with him, Douglas slid his hands up, taking the shirt with him. Before it had cleared Mav's head, Douglas was feasting on his lips. He was tempted to leave the shirt covering Mav's eyes but thought Mav might have had enough of being unable to see, and he tugged it off and threw it to the floor. With methodical precision, he divested them both of their clothes and pulled Mav under the spray, wrapping his arms around Mav's waist and splaying his hands across his stomach and chest. Positioned with Mav's back to his chest, Douglas could kiss, lick and nip at Mav's shoulder, neck and jaw.

Douglas slid his hands over Mav's skin, washing away the sweat and come still lingering. Grabbing the shampoo, he washed Mav's hair, swapping it for body wash and moving onto his body when his hair was bubble-free. His hands roamed Mav's body, the soap slicking his way, and he touched every inch of him.

Once he was happy that they were as clean as they could be, Douglas held him close again, and Mav linked their fingers over his stomach, pulling them as close as they could get. Mav leaned his head back on Douglas's shoulder, eyes closed, and sighed.

"Are you okay?" Douglas didn't want to break the silence, but he wanted to make sure Mav wasn't regretting his decision to stay.

In response, Mav rolled his head towards him and licked his jaw and followed it with a graze of his teeth. Douglas smirked and thrust his hips against Mav's ass, his cock nestling in his crack. Mav arched and exhaled.

"Do you want something?" Douglas nudged Mav's head to the side and nibbled on his earlobe. "Use your words."

Mav repeatedly arched, Douglas's cock sliding between Mav's cheeks. "You. I want you. Please."

Douglas needed to be sure. He spun Mav around, receiving a squeak from the man, and pulled him close, face to face. When their gazes met, he said, "Are you sure?"

Mav licked his lips and wrapped his arms around Douglas's neck. "Yes, Sir. I need you."

Douglas grabbed Mav's thighs, lifting him and encouraging him to wrap his legs around him, then switched off the shower and strode to the bedroom, unwilling to waste time drying off. No doubt they'd be back in the shower after this next round.

He kneeled on the bed, moving them higher before resting Mav down on the covers and blanketing him with his body. Resting on one elbow, Douglas ran the back of his hand over Mav's cheek, and Mav's eyelids fluttered. He smoothed a finger across Mav's bottom lip, and Mav sucked the finger into his mouth. Douglas felt it in his groin and pulled his finger out, taking Mav's mouth with his own.

He swiped his tongue along Mav's lips and dipped inside when Mav opened. Their tongues tangled, sliding alongside each other's. Douglas tilted his head, going deeper and harder, breathing through his nose because he didn't want to part from Mav. Their hips thrust rhythmically, heightening Douglas's arousal. He transferred his lips to Mav's jaw, pressing kisses along the contour and down the column of his neck.

Knowing it wouldn't take much for him to come, Douglas lifted himself off Mav and reached for his lube and a condom from the bedside table, hesitating when he saw the blindfold. Mav whimpered and fidgeted beneath him, and Douglas ignored the black satin and slicked his fingers, leaning over Mav while his finger sought his entrance. Breaching the ring of muscle, Douglas pressed forward carefully, feeling how tight Mav was.

He took plenty of time to get Mav prepared, not wanting to hurt him at all. Once Mav was panting with a dark flush all across his neck and chest, Douglas rolled on a condom, lubed it and rested against Mav's hole. He lifted Mav's legs to his own shoulders as Douglas came down over him.

Mav's eyes rolled back in his head when Douglas pushed into his channel, and it took everything in Douglas to hold back—both the need to climax and to ram into Mav. He inhaled, clinging to the control he'd learned he needed.

By the time his hips met Mav's, Douglas was panting as much as Mav was. He dropped to his elbows, bending Mav in half and gave small thrusts to allow Mav to get used to his size.

"Please! Move!" The words were torn from Mav's throat, and Douglas was helpless to resist.

Douglas rose to his hands, withdrew and slammed forward, Mav's voice calling to the ceiling for more while he grappled for Douglas's forearms. Mav's nails bit into his skin, but Douglas didn't care. Sweat beaded on Mav's skin, and Douglas wanted to lap it off, but he kept his rhythm, hoping to take Mav closer to his orgasm.

Each thrust into the heat of Mav's ass had Douglas gritting his teeth. He spread his knees and changed position until Mav's noises turned to guttural shouts of completion.

Douglas watched Mav's cock empty onto his chest, then picked up the speed and followed him over the edge. He kept moving his hips, but he wasn't sure whether he was trying to get closer or further away from the bliss tensing and releasing him, repeatedly, as sensitive as he was.

He exhaled and dropped to his elbows, sliding his dick free from Mav, unable to miss the wince from the other man. Douglas kissed him and shuffled to the bathroom to get a cloth. Returning, he found Mav in the same position, splayed in a star shape, and fast asleep. Douglas chuckled. He gingerly wiped Mav clean, then himself, and threw the cloth into the wash basket. Climbing into bed, he rearranged Mav's body so that he draped over Douglas's right side. Douglas pulled the cover over them and settled in for a nap. Another shower could wait.

What they'd done had less to do with teaching Mav about sensation play and more to do with Douglas's instincts.

As much as Douglas had told Mav he was teaching him,

he found the lines were blurring for him. What was he going to do about it?

◆

"Sure. Come on up."

Mav glanced at him, wide-eyed. Douglas didn't know if this was a good idea or not, but if he turned Katrina away, she'd wonder what was going on.

Mav stood, gathering the papers they'd been going through. "I'll get going."

Douglas held out his hand. "No, you don't need to. Katrina won't mind about us."

"Katrina?" Mav frowned.

Douglas smiled. "She's a Domme but from a different club. We were friends at Oxford and found out early on we had similar extra-curricular activities. We've been best friends ever since."

"I think I should go."

Douglas's heart raced. Mav was right, but Douglas wanted Mav to meet Katrina. He'd never felt the need to introduce his best friend to his play partners before, but he wanted to do this. He couldn't explain things to Mav, but Katrina would understand as soon as she saw them together. She'd understand what Douglas couldn't admit to himself, either in his head or out loud.

"You can if you want to, but I'd like you to stay and meet her. I think you'll like her."

Mav stared down at the papers in his hands, and Douglas allowed him the time to decide. They'd spent several more hours in bed, Douglas introducing Mav to silk and satin, and had eventually made it into the shower again. After, Mav had explained he'd brought some paperwork for them to go through, and they'd grabbed a snack and sat to go through it, giving each of them a breather from what had happened over the last few hours. Douglas had a feeling it would take them both a little while to figure out where they stood.

The lift doors opened, and Douglas raised his eyebrows at Mav. "Stay or go?"

Mav stared at him, and Douglas could see his hands trembling. "Stay," he whispered.

Douglas smiled and pulled him into the seat next to him, pressing a kiss to his temple.

"I'm here! Have you missed me?" Katrina rounded the corner and stopped, mouth flapping.

Douglas smirked. "Mouth closed, dear. It's not a pretty image of you." Mav backhanded his chest, and Douglas laughed. "What? She's used to me saying worse. Isn't that right, Katrina?"

Closing her mouth with an audible snap, Katrina breezed into the room, holding a bottle of wine. "Well, well, well. What do we have here? Good job I brought several bottles."

Katrina put the bottle down and lifted the bag from her shoulder, the sound of clinking filling the room. She pulled out three more bottles and dropped onto the seat opposite them.

"How did you know I wasn't working?"

"I didn't. I took a chance. If you weren't here, I would've wallowed and drank all four bottles by myself." She winked at Mav.

"They have relieved me of my extra duties as of tonight. Thankfully." Douglas stood, pacing to the kitchen to retrieve glasses and a corkscrew.

"Pfft. You love the club. Stop pretending you don't."

Douglas placed the glasses on the table and picked up one bottle. "I do, but not *every* night." He filled the glasses, holding one out to Katrina, passing another to Mav, then sitting back with his own and sliding his arm around Mav's shoulders.

Katrina raised one perfectly shaped eyebrow. "Are you going to introduce us, or are we going to play charades until I get it right?"

Mav snorted beside him, and Douglas squeezed his shoulder.

Douglas glanced at Mav, who nodded minutely. "This is Maverick."

Katrina peered at the table, no doubt taking in the paperwork scattered across the top, and stared at Douglas before leaning forward with her hand outstretched. "Nice to meet you, Maverick. If this bozo gets on your last nerve, hit me up. I'll put him back in his place."

"Hey!"

Mav chuckled and grasped her hand. "Nice to meet you, too."

"So…how is this relationship triangle working for you?"

"Katrina!"

MAVERICK

$\mathcal{M}$av spluttered the drink he'd taken, spilling it down his shirt. Douglas jumped up and grabbed a napkin from the table, helping Mav to mop it up.

"God, I'm sorry, Maverick. My mouth has been known to say stuff before my head has finished deciding if it was a good idea or not. I was only wondering how you were going to manage your relationship while Maverick works for you, Doug."

Katrina wasn't what Mav had expected when Douglas had described her. He was stereotyping a royal friend, but he'd expected a tall, slender, high-fashioned woman, but Katrina was much different. She was five-foot-five, if that, had a head full of curly brown hair and was overweight. Somewhere in Mav's mind, he'd obviously put real-life Dommes in a box with the ones he'd seen on porn sites. This feisty, opinionated woman was not at all like he'd expected.

"It's fine." Mav smiled in her direction, forgiving her.

"You can stop pawing at him now, Douglas. I think he's as clean as he's going to get."

Mav shook his head, laughing. "I think drinking—any kind of drink—around you might be a bad idea."

Douglas threw the wet napkin at Katrina. "Shut up, Kat."

"What did *I* do?"

Douglas sighed. "Mav is my media manager and sorts out my schedule, along with other stuff."

"I know who he is, Doug, but that's my point. How are you keeping the relationship separate from the work?" She gulped her wine, finishing half the glass in one go.

Mav stared at Douglas, who glanced at him with a small smile. "We're working on it."

Mav raised his eyebrows. *Working on it?* What were they working on? Mav had assumed they were on the same page when King Andrew had interrupted them earlier that evening, but had Mav misinterpreted something?

They had blurred some lines when they'd "played" in Douglas's rooms at Windsor, but now that they could do it here, it would be easier to keep the different aspects of their relationship separate. Wouldn't it? It wasn't as if they were in a romantic relationship. It was purely sex or sensation play, anyway. It's not as if he had to worry about anything long-term.

His phone chimed, and he excused himself to check it.

ZARA: Crossed the line yet? ;-) x

Mav shook his head. He was sure she was telepathic. She always seemed to send him messages when he'd been thinking something about the same subject.

"Everything okay?"

Douglas's hand was warm on his back, and Mav smiled

over his shoulder at him. "Yeah, a message from a friend." He refocused on his phone and replied.

MAV: Several of them x

He shoved his phone back into his pocket and tuned back into the conversation, which appeared to have changed from their situation to the charities Douglas was supporting. Mav listened as they talked through each one and what they were about, Mav throwing in his thoughts as they considered the best options. Finally, between them, they'd chosen three charities for Douglas to focus on for the time being.

Mav cleared away the paperwork, tucking it into his bag. When he stood, Douglas caught his hand.

"Are you not staying?"

Mav's heart pounded with need, but he shook his head. "No. I'm going to go home. Rest up for tomorrow." It was past midnight as it was. He needed space to figure out what the hell was going on between them.

Douglas sighed and stood, threading their fingers together. "I'll be back in a minute, Kat."

"No rush on my account. See you soon, Mav."

Mav grinned over his shoulder. "I'm sure you will. Have a good evening, Kat."

His smile faded the closer they drifted to the lift. Mav put the bag on the floor while he slid his shoes on, then flung it over his shoulder, not wanting to meet Douglas's eyes.

"Look at me."

Mav inhaled and lifted his head, staring into those crystal blue orbs. Douglas was a classic fairy tale prince in appearance, and anyone would appreciate him on their arm, but he hid something else behind those eyes. Something few people got to see, and it scared Mav. It would be too easy to fall for Douglas's charm and ignore everything else, but he'd experienced too many close calls in his past to ignore the voice telling him to be careful.

Douglas cupped his cheek, his thumb brushing over the skin beneath his eye. "Are you okay with everything that happened today?"

The question shouldn't have surprised Mav, but he was. "Everything except your father."

Douglas grimaced. "Understandably." He drew in a long breath and leaned their foreheads together. "We will do whatever we want to do, Mav. My father can deal with it if he doesn't like it."

Mav pulled away. "No! I won't become fodder for the media so you can put your middle finger up to your father."

"That's not what I meant. Why should he choose who I can and can't see?"

"Because it's not just about you. You have a responsibility to the cr—"

"I have a responsibility to be who I want to be! I'm sick of being shoved into this mould that I don't fit in." Douglas gripped his hair with both hands, pacing in front of Mav, then stopped and stared at the floor. "Sorry. Not your problem." He rubbed his hands on his thighs. "I can understand not wanting to be in the media. We can do this however you want."

As much as Mav thought distance was the best option, he couldn't help but be drawn to Douglas, stepping closer until he could cup the back of his neck. "Day by day, okay? Nothing more, nothing less. One day at a time." He lifted his head, brushing his lips across Douglas's mouth in a soft caress. "See you tomorrow."

He pressed the lift button, and it opened immediately. Facing forward, he gave a small smile and kept eye contact with Douglas until the doors closed. Then he sighed and stared at the floor, trying to sort through the thoughts bouncing around inside his head. He was no closer to it when the ding of the lift reaching the car park sounded. He threw the bag into the passenger seat and climbed into the car, starting the engine and sitting for a moment. Everything felt like a dream.

Rubbing his hands over his face, Mav groaned and drove home. By the time he dropped onto his bed, his brain had gone on hiatus. There were too many conflicting thoughts battling it out, and he had no hope of figuring it out that night. Instead, he pulled the covers over him and slept.

Mav stared at the grainy photograph, rubbing his fingers across his mouth, unable to look away. Douglas leaned against a doorframe with one hand, the other cupping the guy's jaw. Douglas's lips were on the man's cheek, and a smile played around both their mouths.

Mav's stomach churned, roiling like he'd eaten bad eggs, but he couldn't stop. He'd believed every word out of Douglas's mouth, but as the saying goes, "A picture is worth a thousand words."

Eyes burning, Mav closed the website and blinked rapidly, breathing heavily to assuage the nausea. He needed to work on a rebuttal or something to stop the rumours, but he couldn't do it right then. He needed a minute.

Coming to a stop in front of the window, he gazed across the enormous expanse of grass and flowers, not seeing anything but a slideshow of what he and Douglas had shared two nights ago. Mav was deluding himself if he thought it had meant something to Douglas. Why he was so bothered when he'd already decided nothing more could happen between them, he didn't know. His brain had made it into something more.

He spent several long minutes staring outside before his phone chimed, and he peeled himself away from the window. Mav's stomach became a mass of butterflies when a message popped up saying King Andrew wanted to see him in an hour. He replied in the affirmative and sat down at his laptop. He had less than an hour to do some damage control.

Mav posted a few photographs of Douglas at one of his chosen charities—an LGBTQ+ shelter that helped abused and homeless people. He didn't point out any correlation between the two, but for those who invested their interest in the royal family or Douglas, they might figure it out.

Once he'd covered all the social media platforms the prince was on, he flipped to the schedule. Douglas had been busy in meetings between the new charities, the events his parents wanted him to attend, and the club, but he hadn't complained once, which was refreshing. They hadn't spoken about what happened between them, and Mav was inclined to ignore it from that moment on.

He refused to be a fool once more, and staring at the photo, Mav was sure Douglas had been leading him on. It didn't appear to be a wellbeing check on a sub, as Douglas had explained before.

Checking his watch, he scrambled to retrieve his tablet while smoothing down his shirt and waistcoat and headed out the door. When he arrived at the king's rooms, he knocked and waited, breathing deeply and slowly to calm his nerves. As he received the word to enter, his hand trembled while reaching for the handle. One final deep breath had him entering and closing the door behind him.

He bowed to the king and queen. "Your Majesties."

"I'm assuming you've seen the most recent picture." King Andrew was a force to be reckoned with usually, but today, his words whipped across the room with more force.

"Yes, Your Highness. I have added some photographs and information regarding Prince Douglas's recent charity visits to the different social media accounts. I have a statement ready for you to check over if you require one at any point."

King Andrew rested his arm along the back of the sofa he was sitting on. "Have you spoken to Douglas this morning?"

"Not yet, Your Highness." And he wouldn't unless he had to.

"I think I need to have another chat with our son about his behaviour." King Andrew faced his wife.

"Why don't you let Maverick deal with this? He seems to have the social media aspect sorted, and he's done wonders with getting Douglas involved with the charities. He might be an excellent influence on him."

Mav swallowed hard and refused to glance at the king when he knew what kind of influence Douglas had been having on him the other night.

The silence was complete, and Mav had to tense his muscles to stop himself from fleeing the room.

"Agreed. Maverick, please speak with Douglas about this situation. I thought we had stopped these…visits of his, but obviously not." Mav's heart slowed. "A private meeting might be beneficial for you both."

Mav darted his gaze to the king, his jaw dropping. He had an idea what the king was implying, but he cleared his throat. "I think the extra duties at the club helped, Your Highness."

"I doubt that was all. See to it."

Mav nodded, palms sweating. "As you wish."

"It seemed to have stopped these visits before; it might again."

Mav glanced at the queen, who wore a faint frown as she stared at her husband. He licked his lips. "Yes, Your Majesty."

King Andrew stood. "All arranged then. Please give us an update tomorrow afternoon. Check with Randall for an appropriate time."

"Of course, Your Majesty."

Mav did an about-face and left the room, exhaling as the door shut behind him. Shaking his head, he strode down the corridors to Douglas's room. This job would be the end of him, he was sure. He knocked.

"Come in!"

Douglas sat in his usual seat as Mav entered. He was freshly showered if his wet hair was any indication, but he wore a navy suit with a crisp white shirt and a pale blue tie. He had a tablet perched on his crossed legs and was holding a cup.

"Mav! I wasn't expecting to see you this morning." Douglas's smile radiated warmth, but Mav didn't have it in him to respond.

"The king has requested I speak with you regarding your continued extra-curricular activities." Mav lifted the tablet to bring up the latest picture and spun the tablet around for Douglas to see. "The king wishes these visits to stop." Mav clenched his jaw.

"Fuck! I checked to make sure there were no photographers around before I left the house. How the hell did they get this photo?"

"It's next to impossible to hide from them. With cameras built the way they are now, they could be several streets away and have a picture seeming as if they were right next to you."

"I can't stop visiting the subs. I need to make sure they're okay."

Mav said nothing, not meeting Douglas's gaze. "The king has requested…" His heart pounded, and he wasn't sure he'd be able to explain. "The king has requested that our…private meetings continue in the hopes these visits will end."

Douglas was silent, but Mav could feel his stare burning into him. The prince stood, drifting over to the window, and Mav realised he was staring at him and averted his gaze.

"You don't believe me."

The words were softly spoken, scarcely audible despite the silence.

"It doesn't matter if I do. The king has made a request."

Douglas snorted. "Yeah, and everyone has to obey the king." The tone was uneven as if he only just held his emotions in check. "If there is no trust in a relationship, there is no relationship."

Mav frowned. "What do you mean?"

Douglas faced him with his arms crossed and a neutral expression. "Trust is a huge aspect of the BDSM lifestyle. If there is no trust, neither participant will feel comfortable." Douglas took a step closer, though he was still halfway across the room. "You don't trust me."

Despite the monotone delivery, Douglas's voice held a tremor, and Mav could tell the idea hurt him, but what did it matter? Douglas had plenty more people he could teach, and it was no issue for Mav.

"I want you to come with me tonight."

"What? Where?"

"We're going to visit a sub."

Mav shook his head. "You shouldn't be doing it when there's a recent photo, Your Highness."

"Fuck the 'Your Highness' crap, Mav. We've been closer than many people get. If you can't call me Douglas in private, we have no hope."

Mav sighed. "I have never called you Douglas anywhere except in my head."

"Well, start."

Mav transferred his gaze to the tablet in his hand, and he fiddled with the cover. "I don't think visiting a sub is a good idea at the minute."

"It's the only way you'll see what I see. Otherwise, you'll use it as an excuse to push me further away than you already have. I want…" Douglas wandered towards him, stopping the sofa's length away. "I want more than I'm allowed, and it's not fucking fair."

Mav didn't know what Douglas was talking about. "What do you want?"

Douglas shook his head, staring off to the side. "Doesn't matter. It's out of reach, even for me."

Mav traced Douglas's features with his gaze. His posture wasn't as straight as it usually was, and his demeanour screamed "leave me alone." Mav had no idea what to do or think.

"I'll pick you up at eleven." Douglas stormed away, crossing into his bedroom and shut the door.

The physical barrier between them caused an ache in

Mav's chest, and he rubbed at it distractedly. Visiting a sub was the last thing Douglas should do, but Mav didn't have it in him to stop it from happening. He was curious about them and wanted to see what Douglas was so worried about.

Mav retreated to his own room, sitting in front of his laptop and staring at the photo. He picked up his phone when it rang, answering before he'd checked who it was.

"Maverick. I see you have another problem on your hands. If you can't do the job, I'm going to have to rethink your role with the company. I know plenty of people who would kill to be in your shoes."

Bert's nasal tone irritated him beyond belief, and he clenched his jaw. "I'm sure many would, but they also wouldn't put up with as much shit as you give me." He knew the minute he'd spoken, he'd made a mistake.

"After everything I've done for you and your father, this is how you treat me? I'm sure Ron would love to know how you've been behaving. He'd be mortified by how you speak to me."

Mav raked his fingers through his hair. "Dad doesn't need to know anything. I'm sorry, Bert. I've had a trying day." Apologising pained him, but he refused to cause problems for his father. Despite being old enough to take care of himself, his father would not easily find another job at his age.

"Regardless, you don't take it out on me. You're using a lot of your chances, Maverick. Be sure to temper your words in the future. Sort out this problem quickly; otherwise, it won't just be your job on the line."

The phone went silent, and Mav pulled it from his ear. He laid it on the table instead of throwing it across the room like he wanted. Once more, his gaze caught on the photograph. Mav couldn't decide what his head was telling him.

Did Douglas have a heart of gold, or did he use anyone and anything to get what he wanted?

17

DOUGLAS

ouglas waited in the car outside of Mav's building that night, Eric and another bodyguard in the car behind as was routine when he visited the subs. His tinted windows wouldn't show who was inside, especially as he'd turned off the interior lights; therefore, when Mav opened the door, the light wouldn't illuminate who was picking him up.

He tapped his fingers on the steering wheel and gazed at his surroundings while he tried to bury the feelings of inadequacy. When he'd closed the door behind himself that morning, blocking Mav out, his chest had ached, and he'd had trouble swallowing. Trust was important for Douglas, not only in the BDSM lifestyle but everywhere. He wanted to be trustworthy and kind and caring and helpful. The media, as well as his parents and Mav, saw him as the opposite.

Huffing a laugh, Douglas shook his head. He didn't know why it upset him. After all, the whole point of the visits was to check on the subs and not show what he was doing. The visit the previous night had been the first where the media had found him before he'd left the property. They had identified none of the other subs. Previously, the photographers had found him as he'd raced to his car, which was always parked a distance away from the sub's house.

He'd been in touch with Xan this morning and apologised. Xan had said it was fine and explained he'd told his Dom he'd asked for a private lesson as a surprise for him. Luckily, Xan knew a few things he could use. It had never been his intention to cause problems for the subs, but if it did, he'd have to figure out a better way of speaking to them without their Masters being present.

The passenger door opened, startling him, and Mav climbed in. No words were spoken, and as soon as Mav had clicked his seatbelt into place, Douglas drove towards their destination. Parking several streets away, he switched off the engine, listening to the clicking as it cooled.

"We have a couple of streets to go before we get there."

"Okay."

"If anything happens, get out of there."

Mav tensed. "You're scaring me now."

"I shouldn't have brought you, but I don't know how else to get you to believe me. Quinn's Dom is at work on a night shift, but there is always the chance he'll return early. If that happens, get out of the house as soon as you can. Don't wait for me."

"I can't leave without you!"

Douglas stared at him. "Yes, you can and will."

Mav sniffed, fidgeting with his coat cuff. "Okay."

They exited the car and strolled down the street as if they were trailing home after visiting a pub. Douglas studied their surroundings along the way, as did Mav, then Douglas pointed to a house on their left. He knocked quietly, and a tall, slender man, who had a shock of red hair, immediately opened it.

They entered the house, and Douglas introduced him. "Quinn, this is Mav, who I mentioned in my message."

"Nice to meet you, Mav."

"You, too."

"Come on in. I've made some tea."

Quinn led the way through the modestly decorated house, indicating for them to sit while he fetched the drinks. They sat next to each other to allow Quinn to sit opposite when he returned.

Once they settled with drinks, Douglas said, "You know why I'm here?"

Quinn tilted his head. "I don't know for definite, but I've heard some rumours."

Douglas glanced at Mav with a frown, noticing he, too, wasn't happy with the news. "Where are the rumours from?" It wasn't Mav's place to ask, but he couldn't find it in him to care.

"Subs talk between themselves, as I'm sure Masters do. We know when to keep quiet."

Douglas continued; he was already here. It wouldn't make much more of a problem whether he left now or later.

He leaned forward, placing his cup on the table. "I wanted to check up on you and make sure you're doing okay. As you said, subs know when to keep quiet, and it's not always a good thing. I need to make sure you know you can talk to me or any other person if you're having problems you can't talk to your Master about."

"I'm doing fine, Your Highness. Thank you for checking. Master is…" Quinn sighed. "Master is everything I'd ever dreamed he could be." Quinn frowned.

"What is it?"

"While I'm doing okay, I don't think Kendal is."

Douglas threaded his fingers and rested his elbows on his knees. "What do you mean?"

"I've seen bruising that doesn't appear to match the activities he says he takes part in." Quinn returned his cup to his saucer and crossed his legs. "At first, I brushed it off, but last month, he was walking gingerly and refused to talk about it. He's not been back to the club since."

Douglas tried to bring the sub's face to mind, but he couldn't. "I know he's on my list to check. I'm slowly getting through everyone."

"And we appreciate it more than you know. I know you've helped several people remove themselves from unpleasant situations."

Douglas didn't confirm or deny the words. He couldn't. Those subs would go through a tough time for several months or years to come because he hadn't seen what was going on early enough. He wasn't taking the praise when he wasn't doing a good enough job.

"I'll ensure Kendal is next on my list."

"Thank you."

"Anyone else you worry about? Sub or otherwise?" Douglas asked.

"Not really. I'll keep my eyes open."

"Thank you." Douglas stood. "We'll leave you to your evening. I'm sorry for the intrusion."

Quinn chuckled. "It's not an intrusion at all when it's someone who cares about your wellbeing. More people should take a leaf out of your book, Your Highness."

Douglas's cheeks heated. "I've had a few issues with

leaving houses lately." He glanced at Mav. "Would we be able to exit at the back?"

"Of course. No house overlooks the back garden. It should be clear."

Mav stepped forward. "Let me go first. I can check it out. If I'm seen leaving the house, it won't be an issue because I could be another sub."

Douglas studied his expression for a moment before nodding, and Quinn led the way to the back door. Mav stepped out and pulled the door shut behind him.

"He's good for you, Your Highness."

Douglas raised his eyebrows. "Sorry?"

Quinn lowered his head, though his smirk was visible. "It's not my place to say, but I can see the pull between you. You're an excellent match."

"We're not...I'm..."

The door opened, and Mav popped his head back in. "All clear."

Douglas cleared his throat. "Thanks."

"No, thank you."

Douglas exited the house and heard Quinn lock the door behind them. They slid out of the back gate, following the path to the end of the street before coming out of an alley onto the original road he had parked on.

Silence reigned, but it wasn't as uncomfortable as it had been during some of their past encounters. Once they settled in the car, Mav grabbed his coat and dragged him into a kiss. The gear stick stopped them from getting too close, but Douglas feasted on Mav's mouth. He threaded his fingers into Mav's hair and gripped tight, moving Mav's head in the direction Douglas wanted it to go. Their tongues duelled, and their lips smashed, their breathing loud in the small space.

Douglas softened his hold, stroking his hand through Mav's hair, and licked and sipped at his lips until they stopped, their foreheads resting together. It seemed to be a ritual for them—staying close but not too close.

"I'm sorry I didn't believe you."

Mav's words whispered into the air, and Douglas smiled into the darkness. "It's okay."

"No, it's not. I shouldn't assume you're like the other losers from my past. It's hard to get rid of sometimes."

"You don't have to explain." Douglas cradled Mav's face and kissed him softly.

"I want to, but not here. Can we go back to your place?"

Douglas kissed him again. "Of course."

Pulling back was hard, but they soon parked in the underground parking of Douglas's building and in the lift after a wave at Eric. Once the doors opened to the penthouse, they slipped off their shoes and coats and wandered into the main room.

"Would you like a drink?" Douglas aimed for the kitchen.

"Water or juice would be good."

Douglas pottered around, all the while tuned into where Mav was and what he was doing. Once he had two glasses filled with apple juice, he shuffled over to where Mav was leaning against the counter and held out the glass.

"Thanks."

"You're welcome."

They sipped in silence until Mav said, "It's difficult for me to talk about this without being reminded of how I felt then. I suppose I still feel that way sometimes. It's a tough thing to forget about."

Douglas slid an arm around his shoulder and guided him to the sofa, sitting with his back to the corner of the sofa and allowing Mav to sink next to him. That way, he didn't have to look at him while he talked if he didn't want to.

"I was twenty when I had my first boyfriend. Gareth was the same age but larger than life. Complete extrovert, partying whenever possible, but he always managed to get his work done, too. I was so jealous." Mav huffed a laugh and shook his head, running his finger around the lip of the glass. "I have no concept of how we fit together, but somehow we did. We were together for several years and ended up living together after uni finished."

Douglas didn't enjoy listening to Mav's past relationships, but he assumed there was at least one man he needed to find and beat the crap out of.

Mav sniffed and cleared his throat. "We'd been together for six years when I came home from work to find him in bed with another guy. The guy ran like his ass was on fire, which left me with Gareth." He exhaled and carried on in a quieter voice, "I remember his words as if they have just happened. *'What did you expect me to do? You've been dangling a life of love and fun in front of me for years, and I kept giving you time to let go, to find your feet, to love me back. I realised you never would.'* I don't know what I did wrong. I loved him. At least, I thought I did. He obviously wasn't feeling it."

Douglas put down the glass that he'd been holding, afraid it would shatter in his grip. He did the same for Mav's glass before gripping him, refusing to push him into eye contact when Douglas knew he felt vulnerable from exposing his past.

"He was wrong. He was using your feelings of inadequacy to cover how much of an asshole he was. No matter what happened in your relationship, he should have talked to you about it, not jumped into bed with someone else. Don't allow his words to haunt you. They're not true."

"Then why did my next boyfriend say nearly the same thing?" Mav pulled out of his embrace and stood, pacing to the windows. "I met Nico when I was twenty-nine. He swept me off my feet, and I fell hard. The words Gareth had thrown at me were always in the back of my mind. I tried to do better, to show Nico I loved him, to encourage nights out and social visits." He waved his hand. "We were out one night when someone came up to Nico and kissed him. Nico didn't push him away, and when they parted, the stranger said, '*I didn't realise you were coming tonight, sweetheart. I would've waited for you.*'"

Douglas fisted his hands, wanting to find these two imbeciles and throw them in the Tower. It was an old punishment, but he thought it would fit. He opened his mouth to speak, but Mav continued, "Nico faced me and said, '*You need to share yourself, Mav, not throw out pieces of a puzzle for someone else to put together.*' Apparently, I can't open up to anyone."

Douglas wanted nothing more than to wrap his arms around Mav again, but he knew how it felt to be raw and exposed. Being held was the last thing the other man needed, but he stepped over and pressed a kiss to Mav's temple with a whispered, "They don't know the real you, Mav."

He wandered to the kitchen, giving Mav some time to get himself together. Waiting was hell on Douglas, especially as he wanted to hold him and square off with Mav's battles himself. Instead, he added some chips to the fryer and grated some cheese. Comfort food was not the solution, but it was a bandage that would help for now.

"What are you doing?"

Douglas smiled over his shoulder. "Making some supper."

Mav raised his eyebrows. "It's two in the morning."

Douglas shrugged. "There's never a bad time for supper."

"What are you making?"

"Cheesy chips."

Mav stared at him for so long, Douglas turned away when his cheeks heated. He was a bloody BDSM Master, and he was getting embarrassed because he knew he was making Mav's favourite comfort food.

He cleared his throat. "Do you want to put some music on?"

Douglas jumped when hands slid around his waist and chest and stood still, not wanting to make the wrong move. Mav's hands stilled on his stomach and over his heart—intentional or not, he closed his eyes in relief. Mav buried his head in Douglas's back, and Douglas felt the heat from him. He wiped his hands, then covered Mav's hands, interlocking their fingers and bowing his head.

He bit back the words that wanted to escape. The words his father had assured him wouldn't be allowed. The words Mav hadn't encouraged. The words Douglas hadn't expected.

He was in deep shit.

Breathing deeply, he stayed with Mav in the embrace for as long as he could. Unfortunately, the chips wouldn't wait. Douglas lifted one of Mav's hands to his mouth, kissing his knuckles, and pulled away, lifting the basket from the fryer. When he turned to Mav, the man had already disappeared from the kitchen.

Douglas exhaled and refocused on the food, plating the chips and spreading a generous amount of cheese over the top. He carried them into the living room, finding Mav cross-legged on the floor by the coffee table, staring at the fireplace with soft instrumental music floating in the air. Focusing on the plates, he put one in front of Mav, the other where he would sit, and dropped to the floor beside the man who was fast becoming more to Douglas than anyone else ever had.

They didn't speak as they devoured the warm comfort food. Douglas was enjoying the company without feeling the need to fill the silence. It was something he rarely got in his role as the spare heir. Most people seemed tense and uncomfortable if they were not talking, and he found himself on the end of many rambling recitations of childhood stories and events Douglas would've been happy not to know.

With Mav, there was a comfort to the silence, a relaxation of needing to speak, to listen, to watch.

And Douglas hadn't realised how much he'd needed it.

After they'd finished and cleared up, Douglas led Mav to bed. The silence continued as they undressed each other with slow movements, in no hurry. When Mav was naked, Douglas picked him up, lay him in the middle of the bed and slid in beside him. As he pulled the covers over them, he caught Mav's creased forehead and hid a smile. He wrapped his arms around Mav, pulling him partially over him to allow Douglas to hold him through the night.

As he held his lips to Mav's head, he felt a wetness on his neck but said nothing, only tightened his arms, his own tears trickling into his hairline.

He had never said and yet heard so many words in the silence before.

18

MAVERICK

Mav woke, cocooned in warmth, and he rubbed his face against the heat. When he realised the strands of his hair moving in time with the breaths of someone, he tensed. Seconds later, he relaxed again when he realised it was Douglas, then tensed again when he realised it was *Douglas.*

A rumble of laughter vibrated from Douglas's chest to Mav's jaw, and he bit his lip at the shiver working its way down his spine.

"Good morning." Douglas's hand slid to Mav's shoulder and squeezed. His fingers began creating a delicate pattern on Mav's skin.

"Morning."

"Stop thinking so hard."

Mav couldn't. The previous night was like a slideshow through his mind, and he grimaced at what he'd revealed. There was nothing more off-putting than having someone verbally vomit their issues to another person. What must Douglas think of him now?

Mav frowned when his slideshow showed the last scenes of the night before he fell asleep. Douglas had held him tightly, and Mav had never felt more cared for and safe. It was an illusion of the night. It had to be. No one would want him when all he did was push people away and ignore their needs.

"I'm sorry for last night. I didn't mean to—"

He squeaked as he was flipped onto his back, caged and covered by Douglas's body. Douglas paused, stared at him and slid his hands under Mav's shoulders until he could cup Mav's head. Their faces were close, and Mav could see every fleck of blue in Douglas's eyes.

"I'm glad you told me, but they were both wrong about what they said, and they were wrong for you. If someone means something to you, you work for it. You work to fix what's wrong; you work to make things right. If things can't be fixed, you end the relationship. You don't cheat and lie and blame the other person. That's not how relationships work."

Douglas's thumbs were distracting, smoothing along Mav's cheeks, but he understood what Douglas was trying to tell him; however, understanding was not the same as believing. He swallowed hard.

"It's difficult…" His voice broke, and tears filled his eyes.

"I know. One day at a time." Douglas leaned down and kissed away the tears that had leaked out. "You're you. You don't need to change for anyone."

"Show me. Show me who you see."

The corner of Douglas's mouth lifted, and Mav's breath caught. "What are your safe words?"

Mav's heart raced. "Red for stop, yellow for slow down and green for keep going." He could hardly speak.

"Good." Douglas trailed his lips along Mav's jaw to his ear. "Hold on to the headboard."

Mav shivered again as Douglas nipped his lobe. He slid his hands under the pillows and gripped the slats, his entire body tingling. Douglas continued his kisses, mapping out a path down Mav's neck when Mav tilted his head to the side. Douglas scraped his teeth along his shoulder, and Mav's eyes fluttered.

"Close your eyes."

Mav allowed his eyelids to close, surrendering to the sensation of Douglas's mouth as it travelled down his chest to his nipples, which were reaching for Douglas's touch before he arrived. Douglas's tongue flicked over one straining bud, and Mav arched his back and moaned. Fire lit his nerves and arrowed to his groin, hardening his cock further. When his nipple was wet, Douglas blew cool air over the tip and gave the same treatment to the other side. By the time Douglas stroked his tongue down Mav's abs, Mav was squirming beneath him, wanting to see what Douglas was doing, but he'd been told to keep his eyes closed. It was becoming harder and harder to do the more Douglas touched him.

"Sir, please!"

"Colour?"

"Green! Please! My eyes…I can't…I want…" Mav couldn't figure out what he was trying to tell Douglas while Douglas was rolling his balls in his hand.

"I think you need the blindfold."

Mav sighed and settled further into the mattress. His Master knew what he needed. Mav would be fine.

The bed dipped and rolled several times, and Mav resolutely kept his eyes closed, though he ached to see what Douglas was doing.

"Here we go."

A silky-soft fabric settled over his eyes and rested behind his head, and Mav relaxed into it. It blocked all the light that streamed through his eyelids and gave Mav the feeling of being alone. He couldn't see anyone or anything. The idea should've worried him, but he trusted Douglas despite what he'd thought before. He did trust Douglas, at least with his body. With his heart, it was another matter, but it wasn't a concern because they were only playing.

Mav was startled when something extremely cold swiped across his belly button. His abs jerked with each touch, and Mav pushed his head into the pillow, mouth open as he panted. His legs were pushed wide, and the bed dipped between them. He assumed Douglas had settled in the middle, which was confirmed when the cold—an ice cube from what limited information Mav could gather—found the crease of his inner thigh and groin. The ice followed a path down to his taint and across to the other side, rising to his hip. A gentle stream of cool air trailed behind.

The ice and cold air disappeared, and Mav writhed, feeling the coolness on his skin despite nothing touching him.

"Ah! Fuck!"

Mav couldn't stop his shout when the ice rested against the tip of his cock, the melting droplets trickling down the length and pooling in the hair at its base. The ice was a constant presence, never wavering, though Mav twitched and thrashed beneath it. With each movement, it slid the ice across the head, then Douglas moved it to the sensitive bundle of nerves on the underside of his shaft, rubbing in circular movements.

Mav gasped, alternating between wanting it gone and needing more. It was a strange feeling. The ice disappeared again, but Mav didn't relax. He tensed, knowing something else was coming and unsure what. He strained his hearing: a rustle of fabric, a quiet thump.

His heart pounded, and he tightened his grip around the headboard. Seconds later, extreme liquid heat surrounded his cock.

"Sir!"

The heat reduced until it was a warmth caressing him as Douglas's mouth lifted and dropped on his shaft. Douglas must've swallowed whatever he'd been holding in his mouth because the liquid feeling vanished, replaced by Douglas's tongue flicking against his nerves.

"Fuck, fuck, fuck," he chanted, bucking his hips into the waiting mouth.

Douglas pressed against Mav's hips, stopping the movement, and continued his ministrations, sending Mav flying but not enough to climax. When Douglas pulled off, Mav whimpered.

"Please, Si—Oh, god!"

The ice had returned. Douglas held Mav's dick upright at the base and spread the ice along the length, no part of his skin being left out. Within seconds, heat encased him again, and he thrashed beneath the onslaught. Douglas alternated between the two temperatures several times.

Mav caught his breath when both stopped. He felt sweat dripping from his body onto the bed beneath him. His cock was so hard, it hurt, and he babbled incoherently. What was he saying?

A hand returned to the base of Mav's cock, and he waited in anticipation of something happening. When nothing did, he released the tension and immediately tensed again when dual sensations rocked his balls. Douglas sheathed one ball in liquid heat, the other surrounded by ice-cold, which travelled down to his taint and pressed against it.

The liquid disappeared, and Douglas licked a stripe up Mav's cock, sucking the head into his mouth for a second.

"Jesus!"

Mav rolled his head on the pillow, unsure if he could take any more.

"Colour?" Douglas's voice pierced the silence, hoarse and deep.

"Green." Mav licked his lips. He needed to come. "Please, Sir?"

Douglas didn't reply. The bed dipped, and Mav felt a cool presence by his hip. He knew more ice was coming, but he didn't know where. His breathing sped up again.

"I need you to stay still now. If you squirm too much, these will fall off, and I don't want that. Do you think you can do it?"

Mav swallowed hard. "Um, I think so. Sir."

"Try your hardest for me, and you'll get your reward."

An ice cube settled on his chest, another an inch or two below that, another on his sternum. More followed, leaving a trail of ice from chest to groin. He was so focused on them, he twitched when a finger pressed against his pucker. It was all he could do to bear down as he concentrated on keeping still to stop the ice from falling off. He had no control over his breathing, though.

While Douglas slid a finger deep inside him, Mav focused on the ice and the drips spilling down his sides and up to his throat with how he lay. He tensed as the cubes swayed in their own liquid, worried they would slide off him. A slight burn caught his attention, and he concentrated on the two fingers breaching his hole.

"Come whenever you want to."

The whispered words slid over him, and Mav frowned. He was feeling close to climax, but not enough to go over the edge yet.

As soon as the thought crossed his mind, three things happened at once. His cock was surrounded by intense heat, hotter than before; ice pressed against one nipple, and Douglas's fingers crooked inside him and hit his prostate. Mav saw stars as his orgasm exploded through his body, spasms wrecking their way through him from head to toe. He wasn't aware of anything else except the pleasure detonating inside him.

When he came back to himself, his body ached, his breathing ragged, and he had no energy. He acknowledged his hands being removed from the headboard and a massage starting at his fingers and continuing down his hands and arms as they lowered to his sides. The massage carried on to his shoulders and neck, Mav moaning at the feel of the aches abating somewhat.

The hands smoothed down his body, working on the aching areas like his hips and thighs. Once his calves and feet had surrendered to the heaven of massage, a cover was pulled over him, and a weight dipped the bed beside him.

Douglas pulled him into his embrace, the man's firm but gentle hold settling something inside Mav. Douglas removed the blindfold Mav hadn't realised he still wore, and he blinked in the bright sunlight, taking several moments to allow his eyes to adjust before glancing at the prince.

The minute he saw Douglas's face, he slid a hand to his cheek and lifted for a kiss, which he granted him with a smile.

"Thank you." His voice was hoarse and used. He could only assume he'd been shouting or screaming at one point.

"You're welcome. Sip this." Douglas reached for a cup of orange juice and helped Mav to rise a little to drink, then moved them both back into their positions.

Mav closed his eyes and revelled in the peace he felt in Douglas's arms. He had never, *ever* felt this before. Nothing had ever been as intense as that orgasm had been. It was more, though. The connection to Douglas was strengthening, and Mav wasn't sure if it was a good thing or not. He'd wanted to open himself to Douglas, but what would come of it if he did? Heartbreak? For sure because he'd heard what the king had said. They could play, but no relationship would ever be allowed.

He pushed the thought aside, not wanting to dampen his euphoric mood. Allowing Douglas to soothe him and bring him down, Mav drifted off.

With his eyes shut, Mav let his fingers work along the strings as he played and crooned *Can't Take My Eyes Off You* by Lady Antebellum. Everything that had happened with Douglas kept playing on repeat in his head as the lyrics passed over his lips. He didn't know why the song came to mind when he'd picked up his guitar, but there was some truth to the words. He couldn't stop playing it.

The song reminded him of how he'd woken the previous morning—late morning—wrapped once more in Douglas's embrace. When he'd glanced at the clock, he'd scrambled out of bed and dragged on his clothes, despite Douglas telling him not to worry. Mav had slowed down and taken a breath when Douglas had rested his hands on his shoulders and ordered him to.

As he'd headed for the lift, Douglas had followed, giving him a mind-blowing kiss before Mav had staggered onto it, panting. Douglas had smirked, and the image was burned into Mav's retinas. Every time he closed his eyes, all he could see was the confident smile and sparkling blue eyes of a man he couldn't have.

His fingers paused when his phone rang, and he was tempted to let it go to voicemail, but he didn't. Putting the guitar on the sofa next to him, he reached for the phone, smiling when Zara appeared.

"Hey, handsome… What's up? You look like someone has changed your password to your media accounts."

Despite the headspace he was in, he snorted. He rested the phone in a holder on the table so she could see him without him having to hold it, then sat back, rubbing a hand over his mouth. "Why am I putting myself through this, Zara?"

"With Douglas?" At his nod, she continued, "Because he's given you the chance to be yourself and learn more about what makes you tick."

"There's nothing at the end of it."

Zara stared at him, and her eyes widened after several seconds. "You're falling for him."

Mav gave a rueful smile. "There is no 'falling,' I'm afraid."

"Holy shit, Mav. You're in love with a prince."

He huffed a laugh. "It doesn't matter. There's no happily ever after despite what fairy tales tell us."

"Why not? Stranger things have happened."

"What? Even when the king himself says a relationship will not be allowed?"

Zara's mouth dropped open. "He said that? When? Why?"

"You know I was meeting up with Douglas the other night?" She nodded. "I'd put it in his diary as a meeting with Prince Frederick. King Andrew turned up wanting to speak to his sons."

"Oh, shit."

"Yeah. I was in the bedroom, but I heard every word he said. Douglas and I may play behind closed doors, but nothing else."

"Does Douglas know how you feel?"

Mav laughed. "No, and I intend to keep it that way. I don't know how the hell it happened. One minute, I was thinking he was sleeping with other people, and the next, I trusted him with everything I am." He rubbed both hands over his face and groaned into them.

"How's the sex?" Keeping his hands steepled over his mouth, he stared at her and raised an eyebrow. "Ooh, that good."

"I need to get out of there. For good." He sighed.

"What about your job?"

Mav stared at the windows of his apartment. "I don't know. I have to be careful, as you know." Zara knew all about what Bert was like. Mav had blurted it all out one night when she had been visiting and noticed he was withdrawn and grumpy. She'd been furious.

"There has to be a way to protect your father and allow you to give the middle finger to Bert. There *has* to be."

"Well, if you think of something, let me know."

"What if you told Douglas?"

"No! He needs to stay as far away from this as possible. I wonder if I can persuade Dad to retire early." He pulled on his lower lip, pinching it between his fingers as his thoughts followed the train the idea had brought up. "It might work, you know."

"Speak to him. The worst he can say is no." She cleared her throat. "The same goes for Douglas, you know."

Mav glared at her. "It won't happen, Z. Would you expect an heir of the crown to go against his father, the king?"

She pouted. "I would if it was a fairy tale," she grumbled.

"Yeah, me too. Unfortunately, my life is as far from a fairy tale as I can get."

The worst thing about his situation was that his fear of being alone forever would come to fruition because he didn't think he'd be able to replace Douglas in his affections any time soon.

Goddamn traitorous heart.

19

DOUGLAS

"**Y**our Highness!"

Douglas pivoted to the voice and waited for Clarice to catch up with him. He had left the changing rooms of the club and was aiming for the main room.

"Are you okay?" Clarice was usually so unruffled, but her frantic demeanour had his instincts firing. "What's happened?"

Clarice stepped close and lowered her voice. "I received a phone call from Quinn. He needs your help."

Douglas glanced at the few people who were around and edged her closer to the wall with him. "What did he say?"

"He asked me to tell you, 'Kendal's house, now.'"

"Fuck." The expletive was low, but Clarice's eyes widened. "I need you to get a Monitor to replace me. I have to leave immediately."

"Yes, sir. I'll call in Prince Albert."

"Thank you, and please message Eric for me to let him know what's happening."

He strode for the lift, but Clarice's voice called him back. When he reached her, she said, "I think you better change first, Your Highness."

Douglas glanced down at his outfit and cursed again. Thanking her once more, he jogged to the changing room and redressed hastily. As soon as he was in his car and heading for Kendal's home, he called Freddie.

"I thought you were—"

"Sorry, Freddie, but I need some backup. Something's going down with one of the subs, and I have no clue what to expect. Can you meet me?" He gave Freddie the address and rang off, knowing his brother would back him up.

They wouldn't get into a fight in public unless there was no other option, but hopefully, whatever was going on was happening inside the home, not outside.

Douglas forced himself to keep to the speed limit, but it was difficult. By the time he reached his destination, Freddie was already there with Damon, his best friend.

"What's going on?"

Douglas shook his head. "I don't know." They were several houses down from where Kendal lived.

"We have time to help him, Doug. Just as you've been helping the other subs, you can help this one too."

Douglas snapped his gaze to Freddie. "You know what I've been doing?"

Freddie rolled his eyes. "You're my brother. I know you better than anyone."

"Why did you never say anything?"

Freddie shrugged. "No harm was coming from it. I assumed you'd tell me when you wanted to."

"We need to get in there. Another sub told me he worried about Kendal. I was planning on visiting him tomorrow night, but the sub rang me at the club tonight, telling me to get to Kendal's ho—" A scream rent the air. "Fuck!"

Douglas raced down the street to the sub's house, not waiting for anything except to check if the door was locked. It was, so he kicked at it several times before it caved. The minute he entered the property, rage filled his body, and he stopped, staring at the scene. Freddie, Damon and several of the security team ran past him, and Douglas saw someone racing for the back of the house, Freddie close behind.

Douglas focused on the sub, who was naked and bound over a coffee table with bleeding lashes littering their back, ass and legs. Kendal whimpered, and Douglas rushed over.

"You're going to be okay, Kendal. I'm here." He mumbled soothing words to them while he fiddled with the ropes on their wrists. They were extremely tight, and undoubtedly, Kendal would be in discomfort with them as well as the lashes, which appeared to have been given to cause pain and suffering, not because the sub wanted it.

When Kendal was free, Douglas moved them into his arms and cradled them as best he could without causing more pain. The lashes would need cleaning and covering before Kendal could settle down. Tears soaked into his shirt, and Douglas vowed that whoever did this would be taken care of, one way or another.

He saw Freddie enter the room but stay back. They understood a sub would not want to be crowded when something like this had happened to them. Freddie crouched, making himself smaller, and whispered, "We have him contained in the kitchen. I've called for backup."

Douglas mouthed, "Who is it?"

Freddie mouthed, "Talon."

Douglas clenched his jaw as fury swept through him

again. When he'd kicked Talon out of the club, the man had been angry, but for him to do this...Douglas would make sure he suffered.

Kendal sobbed, pulling him back from the edge, and he whispered in their ear, trying to calm them again. Once the tears had slowed, Douglas cupped Kendal's face and pulled them back. Meeting their gaze, his heart broke. "We need to clean your wounds, and we'll find somewhere safe for you to stay."

Kendal closed their eyes and nodded, tears spilling over. Douglas helped them onto their stomach on the sofa, then stood, asking Kendal where the first aid kit was. Once he'd retrieved it, he knelt beside Kendal and began tending to their wounds. It was going to take a while.

He wasn't halfway through when a knock sounded, and Kendal tensed. Freddie came to stand beside them, fists clenched but relaxed when their father entered with Uncle William shortly behind. Douglas placed a hand on Kendal's nape, soothing them as best he could without saying words.

"Father, Uncle William. We have the assailant in the kitchen."

Both men stepped past Douglas, but King Andrew rested a hand on Douglas's shoulder, and when he lifted his gaze, his father gave a smile and a nod to him. It seemed like his father was proud. Douglas shook his head and returned to Kendal. It took many long minutes before the wounds were cleaned and covered, but once they were, Douglas helped Kendal to stand.

"Is there somewhere specific you would like to go?"

"Quinn," they whispered.

"I'll see to it, personally," Douglas said. Freddie stepped

into the room, and Kendal curled in on himself. "I'm here. Nothing will hurt you now."

"They took him around the back." Freddie glanced at Kendal. "I'm sorry for what happened. If there is anything I can do, please, let me know."

Kendal nodded once and returned their gaze to the floor. Freddie motioned to Kendal, and Douglas knew what he was asking.

"I'm going to get Kendal situated at Quinn's house, and we can talk through everything. Is that okay with you, Kendal?"

"Yes, Master Douglas."

"Bear with me one minute, Kendal." Douglas made sure Kendal was steady on their feet before approaching Freddie. "If the piece of shit doesn't pay for what he did, I will personally see to it he never has the chance to do this again."

Freddie's eyes hardened. "I don't think you need to worry about it."

Douglas gave Freddie Quinn's address and helped Kendal from the house. He knew his brother would see they secured the house before he left. Helping Kendal into his car, Douglas encouraged them to lay on the back seat with their face towards the back of the seat. It would, hopefully, stop their back from touching anything as Douglas drove them. It wasn't ideal, but he couldn't think of any other way of transporting them without hurting them too much.

The journey was around twenty-five minutes with the traffic that had accrued on a Saturday night, but once he parked the car outside Quinn's house, the man himself flung open the door and raced to the car.

"Is Kendal okay?"

Douglas climbed out of the car and shut the door before

responding. "Not great." He opened the back door, helping Kendal to slide out. Instead of holding Kendal as he would a sub he was caring for, he told Kendal to hold onto him. It meant Douglas wouldn't hurt them unintentionally.

When they were in Quinn's front room, Kendal lying on the sofa and Douglas and Quinn in armchairs, Douglas asked Kendal if it was okay for them to wait for Freddie to arrive. They agreed, and Quinn made drinks for them. Douglas helped Kendal to take small sips of orange juice and small bites of a biscuit. He hoped the sugar in it would help Kendal counteract the potential sub-drop they might feel.

A knock sounded, and Quinn answered the door, coming back with wide eyes, and Freddie followed by Douglas's father.

"I wasn't expecting you, Father."

"It's the least I can do when a sub has been hurt." King Andrew went to his knees next to Kendal, who murmured in denial but hissed when they tried to stop him. "Calm, Kendal. All is well."

Douglas watched as his father cupped Kendal's jaw and stroked his hand through Kendal's hair. Without changing position, his father focused on Douglas. "What happened?"

He explained receiving the phone call, racing to Kendal's house and what he saw. His father's mouth turned white the more Douglas spoke.

King Andrew turned to Kendal. "Can you tell us what happened, little one?"

At that moment, Douglas saw what his father must have been like as a Dom in the club when he was younger. The kindness, softness, easiness with which he spoke and held Kendal was apparent. At sixty-five, his father no longer frequented the club unless it was a special occasion.

Kendal wiped their eyes. "I've been seeing Master Talon—"

"Just Talon. He no longer uses Master." The king's voice brooked no argument.

"I've been seeing Talon for several months on and off. I hadn't been able to visit the club this last month because of work, and we came to an agreement. We would scene at my house during the day when I needed it. He's been training someone to be a Master, and I agreed the guy could watch and sometimes take part." Kendal inhaled shakily. "He's been pushing my boundaries further and further each time, but I called him on it three days ago. He apologised, and they left."

Kendal didn't seem like they wanted to continue, but the king prodded them, "Why was he there today?"

Kendal closed their eyes. "He wasn't supposed to be. As I said, our scenes were during the day, not at night. I was getting ready to go to work when he arrived. We got into an argument when he refused to leave so I could get ready. He… slapped me, and I fell to the floor." Kendal huffed, "He has more muscles than me. It didn't take him long to position me as you found me."

"Was he alone?"

"Yes. Harvey hadn't been there the previous session either." Douglas made a mental note of the guy's name to check it out later.

"Did he say anything in particular?"

"I couldn't understand his words. Although he mentioned…" Kendal's gaze darted to Douglas's.

"He mentioned me." Douglas knew throwing Talon out would come back to bite him in the ass, but he never expected it would involve another sub.

"Yes, sir. I heard your name several times, along with

Prince Christian and Prince Patrick, but I couldn't understand what he was saying about you."

"What happened once he tied you down," the king asked.

"He pulled out a whip from a bag I hadn't seen him bring in."

"Premeditated," Freddie mumbled, barely audible.

Kendal's breathing increased. "He started hitting me, again and again, no respite between."

Douglas frowned. "How did you know Kendal was in trouble?" He faced Quinn.

"Kendal rang me, but there was nothing on the other end. I was about to hang up when I heard what I assume now was the slap and the phone dropping to the floor. The call was still connected when…" Quinn swallowed hard, and Freddie settled onto the arm of the chair, sliding his arm around Quinn's shoulders. "I had to hang up to call the club." He glanced at Douglas. "I knew you'd help, though you were working. Sorry."

"Never be sorry for that, Quinn. You did a great job."

Douglas hadn't wanted to leave Kendal, but his father assured him he would take care of Kendal himself, and they would be protected. He and Uncle William would deal with Talon as well, and it left Douglas with nothing to do.

After aiming the car for the royal household, images of what happened flitted through his mind, and he clenched his hands on the steering wheel and gritted his teeth. Talon had crossed the line between the pain intended for BDSM and the pain for the sake of hurting someone. When it had happened, Douglas didn't know, but it was before the initial incident with Eddie.

When he parked the car, he stared around him, surprised to find himself somewhere other than his intended destination. He tried to decide whether to leave or continue where his head wanted him to go. Sighing, he climbed out of the car, received a nod from Eric and headed for the entrance. As he stood in front of the door, he spun his keys around on his finger, catching them in his palm each time while he tried to figure out if this was a good idea or not.

He knocked, the keys jangling.

The door opened, and Douglas stared at Mav. Something must've shown on his face because Mav ushered him inside and closed the door behind them. Mav rested a hand at Douglas's lower back and led him to the sofa. Douglas dropped into the cushions and lay his head back, staring at the ceiling. Images bombarded him once more, and he rested his hand over his eyes, trying to push them away.

"Here."

Douglas lifted his head and found Mav standing beside him with a glass of orange juice. He gave a small smile and drank, finding he was more thirsty than he realised. When he finished, Mav removed the glass from his hands and placed it on the table, sitting beside him with one leg bent to face Douglas.

"What happened?"

Douglas shook his head and stared at the blank TV. "A sub—" he croaked, then cleared his throat and started again, "A sub was hurt. Intentionally. It's my fault."

"I doubt that."

Douglas scoffed at the conviction in Mav's voice. "I threw a Dom out of the club a few weeks ago for hurting a sub. He turned on another sub tonight. Hurt them badly. I can't help but think if I hadn't turned him out as I had, this never would've happened."

"You don't know that. Have you investigated the guy's background? How do you know he hasn't been doing it before you threw him out?"

Douglas's breath caught against the unintentional pain those words caused in him. He hadn't checked into anything regarding Talon, and he didn't know if Freddie had. He'd dropped the ball on this one. If he'd checked, he would've been able to figure out how likely it was of Talon doing it again. Instead, he was more focused on himself. And Mav.

Leaning forward and resting his elbows on his knees, Douglas dropped his head into his hands. What was the point in him being the spare heir if he couldn't take care of the people he needed to? He'd have a lot more to look after in the future, and if he ever became king—which was highly unlikely—he'd have more to do. If he couldn't manage his responsibilities now, what was the point?

The sofa dipped, and Mav's hand rested on his shoulder. "You're not to blame. You can't be everywhere. You can't expect to know everyone's intentions. You're one person."

Douglas stood, Mav's hand sliding off him, and he missed it immediately. "I might not know people's intentions, but I know what my eyes tell me. They have taught me to read body language, for fuck's sake. How could I have it so wrong?" He stared out of the window, watching the lights of the city.

Mav's reflection appeared beside his in the window. "People are good at hiding. It's not your fault."

"But Kendal is—"

"It's not your fault."

"It—"

"It's not your fault."

Douglas lowered his gaze, feeling a tear overflow and roll down his cheek. He wiped it away and sniffed. "Sorry. I shouldn't have come. I'll leave you alone." He pivoted towards the door, stopping with his hand on the handle when Mav called his name.

"Stay."

Douglas bowed his head and closed his eyes when hands smoothed up his back and around to his chest. Mav's body warmed his back, and his arms gripped him. Douglas released a long breath and gripped Mav's hands.

"Let's get some sleep."

Douglas nodded and held tight as Mav tried to release him. They stayed in the position for several minutes. When he found his equilibrium, he let go of Mav, though Mav kept hold of his hand and dragged him towards the bedroom.

He wasn't used to being taken care of, and he found himself at a loss of what to do. Usually, he was the one caring for his subs, but he found he liked not having to think for a while. He wouldn't be able to do it all the time, he knew, but for tonight, he would take whatever Mav gave him.

When Mav tugged him into the bathroom and washed him clean, Douglas felt his heart expand. He understood where his father was coming from when he'd said they couldn't have a public relationship, but he also knew his father was abiding by the rules of his ancestors. It was the twenty-first century, and rules changed.

His mind settled further while Mav dried him with a huge fluffy towel, and he finally felt some measure of relief. Mav led him to the bed, pulling the covers back and indicating for Douglas to climb in. He did, lying on his back and expecting Mav to climb on top of him. When he slid in next to him and dragged the covers over them both, situating himself against Douglas's side with their legs entangled, Douglas finally realised Mav had been serious about sleeping.

Despite knowing he wouldn't be able to sleep, he was content being able to hold Mav close. He pressed his lips to Mav's head, inhaling his unique scent and closing his eyes in bliss.

20

CHRISTIAN

"What the hell! I knew we should've kept eyes on him." Christian slapped his hand on the table, making Freddie raise his eyebrows. "I told Patrick when we threw Talon out, we should've kept him within the club so we could keep a leash on *him*. This wouldn't have happened—"

"Can you guarantee that?" Freddie asked, crossing his ankle over his knee and resting an arm on the chair next to him. "Can you guarantee he wouldn't still have done this? Because I couldn't."

Christian growled and raked his fingers through his hair. Most of the time, he could control his emotions and hide them behind a blank facade, but when something like this happened, he felt it to his core. He felt responsible for Kendal getting hurt. He should've monitored Talon himself; he had enough training to do it.

"Chris, no one could've predicted this would happen, and if we did, we couldn't have said who it would've happened to. Talon could've chosen any sub, and we're only a few people.

None of us would've been able to check in on them all every single day. Let it go."

Christian closed his eyes and inhaled, pushing aside his emotions and becoming controlled once more. He glanced at Freddie. "What happens now?"

"Father and Uncle William are dealing with Talon. I don't know what's going to happen to him, but at the very least, he'll be charged with assault." Freddie sighed. "As for Kendal, he's staying with Quinn for a few days until he's recovered, then he said he wants to go back home."

"I want to check his house to make sure it's secured properly. I don't want the chance of anyone else coming back to terrify him, especially not that Harvey guy. Have we found him yet?"

Freddie shook his head. "He's in the wind."

"Fucking hell." Christian stood and crossed his hands over his chest. "I definitely want to check over Kendal's house. You know I can secure it as well as anyone, Freddie."

"I know. Let me speak with Father, but I don't see why it would be a problem. The more people who check the place over, the more likely we are to find weaknesses."

Christian headed for the door.

"Christian."

He leaned his head against the wooden door. A hand rested on his back between his shoulder blades, and he sighed.

"Hey," Freddie said, encouraging him to turn around. When he did, Freddie's forehead creased. "What's really wrong here?"

"Nothing. I'm just sick of this happening. Subs are to be protected and cherished, not used as a bloody..." He shook his head, unable to get his thoughts in order.

Freddie gripped his chin, tilting his head up slightly as he said goodbye in their fashion but with a bit more force behind it than usual. Christian understood the undercurrent and acknowledged it with a long blink. When he let go, Christian gripped the door handle.

"I'm going to Kendal's now. I have nothing else urgent to deal with. Ring me if you hear any more."

"I will. Be careful."

Christian nodded and exited Freddie's room. He stalked down the corridors of Windsor and out to his car. He brought up Kendal's address, which Freddie had helpfully sent to him without Christian asking for it. Clipping the phone to his holder, he started the engine and gunned it, driving away. No one should ever go through that. He'd seen enough of it happening within his immediate family; he didn't need to see it outside as well. Within his family, he had no control. Despite being ex-Army, he lost every ounce of respect and training as soon as he stepped foot in his parents' house. It was as if he was five years old again, and he never expected it to change. Outside of that, though, he had control. He had power, he had influence, and he had training. He refused to let that go to waste when someone needed help and support.

He pulled up outside the property and climbed out of the car. He studied the street, the cars, the houses, and then wandered up the path to the door. He could see where Douglas had kicked it down because the repair job wasn't good. It was enough to stop any air from getting inside, but a nudge of his shoulder sent it flinging free. Christian made a note to mention it to Freddie and tell him not to use whoever did it again.

He wedged the door shut and drifted around the rooms.

The furniture hadn't been put to rights, so he could almost see how the event unravelled in his mind. There were bloodstains on the table and floor, there were overturned plant pots, and when he entered the kitchen, there were shattered cups and bowls on the floor.

Anger crawled through his veins, and he tamped it down. That could come later when he'd righted the wrong that happened here. When he'd tidied the place up, he would check what he needed, fetch it, then spend his evening making this house a fucking fortress. Kendal would feel safe in this house again if it was the last thing he did.

MAVERICK

Mav's heart hurt for Douglas. How many people saw how deep Douglas's heart was? When he'd woken the previous morning, it had surprised Mav to find him there. He'd expected Douglas to sneak out in the night, but he'd been there, making breakfast for him. Mav had little food in the apartment, and he'd heard Douglas grumbling to himself about not having much to work with. They'd ended up with a cheese omelette, which was more than what Mav had intended to eat.

Mav had followed Douglas to Windsor, and they'd convened in Douglas's room after Mav had stopped to grab what he needed from his own room. Douglas's schedule had been packed with appointments, but Douglas hadn't complained about it. Mav had been worried he was uneasy about the previous day's activities, but when Mav had asked, he'd been upbeat and seemingly content.

They had slept in each other's arms again last night at Douglas's apartment this time. Mav knew they were taking tremendous risks of being found out, but he couldn't find it in him to care.

Douglas had found out the guy who'd hurt the subs had been arrested and charged with grievous bodily harm, but they had given no other information to him despite his royal status.

As he wandered the corridors of the castle back to his room, Mav decided to ring his father and try to slip into the conversation about taking early retirement. If he could get his father away from Bert's brother, then Bert would have nothing to hold over his head, and Mav could get a clean break. He knew he'd lose his position as Douglas's social media manager, but he needed to get away from his boss. He couldn't take much more.

He made himself a cup of tea and settled on the chair near the window, enjoying the sunshine seeping in and warming him.

"Hey, Dad. How are you doing?"

"I'm good, thanks. How's life treating you? Did you get yourself sorted out since our last conversation?" His dad laughed, the sound taking Mav back to his childhood.

"Life is…interesting. Let's put it that way." He smirked and shook his head as he remembered everything that had happened since he'd last seen his dad.

"Life should be interesting. What's the point if it's not?"

"True. How's work?"

"Ah, same as always. Jimmy has announced his retirement, lucky bastard."

If that wasn't a segue into Mav's chosen subject, nothing was. "You could take early retirement, you know. You only have a couple of years left." He waited for the answer, though he had a feeling he knew what his dad would say.

"Nah, what would I do with myself if I didn't work? I'd be bored to tears staying at home all day."

Mav chuckled, though his heart broke. "You'd find plenty to do. Don't kid a kidder, Dad. You always find things to do, especially if you shouldn't do them."

His dad guffawed. "You wouldn't want me any other way."

"You got that right." He inhaled and pushed away his plans for his father's early retirement with a heavy heart. "Have you been climbing ladders again, Dad?"

"Not since yesterday." He gave a hearty laugh. "You worry too much, Mav. Tell me about your young man."

"He's not my young man! Jeez, Dad."

"Whatever you want to call him. How are things going?"

Mav rubbed his eyes, allowing the sun to heat him further. "Things are good. There have been a few hiccups, but we got over them. It's not... We're short-term, but we're taking what we can get."

"No matter how long you're together, you're living. That's the main thing. Don't let anyone tell you any different."

Mav's phone beeped. He pulled it from his ear to see Bert ringing. Rolling his eyes, he told his dad he needed to take the call, but he'd ring or see him later.

"Good morning, Bert."

"What have you been doing, Maverick? I'm hearing mixed responses about some things you are doing over there. Do I need to replace you with someone else?"

Mav gritted his teeth and put the phone on speaker as he strode to his desk. Opening his laptop, he logged on while Bert rambled on about Mav's apparent transgressions. He was used to the recap and only listened with one ear until he heard, "—your shitty work ethic and making my life harder than it needs to be."

"Wait, what?"

"Were you listening?"

"Yes, but I don't have a shitty work ethic."

Bert snickered. "Really? I'm sure I'm not the only one who can attest that you create more problems than you solve."

Mav's door opened, and Douglas stood there, face red, eyes stormy. Mav was aware Bert was singing Mav's praises —not—and had no knowledge that every word was being heard by someone who could take him apart in one phone call.

"Bert, I'm going to have to go. I'm needed."

"Don't fuck it up, asshole!"

His boss hung up, and Douglas kicked the door closed. His nostrils flared. "Does he always talk to you like that?"

Mav licked his lips and bit his bottom lip as he stared at the table and nodded. "It's complic—"

"I don't give a shit! Who the hell does he think he is to treat you like that?"

"He's my dad's best friend, and his brother is my dad's boss." Mav lifted his head, spearing Douglas with his gaze. "I will not allow my dad to lose his job because I can't take a little ribbing from my boss."

Douglas stepped forward, hands rising from his sides. "That was not a little ribbing, as you say! How long have you been putting up with it?"

Mav shrugged, transferring his gaze to the laptop screen. "Since I started working for him. At least it started small, but when I embarrassed him a few years ago, everything went to shit."

Douglas crouched beside him. "He's been giving you shit for years, and you're allowing him to do so? Would your father be happy with it?"

Mav swallowed hard, knowing the answer, even if he couldn't voice it. "Dad is a couple of years from retirement. If he loses his job now, he'll lose the company benefits. I won't make things difficult for him."

Douglas rested his palm against Mav's nape, and Mav dropped his head forward. "If you weren't doing this, what would you be doing instead?"

"What do you mean?" Mav glanced up at him.

"If you weren't working for that...man, what would you do?"

Mav's cheeks heated, and he glanced away. "I've always wanted to start my own social media company. I have a business plan ready to go as soon as my dad retires, and I tell Bert to shove it up his ass. My problem is that Bert is highly sought after in this business, and I know he'll blacklist me as soon as I leave."

"No, he won't."

"You don't know him like I do, Douglas. He's a manipulative asshole, but he has friends in high places."

Douglas stood, pulling Mav into his arms and surrounding him in a warmth that was different yet similar to the sunshine through the window. Mav tucked his face into Douglas's neck and held him tightly, feeling his muscles release. The easy way they gave and received comfort made Mav's heart skip a beat, but he allowed himself to sink into the embrace, knowing he wouldn't have it for long.

Mav pulled away, smoothing a hand down the lapel of Douglas's black suit. "What brought you to my door, anyway?"

"I wanted to check if you were okay for a visit tonight?"

Mav smiled. "Sure. Apart from catching up with Zara, I've no other plans."

"Say hi to her from me if I miss her."

Mav raised his eyebrows. "You want to meet my friend?"

Douglas tilted his head. "Of course. Why don't you want me to?"

"No, it's not...I didn't think you'd want to if we're keeping this quiet."

Douglas dropped a kiss on his lips and stepped back. "I'm not the one who wanted to keep it quiet, and besides, I trust your friend."

"You don't know her."

"I don't need to. If you're friends with her, then I trust her."

"Why would you trust someone because they were friends with me?" Mav still couldn't understand why Douglas had given him such freedom.

Douglas stepped closer again, brushing the back of his hand across Mav's cheek. "I trust your instincts, Mav. You wouldn't intentionally harm anyone."

Mav felt a mixture of joy and fear at those words. Joy because Douglas trusted him, but fear because Douglas shouldn't take a chance with his life in case Mav was wrong. If Mav trusted the wrong person and Douglas suffered because of it, he'd never forgive himself.

He gripped Douglas's lapels and pulled him close, fusing their lips in a short but hard kiss. "Get going, or you'll be late."

Douglas narrowed his eyes. "I might have let you take care of me the other night, but it doesn't mean you're in charge."

Mav lifted the corner of his lip. "I know, Sir."

"My apartment tonight. I have something for you."

Mav's breath hitched, and he licked his lips. "Yes, Sir."

"Good." Douglas kissed him again and whirled to the door. "Don't work too hard." He winked over his shoulder.

"Be good, and I won't have to." He bit his lip as Douglas narrowed his eyes again, then grinned.

When the door closed behind Douglas, Mav dropped into his chair, unable to contain his smile. It was nice to have someone to banter with. He rubbed his hands over the sleeve of his silk shirt, closing his eyes at the remembered feelings evoked in him when Douglas used different textures on his naked skin. He'd never expected it to feel so…decadent. He scrubbed at his five o'clock shadow, the rough texture scratching his fingers and reminding him of how Douglas had used his own the night before. Rubbing lotion into his skin before they went to sleep had been essential afterwards.

Grinning, he refocused on his laptop, knowing he had some updates to do on the social media accounts.

When he'd finished, he grabbed his things and exited the room, heading for his car.

"Maverick."

He stopped and glanced at the queen. "Yes, Your Majesty?"

"Can I have a word, please?"

"Of course."

Mav didn't know what she might want to speak to him about, but he followed her and her personal guard to a room, entering and sitting when indicated to.

"Would you like some tea?"

"No, thank you."

"Just for me, please, Portia," she told her assistant as she crossed her legs on the sofa opposite him. "Now, Maverick, how are things?"

"Um…good. The public is reacting favourably to the photographs I've been posting about Douglas's recent activities. There has been no further negative media attention, although I'm sure if Douglas keeps as he is, they will dig something up from his past."

Queen Louisa nodded, thanking and dismissing her assistant once she'd been passed her tea. "I know how fickle the media is. Thank you for the update. I was actually asking about you. Personally."

"I'm sorry?"

"How are *you*, Maverick?"

Mav's cheeks lit, and he dropped his gaze. "I'm enjoying what I'm doing."

"And how do you feel about my son?"

Mav's eyes widened, and his gaze shot to her amused one. "I…I…"

"It's not a trick question." She smiled and sipped her tea, placing the cup back onto the saucer with a soft chink.

Mav inhaled. He was in a difficult situation because he couldn't tell her how he felt about her son, but he was reluctant to diminish what they had.

"It might be easier for me to ask how long you've been in love with Douglas?"

His mouth opened and closed several times, trying to formulate a reply before he slumped into the sofa. "Longer than I should've been," he whispered.

The queen's tinkling laughter filled the room, and Mav glanced at her in surprise. She clapped her hands together. "I knew it!" She must've seen something on Mav's face because she leaned forward, clasping her hands together. "Do you not want to be with him?"

It was Mav's turn to laugh. "I want nothing more, but it's not possible, Your Majesty. We're too different."

She waved her hand. "Pfft. Love isn't difficult, Maverick. The things that make life hard are the barriers we put in our own way or other people put in our way. The latter is easier to push aside than the former."

"I can't let Douglas suffer for being with me. It's not fair to him, especially as he has such amazing plans for his future."

She tilted her head. "Why would he suffer for being with you?"

Mav rolled his lips inwards. Although the queen had been present when the king had asked Mav to continue seeing his son, did she know about it? Did she agree to it? Or was she in the dark? He didn't want to implicate the king in anything.

"Ah. I suppose my husband has had some ideas of his own for how his son needs to live his life."

Mav neither confirmed nor denied, but Queen Louisa's mouth firmed. "You let me deal with my husband, Maverick. I have never seen Douglas as happy as he has been these last few weeks. Whatever worries you have about your relationship with him, please don't give up on him."

"I'm not giving up on him, but our relationship won't last."

"How do you know?"

"He's an heir to the throne, Your Majesty. I'm…" He didn't know how to finish his sentence. He wasn't anyone of consequence.

"You're the person my son is in love with."

Mav lifted his gaze to meet hers. "What?"

She smiled and reclaimed her teacup, taking another sip. "You'd be surprised what a mother knows when nothing is said." Mav didn't know how to respond. "Let me handle my husband. You have your hands full with my son." She winked. "Good luck."

Mav stood, bowing to her before exiting the room. When he was several corridors away, he rested back against the wall, puffing. What the hell?

"She said *what?*"

Zara's voice screeched through the phone. Mav should expect that to be her reaction to everything he said instead of being surprised every time. This time, though, it sliced through his head like a knife.

"You heard me."

He had his phone resting on a stand in the kitchen as he cooked his dinner. Douglas was finishing up his last appointment, and Mav knew he would eat at the castle before leaving for his apartment. Mav decided to eat as well; therefore, they would have time to do…other things, as long as his headache let him. A tremor of excitement filled him, despite having no sense of what to expect from Douglas.

"Basically, you're saying the king is against it, and the queen is for it?" Zara's words brought his attention back to the conversation as he poured the pasta into the pan of boiling water.

"Yep."

"I knew they didn't agree on everything. That interview was wrong."

Mav snorted. "They have to be seen in a good light, Z.

What did you expect them to say? *We argue all the time. Neither of us can agree on anything.* I doubt it would go down well with the public."

"I don't see why not. It would show that they were human, not above us all."

"Of course, they're above us. They're the fricking king and queen!"

"But they're always going on about how they want to be seen as normal. How can they when all the public sees are the perfect couple?"

Mav had to admit she had a point, but he could also see how it would seem to the public to see the king and queen as a "normal" couple. There were too many differences between them and the average citizen to make anyone believe them to be normal. It's why his job was so important. Showing the world that, despite their differences in status, they were the same as everyone else wouldn't work.

"Anyway, it doesn't matter. Things will never change. The world wants people to believe in and scrutinise and get frustrated at, and the royal family is one of those groups."

"When you marry into the family, it will make you that, too."

Mav paused in his movements. She was correct…if he married Douglas, he would change, but it would never happen. The king wouldn't allow it.

A knock sounded. "Hold up, Z. Someone's at the door." He switched off the hob and moved the pasta to a cool one before striding to the door. Flinging it open, he got a glance of Douglas, then his lips were covered and arms banded around him. He tensed for a second before his scent enveloped him, and he slid his arms around Douglas's neck.

The door slamming closed gained his attention, and he pulled back, breathing hard.

"Wow." He panted. "I wasn't expecting you for another couple of hours."

"I finished early. Was too impatient to change." Douglas threaded his fingers through Mav's hair, and Mav's eyelids fluttered.

"Mav!"

"Oh shit!" He laughed as he entered the kitchen. "Sorry, Z. Got an early visitor."

"I should've known. Hi, Prince Douglas!"

Mav rolled his eyes at her, then smiled when Douglas slid his arms around his waist and rested his chin on Mav's shoulder so they were both in the camera view.

"Hi, Zara. Douglas is fine."

"I know you are."

"Jesus Christ, kill me now," Mav muttered, returning to his pasta.

DOUGLAS

"Hey! That's not nice, and after everything I've done for you, as well. So ungrateful." Zara fake pouted, and Douglas laughed.

"I can see you're as troublesome as Mav told me you are," he replied.

"Being a prince doesn't make you immune to my retaliations, *Prince* Douglas."

"Zara! Enough. Jesus!" Mav banged the pot on the stove. "At the rate you're going, he's going to leave, and you won't get any of the gossip you're angling for."

"Oh! That's...so..." There was a pause at which Douglas glanced at the phone, thinking it had cut them off, but Zara had a finger tapping her chin with a smirk. She winked and finished, "so true."

"I'd love to see you interact with my brothers, Zara. I think you'd get on well with George. You seem to have the same sense of humour."

"Oh, thank you for the interest, but I'm happily engaged to Tex."

Douglas spluttered. "I didn't mean..." He saw Zara's face and laughed before eyeing Mav. "You told me she was a menace, but you never said how much of one she was."

"You have to experience it to believe it, trust me. There is no way to describe Zara." Mav's eyes widened. "Wait...engaged?"

"You did better than Tex said you would. She bet it would take you over ten minutes to figure out what I'd said. I was kind and gave you the benefit of the doubt, but you took several minutes longer than I thought." She wagged her finger at the camera. "I don't know if I should be sad about it or not."

"Oh, my god! When did this happen?" Mav moved closer to the phone, blocking part of the screen.

"This morning. Tex surprised me with breakfast in bed. Isn't she adorable?" Zara waved and blew a kiss to someone off-screen, her smile so wide it showed how happy she was about the recent development.

"Congratulations to you both."

Douglas nudged Mav, who seemed unable to talk. "Wow, congratulations, you two. I'm so happy for you."

"Thank you! We'll have to get together to celebrate. Are you going to get up here soon, Mav?"

"Well, ask the centre of attention here." Mav grinned and thumbed towards Douglas.

"Hey! No fair! You've mellowed me, sweetheart." He pressed a kiss to Mav's lips, wanting more but knowing they needed to finish dinner and the conversation first.

"Hmm, I'll believe it when I see it." Mav winked.

"Don't take his shit, Mav. Send him to us if he steps out of line." Tex's voice preceded her face, and her appearance surprised Douglas. He didn't think she was going to come on camera. "Nice to meet you, Douglas."

"Same to you, Tex."

They spoke for a while longer before Mav interrupted, "Anyway, girls, dinner is ready, so we're going to let you go. Don't do anything I wouldn't do."

"You're not giving us much of a choice, Mav."

Mav moved his hand in front of the phone and flipped her off. "I'll have you know, my life has expanded beyond my wildest dreams recently." Mav stared at Douglas as he said the words, and Douglas grinned.

"Yeah! Go, Mav!"

Mav's face coloured, but the man ignored it and continued dishing up the pasta.

"All right. Have a good evening, both of you. Douglas, don't be a stranger."

"I won't. We'll come and visit soon. I promise."

Zara's eyes lit up. "That would be great."

They bid goodbye. Zara was awesome, and her partner was nice, too. He'd been a little unsure when he'd first realised Zara was still on the phone, despite what he'd said to Mav earlier, but it had been eye-opening to get to know Mav through her. To find out some of the university stories she had about him. To listen to their banter. To find out he played the guitar.

Once they'd devoured their pasta with chicken and a cheesy sauce, Douglas helped Mav clean up, then dragged him to the sofa. "Play for me."

Mav rubbed his hands over his face. "I'm not that good."

"Doesn't matter. Play for me."

Mav sniffed but reached for his guitar. He fidgeted for a minute and rested the guitar on his lap, his fingers on the strings. Closing his eyes, he breathed, and Douglas took a minute to stare at him unabashedly. There was something about the man that called out to Douglas. When Mav had first started working with him, other than a minor attraction, he had expected nothing like this to happen. Everything about Douglas's life seemed brighter when Mav was around.

Mav opened his eyes, staring at Douglas, and started playing and singing. To begin with, he didn't recognise the song until the chorus came on, and Mav dropped his gaze. It was Mav's version of *In Case You Didn't Know* by Brett Young.

The lyrics slid into him, telling the secrets of the heart, and Douglas restrained himself until the last note flowed through the air. When it had, he leaned forward and kissed Mav softly. Resting their foreheads together, he whispered, "I'm hoping that was an intentional song because I'm crazy about you, too."

Mav moved the guitar to the floor and resumed kissing Douglas, straddling him and holding his head as they sipped and nipped at each other's lips. Douglas held Mav's ass with one hand and slid the other between his shoulder blades, not wanting him to go anywhere. Mav pulled away with a gasping breath.

"Wow."

Douglas laughed. "There's more where that came from."

"Is there?" Mav chuckled but pulled back and reclaimed his seat, snuggling into Douglas's side. "What's happening with Talon?"

The name of the asshole made Douglas's blood boil. Whoever believed they had the right to hurt someone like he had not once, but twice, and potentially more times they were not aware of, was something Douglas could never understand.

"His lawyer is trying to bring things that happen within the club into the conversation, but with the NDAs being signed, they can't say anything about it. Father won't allow it to happen, even if it would strengthen the case against Talon. I can understand why, but it's awful that we can't give the police any more evidence when we know for a fact it has happened before."

Mav rubbed a hand over Douglas's thigh in a soothing gesture and settled closer. "It is a shame, but you need to think about the repercussions on yourself and your family as well. It's not a little thing to brush under the carpet. It's a decades-long business and lifestyle the public wouldn't understand or condone." When Douglas went to protest, Mav squeezed his thigh and continued, "I know it's not fair, but the public has not changed their views enough yet to make this a regular or normal occurrence."

Douglas sighed. "I know. It's so unfair on Kendal. I think it helps that Father was there afterwards. They were able to get a lot of evidence, and with Quinn's statement as well, it will help."

"Will you have to give a statement?"

"I already have. I think they have collected most of the statements already. It's a waiting game now to see what happens to the investigation."

They were silent for a few minutes, then Douglas remembered something he meant to ask. "How is your dad? Still climbing ladders?"

Mav snorted. "Probably. I spoke to him earlier, and he was fine. I'm hoping he will refrain from more home improvements without letting me help him."

"Will he?"

"Doubt it."

They laughed, and the moment was so light-hearted and coupley, Douglas's breath caught. He couldn't resist lifting Mav's head and pulling him into another slow but deep kiss. He explored every inch of his mouth. When Douglas dragged his mouth away, they were both gasping for air.

"I need another drink. You want to choose a movie?"

"Sure."

Douglas watched as Mav stood, collecting their cups and retreating to the kitchen. He was as content at Mav's apartment as he was in his own, which shouldn't have been as surprising as it was. Mav's place felt more like a home, whereas his seemed like a show home, and there was a vast difference. He'd love nothing more than to be settled into a place where he was more content and less sterile.

If they were to stay together, which he hoped they would, despite what his father said, Douglas wanted everything Mav was willing to give him. Some days, Douglas couldn't believe how much his opinions had changed. He'd been so happy being happy-go-lucky and single, getting his rocks off at the club and occasionally somewhere else, but now he wanted more. He wanted everything he never imagined he could have.

When Mav came back in with steaming mugs of tea, he raised an eyebrow at Douglas. "Did you not find anything to watch?"

"Huh?"

Mav's forehead creased as he put the mugs on the table. "The movie? Did you not find one?"

"Oh, sorry, I didn't look." He rested his cheek on his knuckles and gazed at Mav. "I got sidetracked."

The corners of Mav's mouth lifted. "Anything in particular?"

"I'm happy."

Mav dropped into the seat next to him. "Me too." He grinned at Douglas and reached for the remote.

Douglas watched while Mav flicked through the channels, commenting on each one he found before switching over to on-demand. They both had a love of superhero films, so finding something to watch was unlikely to ever be a problem. He had never been as content as he was in that moment, wrapping Mav in his arms as they settled in to watch the villains be beaten by the heroes.

By the time the film had finished, he was as horny as ever. They had spent half the film kissing and canoodling, raising their arousal levels until Mav was straddling Douglas's hips like he'd done earlier that evening. Their kisses deepened until they had no choice but to part.

"You taste so good," Mav groaned.

"You too."

Douglas scooted to the end of the seat and stood, holding Mav. Mav wrapped his legs around his waist with a yelp and a laugh.

"Be careful. I can't afford to injure a prince." Before he stepped forward, Mav halted him. "I need the tablet. I have to check something before tomorrow. It'll only take me a second."

Douglas narrowed his eyes. "A lesser man would worry about why you were thinking about work when you're in his arms, but I understand your need." He slid one arm further under Mav's ass and reached down for the tablet, passing it to Mav before gripping him again and stalking forward.

"You know me better than that."

"You bet I do."

He set Mav on the bed, encouraging him to wiggle until

his head was on the pillow, then Douglas indicated for Mav to get on with his work while he went to *work* on Mav's trousers. They both wore black suits that day, and freeing Mav from the confines of his trousers as he was busy working was a delicious experience. How much could Douglas get away with before it became too much for Mav to concentrate?

Once Mav was in his briefs and his undone shirt, Douglas quickly divested himself of his clothes and climbed between Mav's legs. Sliding his hands up the other man's legs and across his stomach, Douglas blew hot air across his briefs, receiving a minute squirm. He fastened his mouth to the outline of Mav's cock.

"Why was the meeting with the archaeology charity moved to tomorrow?"

Douglas paused, his stomach fluttering. He lifted his head, dragging his bottom lip between his teeth as he decided how to answer. Mav raised the tablet so he could see under it.

"Douglas?"

Douglas tapped a beat on Mav's leg and pulled himself to his elbows. "I requested the change."

"It's not a problem. I just wondered why?"

Douglas was silent for a few beats longer, then glanced at Mav. "I might've visited your boss."

He kept his words quiet, but he knew they would have the impact of an explosion, and he wasn't wrong. Mav sat upright, the tablet dropping to his lap, only missing Douglas's head by an inch.

"What? Why?"

Douglas moved to sit next to Mav, covering his lower half with the duvet. He stared at his hands, not knowing how

Mav was going to react to the news he had but knowing he wouldn't change his actions. He had hoped to have Mav full of endorphins before telling him the news.

"It pissed me off how he had been treating you. I know you can fight your own battles, Mav, but I wanted to help. Dealing with people like that is something I can do. I'm sorry for stepping over the line."

Mav sniffed. "What happened?"

Douglas sighed and explained his visit.

Douglas stepped out of the car Eric had driven them in. It wasn't often he asked Eric to drive him, liking his independence, but this time, he needed backup, as was proven by the three other body-guards who climbed from the backseat. He glanced at Eric, who nodded, and they strode towards the entrance. Having done his homework, Douglas knew where Calverdere Social Management was located. Crossing his arms over his chest as the lift took them to the relevant floor, Douglas braced himself for the confrontation. Having had no interaction with Bert Calverdere prior to this, he wasn't sure what to expect.

Because of the time they'd chosen to visit the man, there was no one present on the floor, though the lights were still on in the main area and in the boss's office. Eric knocked on Bert's door and opened it when the occupant shouted permission.

"Who—Oh, Your H-Highness! What a pleasure! How can I be of assistance?"

The man was built like he had played rugby at one point but hadn't kept up with his training, his buzz-cut adding to the severity of his appearance.

"I would like to talk to you about how you treat your employees, Mr Calverdere."

Bert blinked and held his hands out. "I don't understand, Your Highness."

"I recently witnessed a conversation you had with Maverick Houghton. I have to admit, I was not impressed with the tone you took with him and threatening his family...?" Douglas shook his head, "Not a good impression at all."

"Maverick doesn't listen to what I tell—"

"Does he do the job you've employed him to do?" Douglas crossed his arms over his chest again, trying to intimidate the man.

"Um...yes, but he—"

"Does he ask for more than you give him?"

"Er...no, but he won't—"

"Then I don't understand why you would threaten his father's job when Maverick is doing everything you ask of him."

"It's to keep him doing what he should do instead of messing around and showing me up!" Bert's eyes widened at his words and flicked closed.

"Maverick will no longer be working for you. You will give him three months' pay on top of what you already owe him because I know for a fact he hasn't been taking holidays. On top of that, any thoughts you may have about blacklisting him in the business need to be thrown from your mind right now. You know what I'm capable of, Mr Calverdere, and it won't stop with your business. Ronald Houghton will keep his job until he retires at his chosen age, or my wrath will reach your brother's company as well. Do I make myself clear?"

"Y-Yes, Your Highness." Bert had dropped back into his chair and was wringing his hands. Douglas could see he was shaking.

"I will check to ensure you keep to our agreement, Mr Calverdere. Make no mistake."

· · ·

Once he'd finished talking, he didn't want to see what expression Mav wore. He'd known visiting the man was way over the line, but he couldn't help himself. He wouldn't let Mav put up with that asshole any longer than he had to.

Mav's hand cupped his jaw and turned Douglas's face to his. A small smile played around the edges of his lips, and Douglas's heart raced.

"Thank you." Mav sighed. "I cannot tell you," He shook his head, "how much relief is flowing through me now that I don't have to deal with him any longer. It's a shame I won't be working with you anymore."

Douglas frowned. "Why not?"

"The royal contract is with Bert's company, not me."

"Well, I deem it void."

Mav shook his head. "You can't. I'm happy to keep doing the work regardless, but you need to speak to someone about it if you want me to continue in an official capacity."

"Fuck. I never thought of that."

Mav ran a hand over Douglas's head. "It's okay."

Douglas leaned forward and rubbed his face. "I always leap before I look. I was so...angry at him for what he was doing to you. It wasn't fair. I should've thought of the repercussions, though."

Mav moved the tablet to the bedside table and climbed into Douglas's lap, his hands framing his face. "Everything will be fine. I'm sure I can sort something out fairly easily, as long as Bert keeps to his word about not making things difficult for me." He kissed Douglas chastely. "I would, however, recommend you speak to me before you do something like that again. We could brainstorm before the event to come up with any potential issues."

"I promise. I'm sorry."

"Don't be sorry. Thank you." He kissed each of Douglas's cheeks. "Thank you." He kissed Douglas's nose. "Thank you." He kissed Douglas's forehead. "Thank you, sweetheart."

He kissed his lips, swiping his tongue across the full mounds, then inside when Douglas opened for him. Douglas slid his arms around Mav's lower back, holding him tightly.

"Didn't you say you had something for me?"

Douglas blinked, trying to focus on Mav's words but unable to fully comprehend until Mav repeated the question. "Oh, yes!" Douglas grinned, then deposited Mav on his back on the bed and raced to the living room, grabbing the bag he'd dropped near the front door when he'd first entered. He grinned as he rushed back, hoping Mav would love this experience as much as the previous ones. He'd been taking things further with different items each time they played, and Mav had responded beautifully to everything so far.

Mav was where he'd left him but with his hand behind his head and leg cocked to the side, showing Douglas what he had for the taking. He jumped onto the bed, laughing.

"What have you got today?"

Douglas snuggled down until they were facing each other with the small bag between them. "Okay, tonight, I thought we could try something a little further up the scale. We've done blindfolds, which you seem comfortable with. Is that correct?"

"Yes. It helps me to focus on what you're doing."

"Exactly. I would like to do it again but try you with earplugs as well. I would take away your sight and hearing. You'll only know where and when I'm going to touch *when* I do it. What do you think?"

23

MAVERICK

av inhaled. He liked the idea behind it, but was he ready to have his senses removed? "How will you know if it's too much for me?"

"You'll have your safe words, which you can use whenever you want. I will watch your body language, and if I think you're uncomfortable, I will remove your earplugs to check with you. You will also have use of your hands, so if you can't tell me, you can show me by lifting your hand into the air."

"What will you use on me?" Mav's heart rate increased because the idea that he wouldn't be in control was nice.

"Ah, that would be telling." Douglas winked. "Nothing that will hurt you, I promise. I know it's not your thing."

Mav sniffed, licking his lips as he stared at Douglas. Douglas wouldn't do anything to hurt him, and he trusted him to abide by his limits. Mav's heart skipped a beat. He trusted him with everything he was.

"Yes. Let's try it."

Douglas smiled and leaned forward, kissing Mav with

such tenderness. How was he going to cope once Douglas was no longer in his life?

He moved into the position Douglas showed and waited while he readied a few items out of Mav's eye line.

"All right, I will ask for your colours throughout this, but because you won't be able to hear me, I will tap your chin three times. Okay?"

"Yes, Sir." Mav could already feel the tension releasing from his muscles, his limbs sinking further into the mattress, his gaze softening.

Returning to face him, Douglas smiled. "Okay, let's start with the blindfold." Douglas sat next to him, bringing the black silk fabric to his face and slipping it over his head. Knowing what to expect, Mav sighed as he put it in place. "There we go. How are you feeling?"

"Green, Sir."

Featherlight fingertips danced across Mav's chest and abs, and Mav's breath caught. Mav had to grip the sheets beneath him to stop him from reaching for Douglas's hand and putting it where he wanted it.

"That's it. Now, we're going to try the earplugs. Remember, three taps on your chin if I want to know your colour and safe word or hand in the air if you want to stop immediately."

"Yes, Sir."

"Good. I'm proud of you," Douglas whispered into his ear as he pushed the plugs into place.

There was the initial crinkle of the plugs expanding to the shape of his ear canal, but then the only sound he could hear was his breathing and swallowing. It was extremely disconcerting, and when Douglas rested his palms flat on his chest, Mav jerked before settling again. Douglas rubbed his hands in circles, firmer than he had done when Mav had only the blindfold on. It might be to get him used to it. His breathing sounded loud and shaky as Douglas touched his shoulders and arms, like a massage but not as firm.

Douglas's hands disappeared, and the bed dipped by his hip. When nothing else happened, Mav's breathing increased. A tickle started at his ankle, and he twitched his legs involuntarily alongside a squeak escaping his mouth, which he was sure he would be embarrassed about later.

Three taps to his chin brought his attention to the area. What was…? "Oh, green. Sorry, Sir." A caress to his cheek was gone in seconds.

Mav smiled, biting his lip when the tickle continued its journey up his legs, the air rushing through his nostrils as he scrunched his toes to stop himself from moving away. The soft sensation bypassed his groin, following the crease of his hip and thigh until it reached his side, where Mav arched and pressed his head into the pillow. Just as fast, the feeling disappeared, and it left Mav breathing hard.

Nothing happened for a while, but Mav had no way of telling how long he'd been left with no sensation at all, barring the residual tingle along the path of the item. It could've been a minute; it could've been an hour. Time lost all meaning, but it wasn't a bad feeling. Mav knew he had nowhere to be, and he knew Douglas wouldn't let any harm come to him. It was an eerie feeling.

He jumped when something cold touched his inner thigh. It had a ridged feeling to it when it appeared to be flat against him and was sharper along its edge. Whatever it was, he could feel the path of the cold rising towards his groin, around his balls, around the base of his cock, which was hardening further as sensations bombarded him. When the scratch of the item dragged up the underside of his cock, his hips flexed as much as his shaft did, reaching for what it wanted.

The item slid over the head of his dick, catching on his slit and bringing a moan from his throat that vibrated in his ears.

He gasped. "Fuck." He licked his dry lips as three taps hit his chin. "Green, Sir," he gasped as the sensation continued back down the shaft but on the top this time. How was he going to manage?

Once the object was removed, Mav took a deep breath, which was loud in his head. He wished he could hear or see what was coming next, but it wasn't enough for him to stop what they were doing. It was only because he was eager to know.

Something spiky pressed into the outside of his thigh, and he flinched. It was when he went lightheaded he realised he was holding his breath. He exhaled in a rush, then inhaled quickly. The sharp instrument, which was sharper than the last one by a lot, continued up his leg to his hip and across his lower stomach. He was panting and shaking as he received taps on his chin.

"Um…Y-Yellow, Sir."

The sharp item disappeared, and Mav felt the bed move and dip the full length beside him. Douglas's hands—because there was no denying that was who it was and not because Mav knew he was there; he'd be able to tell Douglas from anyone else—smoothed across the path of the sharper item and slid across his chest. His hand stopped over Mav's heart.

Seconds later, he heard a loud scratching in his ear, and an earplug was removed. Douglas's hot breath fanned across his skin.

"Are you okay, sweetheart?"

"Yes, Sir. I'm fine. I panicked. Sorry."

"Don't be sorry. You did well. I wasn't sure if it would be too much for you or not, but I wanted to try. Thank you for being honest and telling me you were unsure." Douglas's free hand played with the ends of Mav's hair. "Would you like to continue with something else? Or would you like to feel it again while I'm here talking to you? We can try it on your hand if you want to."

Mav couldn't see and only had hearing in one ear. He cleared his throat and swallowed a few times before answering, "Try on my hand, please, Sir. I think it was that I wasn't expecting something so sharp and prickly."

Douglas's hand left his chest, and Mav wanted it back. "Okay, here we are." Douglas lifted Mav's hand to rest against his stomach. "I'm going to run it across the top of your wrist. The skin there is not as sensitive. Ready. Now."

The sharp scratchiness returned but was not as scary. It could be the area of skin, like Douglas said, but also because Douglas was closer to him, and Mav was less isolated. Either way, it didn't seem as daunting as before.

"It's a pinwheel. Think of a pizza slice with fangs."

Mav bellowed a laugh. "I'll have to remember to tell Zara that one."

Douglas chuckled. "It's a versatile instrument because it depends how hard you press it into the skin as to if it hurts. I hadn't planned on hurting you, as I said, but I knew it might be too much."

"It's not so bad now. It reminds me of a spiky stress ball I used to have, only sharper."

"Would you like to try again?"

Mav wavered, although he knew he'd have to be honest. "Could we try it another day?"

"Absolutely. Do you want the earplug back in?"

"Yes, please, Sir."

Douglas replaced the plug, and Mav heard the crinkle of it expanding again before hearing his breathing. It was like being underwater.

Between one breath and another, Douglas took his lips, spearing his tongue into Mav's mouth and exploring as if he had never been there before. The sounds they made as their tongues and lips moved against each other were erotic, and Mav felt himself teetering on the edge of something. He hadn't been given permission to touch, but he also hadn't been told not to. Taking a chance, he rested his hand against the back of Douglas's head, the groan from the man loud and sensual through where they connected.

Douglas's mouth lifted, and Mav inhaled, returning air to his deprived lungs. Douglas's mouth trailed kisses down Mav's neck and chest, flicking over his nipples before continuing the route to his cock. A warm hand encircled the base while Douglas's tongue swiped over the head, collecting Mav's precome.

Mav could do nothing but feel as Douglas brought him to the edge of climax repeatedly with his hand and mouth, only giving him a break to check his colour with the three taps on his chin. By the time Douglas pulled off and didn't return, Mav was breathing so hard, he thought he'd pass out, but he knew he needed everything Douglas could give him.

"Please." The plea was torn from his lips without his consent, but he needed more.

Douglas checked his colour again before kneeling between Mav's legs. His hands smoothed over his skin, then below his balls to his taint. When a wet finger rubbed against his entrance, Mav groaned, and he rolled his head over the pillow. Douglas's fingers prepared him well, and Mav ended up back where he'd been when Douglas had sucked him.

He babbled nonsense when Douglas pressed his covered cock at Mav's pucker. His hands gripped Douglas's forearms, no doubt leaving nail marks, but all Mav could do was hold on as Douglas pressed inside him in slow increments.

Finally seated, Douglas covered Mav's body with his own, and Mav wrapped his legs around Douglas's waist and his arms around his neck. Douglas's arms slid underneath Mav, holding him tightly. It wasn't conducive to deep thrusts, but the small circles Douglas's hips made sent Mav higher.

"Mine." The words were growled next to his ear, and he heard every word.

Mav had no timeframe for how long they were sharing air before Douglas pulled back and began pounding into him. His patience must have snapped because he was taking no prisoners, and Mav loved every minute.

Mav arched into the movements, keeping his hips in time with Douglas's, and they reached the peak at similar times. He could tell because Douglas's hips lost their rhythm, and his hands held him harder. His body melted into the mattress as Douglas withdrew, and Mav floated on air.

Mav sat in front of his laptop and scrolled for social media jobs. As well-meaning as Douglas was regarding Bert, it still meant Mav was without a job. He highlighted a few jobs that seemed promising, then shut down his computer. Grabbing everything he needed, he strode down the castle corridors, lost in his mind.

"Maverick!"

He glanced behind him and found Randall approaching him at a fast pace. "Hey. Everything okay?"

Randall smiled. "Yes. Can I have a word?"

Mav nodded and followed Randall back the way he'd come to Randall's office. Once they settled, Mav said, "Are you sure everything's okay?"

Randall linked his fingers over some paperwork on his desk and stared at Mav. "I heard what happened with your job."

Mav's heart sank. Of course. The king probably wanted him off the premises and out of the rooms as soon as possible to make way for the new person. "It's okay. I'll get my stuff together and vacate the room today." Mav rose, but Randall waved him down.

"No, no. That's not what I mean. Sorry." Randall smiled. "What are your plans now?"

Mav quirked his lip. "I don't know, to be honest. I daren't use my contacts in case Bert, despite his assurances he wouldn't, has sent a blacklist to them. I'd prefer not to know."

"I can understand that. I know someone who might be able to help you. I don't know if she can for definite, but it would be worthwhile speaking to her. If nothing else, she might have someone else who could help."

"I still need to leave Windsor."

Randall licked his bottom lip as if thinking. "I wouldn't be too hasty. Wait until you're asked to leave."

Mav frowned at the pointed stare Randall gave him. "Why?"

Randall studied his fingers. "All I can say is that you have people other than Douglas working behind the scenes to help."

Mav raised his eyebrows. Who would help him? And why? "All right. I'm a little confused, but okay."

"Trust me. For a short time, at least."

Mav nodded, his mind whirling at the different reasons for Randall's request, but he was happy to continue pretending he had a job for as long as they let him. He hated the idea that Douglas would have someone else doing the job he should be doing, but he couldn't expect the royal family to keep him on when they had a contract with Bert's company.

Would Douglas behave for the new social media manager as he would for Mav? He smiled. He doubted it, but Mav could meet them and train them enough to know what Douglas was like.

Randall scribbled on a piece of paper and handed it to Mav. "Contact her. See what she says."

"I will. Thanks, Randall."

"You're welcome. Come and see me if you need anything."

Mav stood and shook hands with him before leaving. He was just as confused by the time he reached his car, but he brushed it aside. Instead, he focused on what he'd experienced the previous night. He'd been overwhelmed by the feelings and sensations bombarding him, but he'd loved every minute. He had never imagined something seemingly so simple as covering his eyes or stopping his hearing would make things as intense as they did. He couldn't wait to try again.

When he reached home, he made a cup of tea and settled on the sofa to call the number Randall had given him.

"Winter Johnson."

"Good afternoon. My name is Maverick Houghton. I—"

"Maverick! I'm so glad to hear from you. Randall wasn't sure if you would call, but I hoped you would."

Mav's eyes widened at the exuberant greeting. "Um, hi?"

"Randall told me you no longer work for that asshole, Bert."

"That's right, yeah."

"Splendid news!"

"Um, is it?"

A light tinkle of laughter sounded down the line. "Of course! It means you can branch out, Maverick. A little bird told me you want to open your own business, right?"

Who had been talking to her? As far as he knew, Randall didn't know his plans for the future. "Yes, it has been a plan for a while."

"Wonderful. I can help if you'll allow me."

Mav sighed. "I...I'm a little overwhelmed, in all honesty, Winter. What's going on here?"

The laughter returned. "Sorry. I'm so excited for you. I've been following your career, and what you've done for the royal family has been beyond anything anyone expected. You might not see it, but they have responded to you better than anyone else."

"I don't..." He tugged at his hair.

"It's a lot, I know. All you need to decide at the moment is if you want to have your own business and if you want my help. That's it."

How could he say no to someone helping him through the densely populated forest of social media management? "Yes, and yes."

"Wonderful! For the moment, continue as you are. The

royal family has not told you to stop working for them, have they?"

"No, not yet."

"Carry on what you're doing then. Act as if nothing has changed."

"Why?" Mav's mind was at maximum capacity.

"Because if the royal family can see you doing your job though you don't *have* to do it, they will see how much better a person you are than they may have originally thought."

"Okay?"

He knew it sounded like a question, but she bid goodbye, and he let his hand drop to his lap. His tea was getting cold, but he couldn't make himself move. What the hell was going on?

24

DOUGLAS

If nothing else had proven how much Mav was coming to mean to Douglas, it was the fact he'd been so proud of Mav slowing things down the previous evening. It never annoyed him when anyone said words to slow or stop the activities, but the warmth that had seeped through him at Mav's words had shown Douglas that he was in over his head.

"Douglas?"

Freddie's voice brought him back to the room, and he glanced across at his brother, who was sharing a grin with his best friend. Damon had been a part of their lives since Freddie had attended pre-school at age three, and they'd been inseparable since. The man was laid back as fuck and went with the flow of things. Nothing ever seemed to faze him, which was probably why they all got on so well. How he and Freddie had become friends was a mystery to Douglas with how uptight Freddie could be at times.

"What?"

"Did you hear anything I said?"

Douglas raised his eyebrows and smiled. "Of course not." He shook his head. "Sorry. Got things on my mind."

"How is Maverick?" Freddie tilted his head from his seat in the corner of the sofa, appearing as relaxed as he ever got with a knee up on the cushion and his arm laid along the back, almost touching Damon.

"He's all right." He hesitated. "I think I messed up a little."

"Just a little?" Damon smirked.

"Shut up." Douglas threw a cushion his way. "I mean, I got pissed at how his boss was treating him, and I paid him a visit."

When he didn't continue, Freddie prompted him. "What happened?"

"His boss was fine. Cowed in a good way, but Mav doesn't work for him any longer."

"You got him fired?" Freddie sat forward.

"No!" Douglas frowned. "Not in so many words. After speaking with his boss, I made him give Mav three months' pay because he hadn't taken any holidays in ages. It ended up with Mav no longer working for him—which is a fantastic thing, by the way—but now he doesn't have a job and can't work with me because his boss has the contract with the royals."

Freddie rubbed his hand over his mouth, staring at the floor. "I wouldn't worry about the contract. I'll speak with Father about it. The company can always stay on for other members of the family, but as for us, they can forget it. If he wasn't treating Maverick fairly, I'm out."

"Why was Maverick putting up with it?" Damon asked, slouching further down the sofa and resting his feet on the coffee table.

"He couldn't see another way out of it. His father is his

boss's best friend and works for his boss's brother. He was worried his father would lose his job before he could retire in a few years."

Douglas could feel his anger building again, but he'd stepped over the line already. He wasn't going to mess up any more than he already had.

"Is Maverick upset?"

Douglas shook his head. "He doesn't seem bothered about it, but he knows he needs to find another job. He offered to keep working for me for free."

Freddie's forehead creased. "Why can't he?"

Douglas dragged his bottom lip through his teeth. "I want him to, but we're..." He wasn't sure how to explain what he felt for Mav. He knew he was in love with the man, but how could he get around what his father had stipulated? Would Douglas have to leave his family behind if he wanted Mav? Could he do it?

As much as it pained him to think about, he knew he couldn't give up Mav. Not even for his family.

"I'm in love with him."

Freddie and Damon burst out laughing, and Douglas waited for them to recover, which took longer than he liked.

"Jesus," Damon said, wiping his eyes. "I haven't laughed like that in months."

"It's because you're not funny," Freddie deadpanned.

"Fuck you." Damon backhanded him, and they dissolved into a tussle, which Douglas then had to wait for them to finish.

"Have you finished?"

Freddie and Damon glanced at each other, smirked and turned to him. "Yeah," they said in unison.

"Wonderful."

Freddie sat forward again. "We know you're in love with Mav, Doug. You've had hearts in your eyes for weeks."

Douglas's cheeks heated, but he held his brother's gaze. "Father is the problem."

"How come?"

"He found us together. You remember the night I asked you to cover for me?" Freddie nodded. "Father turned up to talk to us both but found Mav and me instead. In no uncertain terms, he told me I could play with the staff but not have a relationship with one."

Freddie sighed and sat back, staring up at the ceiling. "It's how—"

The ringing of Douglas's phone ended what Freddie was going to say, and Douglas answered when he saw it was the club calling.

"Prince Douglas, I have a sub requesting help with a new activity. Are you free to have a session tonight?"

He had hoped to spend the evening with Mav, but he couldn't ignore his responsibilities, although he would have to explain to Mav.

"Sure, Clarice. Can you schedule it for eight o'clock?"

"Of course. Thank you, Prince Douglas. Have a wonderful afternoon."

"I need to find Mav," he said once he'd finished the call. Standing, he slipped his phone back into his pocket.

Freddie stood, clapping him on the shoulder. "Things have a way of working out for the best, Doug. Try not to worry about Father. I have a feeling everything's going to be fine."

Douglas tried not to get his hopes up, but it was difficult when he wanted it so much. "Thanks. Anyway, I'll see you morons later." He slipped out of the door before they could retaliate, although he knew that wouldn't be the end. No doubt he'd have some reaction from them over the next few days. He was glad Freddie had grown out of putting frogs in his bed.

He knocked on Mav's door, trying to hide his smile at seeing him before he was behind closed doors, which was becoming harder and harder to suppress. Mav opened his door with a frown, which quickly morphed into a smile. Douglas stepped closer and waited until Mav closed the door before sealing their lips. He never had enough of kissing this man.

"That's a nice greeting. I'm tempted to ask what you've done." Mav's eyes twinkled.

"I've been good, but they have called me into the club for a teaching lesson at eight. It shouldn't take more than an hour, then I'm all yours." He wrapped his arms around Mav's waist.

Mav slid his hands up Douglas's biceps to his shoulders and linked them at his nape. "It's okay. I know you have a job to do."

"It *is* just a job, you know."

"It's all right. I know we're not…exclusive."

Douglas stepped out of Mav's arms. "What?" His heart raced. Had he got it all wrong? Was this nothing but a notch on Mav's bedpost?

Mav had the decency to seem uncomfortable and sniffed several times. "I heard what the king said. I'm not stupid, Douglas. I know we have an expiry date, though I ignore it most of the time." He pivoted away, striding to his desk and dropping into the chair.

"And that means we're not exclusive? Have you slept with other people?" Douglas wasn't sure he wanted to know the answer, but he needed to hear it.

"No! Never!" Mav stood again. "But you have to work at the club and do the lessons. Are you telling me there's no intercourse during those?"

Douglas's heart calmed. He kept forgetting how little Mav knew about the club. There and then, he decided he'd fight tooth and nail to get Mav into the club, either with or without his father's permission, since his father had changed his tune about wanting Mav to visit the place. He wandered over to Mav, placing his hands on his shoulders.

"I promise you, there is no intercourse during those sessions. You are the one I'm sleeping with. BDSM does not have to culminate in sexual intercourse or any kind of sexual activity. The lessons are just that, lessons. Teaching 'how to' to those who don't have the knowledge yet."

Mav sighed and played with a button on Douglas's shirt. "Sorry. I know I'm a complete newbie when it comes to this."

Douglas tucked a finger under Mav's chin, lifting it to meet his gaze. "And I can teach you."

He peppered kisses all over Mav's face and claimed his lips in a fierce kiss, meant to remind them both of what they had. He wanted nothing more than to express his love for the amazing man in front of him, but he wanted it to be in a place that was special to them, not just anywhere.

When Mav pulled away, gasping for breath and looking like he was ready to be devoured, it made Douglas take a step back after ensuring Mav was steady on his feet.

"You test my resolve." Douglas kept stepping backwards, knowing there was nothing between him and the door.

Mav curled the edges of his lips, and Douglas took in everything about him. He wore navy suit trousers and a waistcoat with a light blue shirt. All he needed was a watch strap hanging from his pocket, and he'd be the image of how someone might dress in the 19th century. Douglas bit his lip as his back hit the door.

"I'll be at yours after the lesson. Is that okay?"

"I'll be waiting," Mav whispered.

Douglas fumbled with the handle but managed to get out the door without appearing too much of a fool. He aimed for his rooms and changed into something less formal, though he would change when he got to the club, which he did as soon as he was there. Clarice had explained what the sub wanted to experience, and Douglas mentally prepared himself. The sub wanted to try out the suspension bar and flogging. Clarice had done her homework and found out the sub had experience with other impact play instruments; therefore, this next step for them wasn't out of the ordinary. Some subs didn't have anyone they could experiment with, and some had trouble choosing a stranger from the club, understandably.

He entered the teaching room, which was equipped with many items to accommodate the different aspects of BDSM as much as possible. They packed away the suspension bar in a cupboard after each use, and Douglas set everything up, ready for when the sub would arrive. Checking everything was in place, he exited and grabbed several bottles of water from the bar before returning.

Setting the bottles to one side, he scratched at his chin. As much as he enjoyed the BDSM aspect of his life, he could do without the extras he had to take part in, mainly without the monitoring. The teaching part was great, but now that he had Mav, even that didn't grab him as much as it had before. If it was only part of his private life, he'd be happier.

A knock brought him from his musings, and he stepped

over to the door, opening it wide. A tall, slender man with closely cropped hair stood on the other side, his hands lightly clasped in front of him, eyes lowered.

"Umar?"

"Yes, Master Douglas. Thank you for taking the time to teach me."

"You're welcome. Come on in."

Umar crossed the threshold, never once lifting his gaze, and stopped in the middle of the room.

"I understand you wish to try the suspension bar with flogging today. Is that correct?" Douglas came to a stop in front of him.

"Yes, Master Douglas."

"Look at me." Umar lifted his head, meeting Douglas's gaze. What he saw behind them made him pause, but it disappeared before he could decipher it. "What are your safe words?"

"The traffic lights, please, sir."

"Good. They have given me your aftercare requirements. Are you ready to begin?"

"Yes, sir."

Douglas led him over to the suspension bar where Umar disrobed. "As this is your first attempt at flogging, I will concentrate on your thighs and ass. If at any time you are not happy with what we are doing, what do you do?"

"Say red if I want you to stop, and yellow if I need a breather."

"Good. Let's get you strapped in."

Douglas focused on fastening the buckles into place, then moved to raise the bar until only the pads of Umar's feet were touching the floor. His muscles bunched, and his body tensed for several seconds before the tension released.

"Colour?"

"Green, sir."

Douglas stepped over to the toy cupboard, selecting the leather-tasselled flogger, which was what they used for a first-timer. He squeezed his hand around the handle, the leather squeaking, and waved it from side to side to make a swishing sound. Umar could see everything he was doing, although he had his head lowered.

"Ready?"

"Yes, sir."

Douglas trailed behind Umar, sliding his hands over the area of his legs and ass he was going to be flogging. That minor act made him think of Mav, and he hesitated because he was touching another person who wasn't his lover. Brushing the thought aside, Douglas lifted his hand away and readied himself.

He started slow and light, checking in periodically with Umar to ensure he was with him and talking him through the process and the rights and wrongs of flogging. Douglas believed subs needed to know how the process worked; therefore, they could also understand when things might go wrong.

Douglas's wrist ached, and he stopped, his breathing elevated.

"Colour?"

"Green, sir."

Umar's head hung, but he was panting. Douglas released him from the buckles and carried him to the sofa in the corner, where he praised the man and rubbed lotion into his body. He covered him with a sheet and grabbed a bottle of water and some orange juice. Douglas sat on the floor beside

Umar's head, stroking his fingers through Umar's hair as Umar sipped the orange through a straw.

Each submissive was different in what they wanted and needed from a scene, but also how they needed to be cared for afterwards. Some needed to holding and comforting, some wanted to be left alone, some were in between. Nothing was right or wrong, but Douglas had always struggled with the aftercare of those like Umar. Douglas wanted to cuddle and assure him over and over again that he was an amazing person and worthy, but it wasn't what Umar needed.

Once Umar's aftercare was complete, Douglas helped him into the trousers he'd been wearing when he arrived and guided him to the changing rooms. Umar thanked him profusely and confirmed it was something he enjoyed and would consider in the future. Douglas reminded him to speak with Clarice and update his hard limits list.

Douglas bid goodbye and returned to the teaching room to clean and set it to rights ready for the next lesson, then strode to the Monitors' changing room. Once he'd shut the door behind him, he slumped into a chair and stared at the wall. He had done nothing sexual with Umar, but he felt guilty about touching the man. Mav knew what Douglas's job was, but he needed to speak to him in more detail or find some way to bring him into the club to allow him to see what happened. He was making more of things than he needed to, but for the first time in a long time, he had to contend with thoughts about screwing up.

Douglas jumped into the shower and washed himself clean of the club before redressing in his casual clothes. He checked out with Clarice—she needed a pay rise—and strode to his car, aiming straight for Mav's building. By the time he was knocking on Mav's door, he was breathing heavily again. He couldn't wait to see him.

As soon as the door closed behind them, Douglas reeled Mav in for a kiss. He couldn't restrain himself any further.

"Missed you." His words were muffled against Mav's lips.

Mav pulled away. "I'm glad you're here. Did everything go okay?"

"Yeah, great. I wanted to talk to you about it, though."

Mav stepped away and frowned. "Sounds ominous."

"No, I had a few thoughts as I was doing it and wanted to talk to you about it."

"All right. Let me grab some drinks, and we can chat on the sofa. Go choose a movie to put on in the background."

Douglas leaned forward and pecked him on the lips again, then weaved around him to the sofa. Dropping into the seat, he grabbed the remote and switched the TV on, bringing up the list of movies on demand. Mav hadn't said what he was in the mood for, but they could always change it afterwards. Finding *Spiderman*, he let it start as Mav entered the room.

"Good choice."

Mav passed him a mug of tea and sat close, but far enough away, they could see each other.

"What do you need to talk—" Someone knocked at the door, and Mav frowned. "Are you expecting anyone?"

Douglas shook his head. "Why would I? This is your place."

"I'll get rid of them."

Mav crossed to the door, opening it a little, then wider.

"I'm Commissioner Thomas. Can I speak to Prince Douglas, please?"

Douglas heard the words and frowned. Mav glanced over

his shoulder and invited the person in when Douglas nodded.

He stood. "Commissioner Thomas, how can I—" Douglas froze when his father entered, followed by Freddie, Eric and two other police officers. "What's going on?"

Commissioner Thomas stepped forward. "Douglas Sutcliffe, you are under arrest for the assault of Umar Troche."

"What?"

"Say nothing until we get a lawyer for you, Douglas." His father was every bit the king at that moment, but Douglas could also see something else behind his eyes.

"I don't understand."

"Please come with us."

The two police officers came forward, one pulling out handcuffs.

"Is that really necessary, Commissioner?" King Andrew frowned.

"Yes, Your Majesty."

Douglas swallowed and glanced at Mav. Mav's face had drained of all colour, but Freddie was there, holding him up. He met Freddie's gaze, and Freddie nodded once, flicking his eyes towards Mav. Douglas felt better knowing Freddie would keep an eye on Mav. Whatever the hell was going on, he hoped they would sort it sooner rather than later and, with any luck, with no damage to his relationship with Mav.

The cold cuffs clinked closed around his wrists behind his back, and his mind raced, trying to figure out what was happening.

As they marched him past his father, the man reached out and squeezed his shoulder. "Eric, stay with him. Douglas, remember, not a word until someone is with you. Understand?"

Douglas nodded and stepped out the door, unable to stop himself from glancing back once more to Mav. Would Mav believe his innocence?

25

MAVERICK

Mav watched as they took Douglas away, the king closing the door with a grimace toward the remaining occupants of the apartment. After they left, he stared at the door as if it was some sort of joke, and Douglas would fly back through it shouting, "Surprise!" He didn't, though, and it wasn't a joke.

Freddie's hand squeezed his shoulder. "Father will sort this out, Maverick. I promise he will. There is no way Douglas did this."

Mav didn't reply. His mind was whirling with thoughts, images and conversations, parsing through every interaction they'd ever had, checking every bit of information he knew, then double-checking it.

He rounded on Freddie. "He didn't do this. We need to find out who did." He brushed past the heir to the throne and stalked to his desk, opening his laptop and sitting in front of it.

"What are you doing?"

"Researching. We need to figure out who had enough

motive and opportunity to frame Douglas for this. This Umar guy? Was he the one who had the lesson with Douglas earlier?"

When Freddie stayed quiet, Mav glanced up and raised an eyebrow. Freddie worked his jaw from side to side, then nodded. "He was. I haven't seen the evidence, but apparently, Umar's wounds were lashes of broken skin that hadn't been cleaned or cared for."

Before Freddie had finished talking, Mav was shaking his head. "No way. Douglas would prefer to have taken the lashes himself before leaving a sub in that condition."

"I agree," Damon said.

"That makes three of us." Freddie stepped closer and clenched his hands. "Someone is setting him up, and I want to know who."

"My boss is likely to have a grudge, but I doubt he could've set this up so quickly. Also, I'm not convinced he knows about the royal family's involvement in the club." Mav rubbed his forehead, a headache forming—from the stress, no doubt.

Damon nodded. "Yeah. I'd have made a bet on Talon doing it, but how can he do it from behind bars?" He glanced at Freddie, who shrugged.

"There has to be someone else we haven't thought of," Freddie said.

In the silence that followed, Mav grabbed for a thought just out of reach. When one of them went to talk, he held up his hand, closed his eyes and tried to grasp it. Excluding the clash with the media after the picture of Douglas with his pants down in an alley, there had been another altercation Douglas had told him about, but what was it?

Mav tapped his index finger against his forehead in a

rapid beat. Something had happened at the club. Well, nothing had happened, but he'd argued with someone. He stopped tapping.

"His cousin!" Mav stared at Freddie. "He'd had an argument with his cousin at the club. Something about staying away from his sub and not interfering. I can't remember the name of the guy. Douglas said a server pulled him away, pretending there was an issue, and Douglas could get away from the guy."

Freddie and Damon shared a look. Freddie crossed his arms. "We have many cousins, Mav. At last count, it was something like seventeen."

"How many are men?"

Frowning, Freddie gazed out of the window. "Ten if you only include the ones who frequent the club."

"All right." Mav drew in a long breath. "Tell me their names. It might jog my memory."

"John, Philip, William, Louis, um…Albert, Patrick, Henry, Charles, Christ—"

"Charles! It was Charles. Douglas said Charles approached him at the club in the reception area, telling him in no uncertain terms he needed to stay away from Charles's sub. Douglas pretended he and the sub had been talking about Charles's birthday, but Charles didn't believe him."

Damon rubbed a hand over his jaw, the scratchiness audible in the silence. "We need to be careful if it's him." He stared at Freddie. "They're not ones you need to cross, Freddie."

"Why?" Mav asked. He felt like this little titbit of information was something he should've known about.

Freddie sighed. "Charles's mother is Father's sister. She has vocally opposed the LGBTQ+ community. She has been a thorn in all our sides for many, many years. Aunt Charlotte thinks only heterosexual male members of the family should reign."

Mav stared at him with his mouth open wide. "What the actual fuck? What century is she living in?"

"She's traditional in every sense of the word. If there is a loophole or anything, she will find it no matter what it's about." Damon gritted his teeth.

Mav thought through the new information. "Do you think Talon convinced Charles to set Douglas up?"

"It's not outside of the realm of the possible. There's no way of proving it, though. There's also this other guy that had been involved with Kendal. Harvey someone. He seems to have disappeared." Freddie turned back to the window, staring out of the glass.

"Could you speak to the server? Get their side of the story for the altercation. We can get statements from Kendal and Quinn, too. Anyone else who might help us out?"

"This is all stuff the police will do, Maverick."

Mav pinched the bridge of his nose with one hand and rubbed his forehead with his other. "I know, but I have to do something. The police won't investigate any of this until after they've spoken to Douglas. If we can get some of the information ready to go, we could give it to the lawyer and get him to use it or something. I don't know, Your Highness, but I have to do something."

Freddie snorted. "You can't get rid of the tags even when you're riled, can you?"

Mav smirked. "Nope."

His phone rang, and he jogged to the coffee table to grab it, hoping it was some news on Douglas. His shoulders slumped a little when he saw it was Zara—not that he didn't want to talk to her. He put her on speakerphone.

"Hey, you."

"What the hell happened? I saw on the news sites that they arrested Douglas. What the fuck is going on?"

Mav dropped onto the sofa, resting his head against the back. "I have no idea, Z. We're trying to figure it out. We think he's been set up."

"Who would do that to him?"

"He has enemies, the same as any other member of the royal family, I'm sure." He glanced at Freddie, who frowned but nodded his agreement to Mav's words.

"Well, we're on our way. We should be with you in five or six hours."

Mav sat upright. "You don't have to—"

"I know, but we want to. You need someone by your side."

Mav was close to tears but sniffed them back. "Thanks, Z. I have Prince Frederick and his best friend here."

There was a pause, then Zara squealed. "Seriously? You're in the same room as Prince Frederick?"

Mav rolled his eyes, his cheeks heating at the embarrassing noises his best friend was making through the phone. "Yes, and I have been several times. This is not an irregular occurrence."

"But...he's Prince Frederick!"

"And you are a lesbian. Keep reminding yourself of that. Or better yet, let your fiance remind you."

"Shut your mouth, Mav. I know I'm a lesbian. It doesn't stop me from appreciating what a fine work of art the man is."

Freddie laughed, slapping Damon on the shoulder with the back of his hand.

"Oh, shit. Did he hear? Am I on speakerphone, and you didn't tell me?"

"Loud and clear, and I appreciate your words," Frederick said with a grin.

"Um…hi, Your Majesty." Zara's voice shook, and Mav couldn't help but laugh.

"Zara, get off the phone before you cause more trouble than I know you're already likely to cause when we get there." Tex's voice was full of humour. "Bye, Mav. We'll message you when we're close."

"Thanks, Tex. See you soon."

"They're going to be a handful," Damon said when Mav hung up.

"Whatever you're thinking…triple it," Mav agreed.

They laughed, then sobered. Damon slapped his hands on his thighs and stood. "Right, let me start the kettle, and we can go through everything again before we plan a course of action."

They spent several hours going through what they each knew, getting information from subs that had been involved with Talon, and trying to find more information about this Harvey guy. Freddie's father called with updates. At that moment, it seemed Douglas was being questioned about what happened between him and Umar. Mav knew it would be difficult for Douglas because he had to keep certain things to himself. The NDAs didn't give them much leeway.

Freddie and Damon left Mav in the early morning. The last update had been that they had postponed questioning until the following day, which meant Douglas had to spend the rest of the night locked up. As much as Mav wanted to break down and cry into Douglas's pillow, he made himself keep searching. He knew how to find information on the internet and social media, and he put his skills to good use.

By the time Zara and Tex turned up at six in the morning, Mav was bleary-eyed and exhausted, but several cups of coffee later, he was raring to go again.

"Mav! You need to get some sleep. You will be no good to Douglas unless you're at your best." Zara gripped him by the shoulders and spun him to face her.

"I can't, Z. I need to help him."

"You are. Look at everything you've found out. Now, you need to sleep. I'll wake you if anyone rings, okay?"

Mav slumped and rubbed a hand over his face. "All right. I'm taking my phone—"

"Not a chance. I'll keep it with me, and the moment it rings, I'll come and get you."

Mav glared at her but agreed. As he crawled into bed fully dressed, he grabbed the pillow Douglas usually used when he stayed over and clung to it. As his tears soaked into the fabric by his cheek, he prayed they'd find who had done this. He refused to believe they wouldn't free Douglas.

"Mav!"

The quiet voice and persistent shaking of his shoulder roused him from his sleep. "What?"

It took several minutes to figure out why Zara was standing in his bedroom, then everything flooded into his brain. He scrambled upright.

"What's happened?"

"There's someone here to see you." Zara's voice showed her uncertainty.

Mav stood, stumbling when his legs trembled beneath his weight. "Who is it?"

"Prince Frederick, Damon and two other people I don't know." Mav frowned but started forward before Zara stopped him with an arched eyebrow. "Don't you want to freshen up first?"

He glanced down at his rumpled outfit and knew he needed to do something. "Okay, but I'll be quick."

"They're not going anywhere."

"I know, but if they have information to help Douglas, it might need to be done sooner than later."

He rushed through a shower, decided not to shave, and dressed before he was properly dry. After he'd pulled on some socks, he exited into the living room. Freddie, Damon and Quinn sat and stood in various places around the room with someone Mav didn't know.

"Sorry it took me so long," he said to Freddie, who was standing by the window with his arms crossed and a tense posture. "What happened?"

"Don't be sorry, Mav. Zara has shown me some things you've been working on, and it's great. Thank you." Freddie glanced at the floor, then back at him. "There's been a development."

Mav's heart skipped several beats. "What?"

"Let me introduce you to someone." He indicated with his hand. "Mav, meet Umar."

The man was tall and slender, with closely cropped black hair. Mav glanced at Freddie as a wave of anger swept through him. "Why is he here?"

Freddie held his hands up, palms out. "Listen to what he has to say."

Mav firmed his jaw and crossed his arms over his chest.

He didn't want to hear anything this person had to say, but if Freddie thought it was important, he'd listen.

"I'm sorry for—"

"I don't want to hear your apology. I don't need it. Tell me what you need to." Umar flinched at Mav's words, and he felt a certain satisfaction.

Umar bowed his head, his fingers tangling between themselves. "I lied about Douglas. I was told to request a lesson with him and, afterwards, to go home. Once at home, a man would meet me there to…"

Damon moved to sit next to Umar, and Mav bristled at the comfort he was giving the man who had lied about what Douglas had done to him. When he opened his mouth to complain, Freddie squeezed his shoulder and shook his head.

After several minutes, Umar continued, "The man would meet me at my house and flog me again, after which I was to call the police and blame Prince Douglas." Umar's water-filled gaze met his. "They said they would go after my sister if I didn't do as they'd asked."

"Why are you here then?"

"The second flogging wasn't supposed to be bad, just enough to break a little skin and make it look like Prince Douglas hadn't completed the aftercare. The man didn't use a flogger. It was worse…much worse than I was told it would be, but I did what I was told to do." Umar dropped his gaze again, tears sliding down his cheeks. "How could I choose between my family and pointing the finger at an innocent man?"

"Umar went to Quinn and told him what happened. Once Quinn contacted me, we hid his family. He has no reason to lie any longer. No one can touch his family." Freddie stared at Mav.

Mav dropped into an armchair, weary. "Can we get this cleared up and Douglas free?" he asked Freddie.

"We can, but we need information on this Harvey guy. That's who did this to Umar."

Mav's eyebrows rose. "Not Charles?"

Freddie shook his head, his mouth a hard line. "We can't prove who called Umar. It could've been Charles, or it could've been a third person. We have nothing to link Charles to anything other than our suspicions."

Mav dropped his head in his hands, then straightened, wandering over to his desk where he'd spent several hours of the night. "I've found out some things about Harvey."

Freddie and Damon drifted closer. "How did you find him?" Damon asked.

"Social media is my bitch." Mav cracked a smile. "Harvey Johnson, age twenty-nine, worked several jobs over the past ten years, usually bartending or in supermarkets. He has no family I could find but has plenty of friends, according to his photos. They have arrested him several times over the past five years for GBH, assault and domestic violence."

"Fucker." Damon placed a hand over his mouth. "How did we not know about him?"

"He's been in the BDSM community for two years," Mav added.

"I wonder if he's tried to get a membership at the club?" Freddie said. "It might give him the motive to do what someone else had told him to. They could've offered him a place at the club as payment."

Mav frowned. "Who has control over who is and isn't given membership?"

"Several people, but members can vouch for someone, and if their checks come back okay, they'll be accepted. I know for a fact Harvey wouldn't have been because of the specifics of his police record, but *he* wouldn't know."

"It makes sense. Theoretically, Talon could've contacted Charles and asked him to mete out punishment to Douglas, but from what you've told me, Charles doesn't seem to be a person to do what other people tell him to. Do you think he's behind all of this?"

Freddie shared a look with Damon. "Yes. I have no proof, but it fits. I'm not sure how Charles and Talon connect other than being at the same club, but it's not impossible that he orchestrated it. In my opinion, he seems to have had a hand in what happened with Douglas, Umar and Harvey, though."

"You need to speak to your father." Mav held out the sheets of paper he'd printed with the evidence he'd found on Harvey. "I want Douglas out of there."

Damon took the paper and turned away. Freddie rested his hand on Mav's shoulder again. "Father will come around to you and Douglas, Mav. Fight as hard for your relationship as you have for Douglas's freedom, okay?"

Mav's throat closed up, and he nodded.

"Let's get going." Freddie stepped towards the front door, Damon and Umar following behind, but Quinn closed the distance between them.

"Master Douglas is one in a million. I wish you every happiness, Mav, but could I ask one favour?" Mav nodded. "Please don't stop him from doing the good work he's doing with the subs here. Many would fall through the cracks if he didn't check up on them like he's been doing. There's only so much other submissives can do, but a Master like him can make an enormous difference to their lives. I don't mean sexually. I mean the visits. Please help him continue."

Mav nodded his head. "I intend to."

Quinn wrapped his thin arms around Mav's shoulders in a small hug, and Mav could do no more than reciprocate. "Thank you."

The four men left, leaving Zara, Tex and him standing in silence.

"Well, that was interesting."

Mav glanced at his two friends. "You must be exhausted. Why don't you get some sleep? There's not much else we can do until I hear from Freddie again."

"Freddie, is it?"

"Oh, shut up!"

FREDERICK

Damon slammed the car door harder than usual, his fists clenched on his knees.

"Are you okay?" Freddie asked from beside him. He glanced to the front of the car and nodded at the driver, who pulled away from the kerb.

Damon sighed. "Not really. I can't believe this fucker won't just disappear."

Freddie chuckled. "Yeah, I know the feeling. Unfortunately, Talon is safe where he is, and Charles is untouchable at the moment. We can build a case against him, though. I'm going to collate all the stories and as much evidence as I can against him and Aunt Charlotte and whoever else is involved. It can't be just those two."

"They have many backers, but some are too clever and hide behind the scenes."

The tone of voice showed what Damon thought of those people, and Freddie wholeheartedly agreed. He took the sheaf of paper Maverick had given them and flicked through it. Maverick was bloody good, thorough. If he did that for all other aspects of his job, he would be a force to be reckoned with.

Freddie glanced over his shoulder at the car following behind them, containing Umar and Quinn, and pulled out his phone.

"I'm busy, Frederick." His father's voice was hard, but Freddie knew he'd listen.

"I have some information to help Douglas."

"What?" he barked.

"Where are you? We need to do this in person, preferably with the police present."

His father remained quiet for a moment, then asked him to wait. The phone went silent, and Freddie caught Damon's gaze. His expression was tight, and Freddie knew his would be the same. He itched to remove that look from his best friend, but only ending this case would work.

"Frederick, come to the police station but go around to the back."

"Yes, Father. We'll be there shortly."

He closed the phone and asked the driver to take them to where his father was obviously waiting.

"Do you think Umar will tell the truth to the police?" Damon asked.

It was worrying Freddie, too. Just because Umar had admitted what truly happened to them didn't mean he would do it to the police. After all, he would get into trouble for telling a lie in the first place. Hopefully, his father could stop that from happening. Umar had been punished enough for his transgressions, in Freddie's opinion.

"I think he will. He knows right from wrong, even if he fell onto the wrong side for a short time. If someone threatened my family, I would probably do the same thing. You do anything for family."

Damon twisted to look out of the window, and Freddie frowned. As much as he knew everything there was to know about Damon, the man confused him sometimes. Freddie turned his attention back to the papers. There was a lot of information about Harvey Johnson, and he was sure they'd be able to find him at one of the addresses listed. Maverick would be an excellent investigator.

They arrived at the police station and climbed out, waiting for Umar and Quinn to join them.

"Are you okay?" he asked Umar.

The sub wrung his hands between him but nodded. "I will be. No matter what happens to me, I will make sure Prince Douglas is free. It's not fair to him, and I deeply apologise."

Freddie gave a small smile. "Douglas is the one you need to apologise to, but by telling the truth, you are mending some of those bridges already. The police are waiting for what we have to tell them."

He placed a hand on Umar's elbow, knowing his back would be extremely raw and sore, and guided him into the station. Immediately, they were shepherded through to a room with no windows, where his father, the Commissioner and two police officers waited.

"Frederick, what do you have to tell us?" His father frowned, his gaze flicking to the subs, but he didn't ask them to leave.

"Umar has something to tell the officers in charge of the case."

Andrew raised his eyebrows and glanced at the officers. "Commissioner?"

The older gentleman stepped closer but not too close. "Umar, let's take this into an interview room—"

"No, please, sir. I'm happy to talk with everyone present," Umar said, holding onto Quinn's hand.

The Commissioner shared a look with the officers and the king, then nodded. "Okay. Take a seat. Sampson, please fetch a recorder."

One officer dashed out of the room, and Umar stepped over to a chair the Commissioner had pointed to and pulled Quinn down beside him. The rest of them fanned out around the room, trying not to crowd them.

When Sampson returned, he placed the recording device on the table and started the interview. By the time Umar had finished his amended statement and answered any questions the officers had, Freddie's father looked pleased. Catching his eye, his father nodded his head at him.

"Okay, I've heard enough," the Commissioner said. He stared at Andrew. "Let's get your boy out."

King Andrew held out his hand to the Commissioner. "Thank you."

Freddie stepped closer. "There is one more thing, too." He held out the sheets of paper. "This is some information we found on Harvey Johnson. I hope it will be useful."

The Commissioner raised his eyebrows when he shuffled through them. "You might need to explain your sources for this."

Freddie smiled. "Not a problem. Douglas's boyfriend, Maverick, is a social media manager. He had the social media world at his fingertips. I'm sure he would have evidenced where this information came from, but if he hasn't, he won't hesitate to tell you."

The Commissioner nodded and passed the paper to

Sampson. "Come on, then. He's been in there long enough. Sampson, can you please finish up with Umar? Then he can go home."

"I'll ensure he's taken home," Freddie said.

His father pulled him into his embrace. "Thank you, son."

"Don't thank me, Father. Thank Maverick. You know they're good for each other. Let them be together."

Andrew pulled back and sighed. He nodded but said nothing, then followed the Commissioner out of the room. Freddie blew out a breath and leaned back against the wall next to Damon. They shared a smile, then waited for Umar to finish.

DOUGLAS

Spending the last few hours in a dreary room with only the necessities had not been his plan for the evening, but after several hours of questioning, he was glad of the reprieve. He'd not been able to sleep at all, and he'd spent the time remembering everything about Mav he could. Hearing his voice in his head as he sang to him. Smiling at the expressions on his face in reaction to different things. Anything that took him away from where he was.

He couldn't believe Umar had accused him of lashing him and leaving him with wounds. It hurt to *think* of leaving a sub in that state; he would never do it. He wondered what possessed Umar to do such a thing. Did he want money? Was someone else making him do it? Douglas didn't know, but he hoped Mav was okay.

There was no window in his room; therefore, he had no concept of time when the door to his room—cell—opened, and his father strode in. Douglas fought to stop his tears from escaping as he stood. Someone stepped into the room behind him, but his father didn't care, taking Douglas into his arms and gripping him. Douglas screwed his eyes closed, not wanting to show weakness.

"I'm sorry for everything," his father whispered into his ear. "I've been trying to keep you too close and forgot what it was like to be the recipient of an overbearing father. I want what's best for you, but it's because I'm your father. I have to step back because it's your life, and you get to make the mistakes you need to. Mistakes you learn from. I understand that, but I don't know if I'll be better straight away."

King Andrew pulled back, his eyes as wet as Douglas's. Douglas had never expected any of those words to come from his father, but he'd needed to hear them more than he realised.

"Thank you, Father." He wiped his face. "Not that I'm not grateful, but what's brought you here?"

"You're free to go."

It was the Commissioner who had spoken, stepping from behind his father and into view.

Douglas raised his eyebrows. "What?"

"The victim has rescinded the charges against you."

Douglas stared at his father, who nodded and smiled. "The victim came forward to explain the truth of the matter. We have dropped all charges against you."

"Just like that? I don't understand."

The king clapped him on his back. "I'll explain later. Come on. Let's get you home. Your mother wants to see you."

They went through all the paperwork needed to get Douglas back into the outside world, but instead of exiting out the front door, they went through some back way out to a blacked-out car waiting for them. One of his father's security officers opened the back door for them, and they slid in.

The journey was short but silent, and Douglas hadn't expected any different. His father was a man of silence and retrospection after something like this happened, but Douglas was sure he would have plenty to say once they'd arrived.

"Father, could I freshen up before we talk?" he asked once they were traversing the corridors of the castle.

"Of course, son. Come by my chambers once you're ready."

They parted, and Douglas escaped to his rooms. After a long, hot shower, he dressed in jeans and a polo shirt. He'd thought about checking in with Mav, but he wanted to know what had happened before he spoke with him, then he could pass the information on. He chose to ring him after he'd spoken with his father.

Sliding his phone into his pocket, he strode to his parents' room. When he opened the door, it surprised him to find the room filled with several people.

"Close the door, Douglas. Some people are keeping themselves on the down-low," Freddie said as he approached, giving him a bear hug once he shut the door.

Douglas held onto Freddie and closed his eyes, his body trembling with the emotion he was trying to suppress. When he finally pulled back, he received a similar hug from George, then his mother, who wiped his face before cradling him until more tears escaped.

"My boy," she whispered. "I'm so sorry for what you've been through. We all knew you had nothing to do with it. Never think otherwise."

"I know, Mother," he whispered.

"There's someone who's been dying to see you," she said as she pulled back, a twinkle in her eye. "Don't worry about what anyone else thinks for the moment, my dear. Promise me?"

Douglas nodded, having an idea who it was. She moved to the side, and there stood Mav, wringing his hands. Douglas covered the distance between them in seconds and wrapped his arms around him. Mav buried his head in Douglas's neck and sobbed while Douglas did the same. He was holding Mav too tightly, but he couldn't let go yet. He needed time to make sure this was all real and not a dream from which he'd wake back in the cell.

He had no clue how long they'd been holding each other, but he became aware of conversation around them, and he let Mav go. Cupping his boyfriend's face, he lowered his mouth, leaving a chaste kiss on Mav's lips.

"I love you," he mumbled into Mav's ear as he slid his arms around him again.

Mav pulled back, mouth wide. "What?"

"You heard me." He smirked.

Mav smiled and cradled Douglas's face between his hands. "I love you." They shared another small kiss before a throat cleared.

"I understand you needing to remind yourself he's alive and well, but can we get down to business?"

Mav's expression turned horrified at his father's words, and he jumped back, though Douglas grabbed his hand before he could go too far.

"Andrew, that wasn't nice," his mother admonished. "Leave them be."

"What? I don't mind the reunion, but do I need to see my son with his tongue down his boyfriend's throat?"

Douglas snorted as laughter flowed through the room. How the idea of him and Mav together wasn't upsetting his father was beyond him, especially after their last conversation regarding it.

"Let's go through what we've found out."

Douglas sat on a loveseat, pulling Mav with him despite his protestations. As Freddie began explaining what had happened, Douglas took in the occupants of the room. Freddie, George, Damon and his parents he'd expected, but he hadn't expected Quinn, Kendal and a woman he didn't recognise.

"This was all Talon's doing?" Douglas summarised.

Mav's hand squeezed his, and he noticed the tension running through the room.

"Not entirely," his father said. "We believe Charles is behind it."

Douglas frowned. "Cousin Charles? Why would he…" His voice trailed off as he remembered the argument. "It makes a certain sense. He's always had it in for us. For me, especially."

"That's his mother's doing," Queen Louisa snapped. "The vile woman needs to receive some of her own medicine."

"Now, now, love. Don't go upsetting yourself. I will deal with everything. You have my word."

His mother reached for his father's hand, covering it. "I know. I hate that her part of the family is targeting mine."

"There will be repercussions, but we need to find evidence that points to Charles. Until we have it, we have nothing," Freddie said.

"The key thing is we've cleared Douglas's name, and he's back home with us."

"And we have Mav to thank for that," his father said, surprising them all.

"Don't forget Umar," Kendal added, a hint of defiance showing in his body language as he faced the king.

His father smiled. "And Umar. Douglas, this is Umar's sister, Amaya. She is also a sub at the club."

"Nice to meet you, Amaya."

"Thank you for your kindness, though I know we don't deserve it. We have been told what happened and will speak to Umar as soon as we can. I don't think it's fair for him to be at the club after what he did, regardless of his reasons. We will find—"

"No." Douglas held out a hand. "I'm sorry for interrupting, but we will welcome him back to the club with open arms. He had a hard choice to make, and many people would have faltered. In the end, he spoke up. That's what matters. As far as I'm concerned, this is the end of the matter." He glanced at his father, receiving a nod.

"Thank you, Prince Douglas. You are very generous."

"Right, I think you're all up to speed, so you may all go back to your day. Thank you for being here to help clear things up," King Andrew said. "Douglas, Mav, would you mind staying for a few minutes longer?"

Douglas wanted nothing more than to get Mav beneath him as soon as possible, but he'd wait. A few more minutes wouldn't make a difference. He received hugs from everyone except Amaya before they left, then it was just the four of them. Douglas could feel Mav's hand trembling in his, and he squeezed it, hoping to reassure him.

His father rubbed a hand over his chin repeatedly as he stared at the floor. It was what he always did when he was trying to gather his thoughts.

"Maverick, I want to thank you for everything you did to figure out what happened. I know you spent many hours searching for information to help. Not only with this, but your work ethic has been flawless, too. With that in mind, I would like to offer you the chance to keep your position as social media manager for Douglas. Technically," his father glanced at him with a smirk, "it's a conflict of interest, but I know you work well together, and you have not let your relationship interfere with the work that needs to be done."

When Mav stayed silent, Douglas smiled and prodded him. "Oh, um…yes, Your Majesty. That would be fantastic, but, um…" He took a deep breath and straightened his spine. "Can I clarify, does this mean your opinion about our relationship has changed? Because if it hasn't, I would have to decline."

Douglas stared at Mav, his heart galloping at his words. Why would he say no? Mav wouldn't meet his gaze, choosing instead to stare at King Andrew.

"It has been brought to my attention that my opinion was incorrect." He smiled at his wife. "I have never seen my son as happy as he has been these past few weeks, and despite my initial reservations, I believe we can weather whatever is thrown our way regarding your relationship. All I ask is one thing from you both, *if* there comes a time when you are having second thoughts about your relationship, come to Louisa or me first. It's easier to deal with things when they haven't already made it into the press, as you well know, Maverick."

Douglas and Mav shared a glance and a smile before agreeing to the terms. His heart was ready to burst.

"In which case, you have our blessing. Though you don't need it." The king sighed.

His mother patted his arm with a chuckle. "All our children grow up eventually, Andrew. It's better to stick with them than to fight with them about it."

Douglas couldn't wait any longer. He stood, pulling Mav

with him. Releasing him, he stepped closer to his parents, giving them hugs and watching as they did the same for Mav, despite his shocked expression. As soon as they said their goodbyes, Douglas jogged them through the corridors until they reached Douglas's rooms. When they were inside, Douglas rounded on Mav and pressed him back against the door, ravaging his mouth. He needed to feel Mav. He needed to be in control again.

"Mav, I need you."

"I'm all yours."

Douglas slid his hands under Mav's thighs and lifted him, allowing his legs to wrap around his waist. He shuffled towards the bedroom, barely keeping his eyes open enough to ensure they didn't bump into anything. He didn't want to hurt Mav. He felt the bed at his knees and crawled onto the covers, laying Mav down, all the while twining their tongues together and breathing heavily through his nose.

Mav's hands were roaming his back, but Douglas needed skin on skin. He rose to his knees, dragging the polo shirt over his head and throwing it aside. Mav squirmed beneath him. For a change, Mav was not in a suit. He wore black jeans and a T-shirt. Douglas raked his nails down Mav's chest until he reached the hem, then dragged it up and over his head, throwing it to join his. He leaned down, taking Mav's mouth again. This time, Mav's nails scored down his back until he slipped his hands beneath the waistband of Douglas's jeans. When Mav's hands squeezed his ass, Douglas bucked forward, their cocks pressing against each other.

Douglas needed more. He scooted down the bed, undoing Mav's jeans and sliding down the zipper. His cock strained at his briefs, and Douglas's mouth watered.

"Shift up. Put your head on a pillow."

Mav did as instructed, and as Mav moved, Douglas dragged his jeans down his legs until he left him in his briefs. Douglas slid off the bed, taking care of his own clothes and climbed back on, naked. His cock was hot and heavy and straining for relief. As he crawled up Mav's body, he kissed his skin, intermittently licking and nipping as he rose.

The light flick of his tongue over Mav's nipples had Mav thrashing beneath him. He closed the distance between their mouths once more, taking Mav's gasp into his mouth.

"This is going to be quick, but I promise it will satisfy," he said, pulling back.

He left the bed, striding across the room to the chest of drawers on the opposite side. Sliding open the top drawer, he pulled out two ties and closed the drawer again. He headed to the bottom of the bed, opening the chest at the base and rummaging for a second until he found earplugs. Closing the lid, he climbed over it to the bottom of the bed and crawled towards Mav, who was watching with wide eyes and his bottom lip held tight between his teeth.

Douglas straddled Mav's hips, their groins lined up but not touching. "Okay, my plan is to blindfold you, put the earplugs in and tie your wrists to the headboard. Are you happy to try?"

Mav exhaled, nodded and answered a breathy, "Yes, Sir."

Douglas grinned. "Let me do your wrists first, and you can see."

He reached for one tie, winding it around Mav's wrists and through the slats in the headboard. He could have made Mav grip the slats, but he wanted Mav to feel what it was like to give over control fully. Although Mav had never tried it that Douglas was aware of, Douglas wanted to show him how exquisite he could feel from allowing Douglas free rein.

Once he'd finished tying Mav's wrists, Douglas told him to pull on them. When Mav did, his pupils dilated, and Douglas smirked.

"Now for your ears."

Douglas pushed one earplug in, peppering kisses along Mav's jaw. He moved to the other side, repeating his actions but whispering, "I love you," before putting the plug in. When Douglas glanced at Mav, he had a dreamy look in his eyes and a small smile on his face.

"Now for your eyes," he mouthed.

As Douglas slid the silk tie over Mav's eyes, Mav's body arched towards him. Douglas couldn't remember ever seeing someone as sensitive to sensations as Mav was. He was sure they had many more experiences to take part in over the coming years because Douglas was all in. When the blindfold was in place, Mav repeated a declaration of love over and over. Once he secured everything, Douglas skimmed the tips of his fingers over Mav's chest and abdomen, hooking his fingers into Mav's briefs before sliding his own body backwards and taking the underwear with him. When he reached Mav's feet, Mav curled his body, and Douglas threw the briefs behind him.

He wrapped his hands around Mav's ankles, sliding Mav's legs wider and encouraging him to bend his knees. Once Mav was in the position Douglas wanted him in, Douglas reached over for the lube and condom. Knowing his patience was wearing thin, Douglas slid the condom on before preparing Mav. While his fingers worked to open Mav as much as possible, Douglas licked and sucked at the head of Mav's shaft.

Mav wriggled and squirmed beneath the onslaught, pleas falling from his lips along with the colours when Douglas tapped his chin. Douglas pulled off and inhaled roughly. He slicked his cock and held it against Mav's entrance. A chant of pleas followed his actions, and Douglas pressed forward. Once he was fully seated, Douglas encouraged Mav to lock his heels at Douglas's lower back by pushing against his feet and slid his hands under Mav's back to his shoulders.

Unable to resist, he took Mav's mouth and moved. As high and needy as they both were, it didn't take either of them long to reach the peak and fall over the edge. When he'd released Mav from his restraints, blindfold and earplugs, Douglas wrapped his arms around his boyfriend and held him close, pressing kisses to his forehead and reminding himself they had the future to look forward to.

MAVERICK

av stared across at Zara, unbelieving of what she had asked.

"What? I'm not the only person who would want to know, Mav. Your boyfriend is a prince! What else am I going to ask?" Zara smirked.

"I don't think people want to know whether I'm moving into the castle, Z." Douglas lifted his hand to his mouth, and Mav could tell he was hiding a smile. "Stop encouraging her!" He backhanded him on the shoulder.

"Hey! I didn't do anything!"

Douglas pulled Mav closer on the sofa, and Mav sank into his embrace, closed his eyes and felt the sense of rightness settle into his body. He turned his head to the side and rubbed his cheek against Douglas's shoulder. Douglas kissed his forehead and continued chatting with Zara and Tex. They'd spent the evening talking about everything and anything while they ate takeaway.

"—security guard or bodyguard or something?"

Mav refocused on the conversation, wondering why Zara was asking about security.

"I have a bodyguard, for want of a better word. When I'm here, he sits outside because they have already checked this building out. When I go to other places, he's by my side or a step behind. Around other people, like say you guys, he would be a little further away to give some semblance of privacy."

"I expected them to need you to be in their eyesight all the time," Tex said.

Douglas shrugged. "When we're out in public or at an event, he is more prominent, and there is usually more than one. Otherwise, I'm not wasting resources by having more than one person around me. It's not fair to others who need it more than I do."

Mav's gaze followed the contour of Douglas's face as he spoke, a small smile making its way onto his own face. Despite Douglas's assurances that he wasn't important enough to warrant extra protection, Mav knew otherwise. Douglas was more than capable of looking after himself in certain situations and wanted to ensure those who couldn't had more people for them. It was another hidden factor in his personality, though Mav was beginning to believe Douglas's family wasn't as in the dark as Douglas thought they were.

"Which reminds me, Mav," Douglas continued, "Would you like to come to the charity event with me this weekend?"

"I don't...I...What?" Mav couldn't fathom how he could be on the other side of the coin for royal events like this one. This event was for a children's charity Douglas's mother supported. It was an auction-style event with dinner and dancing.

Douglas grinned and cupped his cheek. "You're so cute when you're flustered." He pressed several chaste kisses to Mav's lips before releasing him.

"You don't need me there, do you?"

"Need you there? No. Want you there? Yes. I don't want to hide our relationship anymore. Not now that we have Mother's and Father's blessings."

Those beautiful words were how he found himself fussing with a tuxedo bow tie an hour before the event started, several days later. Douglas had wanted him to get ready in his rooms, but Mav wasn't ready for that yet, not on Windsor grounds. If they had been getting ready at Douglas's apartment, it would have been a different matter, but at the castle, where there were so many people, Mav felt weird.

A knock sounded, and Mav abandoned his tie and raked his fingers through his hair as he stalked to the door. Opening it, his mouth dropped open. "Holy hell," he whispered.

Douglas grinned and slipped past him into the room. Mav's eyes followed, and he barely remembered to close the door behind him.

"I don't think we should go anywhere tonight. Not with you looking like that. I won't stand a chance against all those other people." Mav wasn't joking either, but some of his insecurities reared up. How could Douglas be happy with him?

Douglas stepped closer, bringing his hands to Mav's cheeks. "You're all I need. You make me whole. You don't expect me to change who I am. You're not after the fame and glory of being with a prince. You want me because I'm me. In my books, it makes you worth a hundred times more than anyone else out there."

Mav rested his hands on Douglas's wrists and closed his

eyes as tears leaked out. How could Douglas so easily express what he thought and felt?

"I love *you*, Mav. No one else. Never have, never will."

Douglas brushed their lips together, and Mav swooned—full-on swooned—into his arms. He had his own prince charming. No matter how long it lasted, Mav was going to enjoy every minute.

"I love you, too." He opened his eyes and blinked a few times to clear the tears. "Sorry, I thought I'd got through all the issues I had with the others."

"Don't be sorry. You're worth everything, and I will remind you every day. You'll have no cause to forget."

Mav smiled and closed his eyes again. "Thank you. Now, stop saying nice things like that; otherwise, I will never be ready in time."

Douglas pressed a kiss to Mav's lips once more, then pulled away. "Have you spoken to your dad?"

Mav headed into the bathroom to attempt the bow tie again. "I've spoken to him, but I'm going to visit him tomorrow afternoon. Although, I should've been to see him before this event. He'll read the paper and find out about us before I can tell him."

Hands came around his shoulders and took hold of the tie. Douglas nimbly tied it and rested his hands on Mav's shoulders. "Regardless, I'm sure he'll be fine about it."

"Oh, I'm not worried about that. I know he'll be happy. I'm not looking forward to telling him about Bert."

Douglas slid his hands further around his chest and rested his chin on Mav's shoulder. "You should tell him the truth. I doubt he'd be friends with someone willing to do that to his son."

Mav sighed. "I know. I don't want him to lose his job."

"You're more important than a job, Mav."

"I know, I know." He rolled his eyes and fiddled with the edge of the counter.

Douglas squeezed him and let him go. "You'll figure it out. I have a surprise for you."

Mav raised his eyebrows. "A surprise? What for?"

"Well, I know you were worried about me leaving you alone when I had to do my royal duties, so I've invited someone to keep you company."

"Who?"

"You'll see when we get there." Douglas winked. "Are you ready?"

Mav exhaled. "As I'll ever be." He wasn't. Not even remotely, but he'd be the best damn partner he could be, despite how scared he was.

Douglas held out his hand, threading their fingers together when Mav joined him and led him out of the room. This was the first time they would be in public as a couple, and although a few of the household staff had seen them holding hands, they still drew attention. Mav pretended they were staring at Douglas because it made it easier for him to breathe.

They wandered the corridors until they reached the exit. Douglas helped him into the Bentley—Mav had no idea what type it was—waiting for them and slid in beside him, retaking his hand once they were settled. Mav tried to settle his stomach by taking deep breaths, but his whole body trembled.

"Are you okay?" Mav nodded. "Words, Mav."

"Yes, trying to remember how to breathe." His smile was

undoubtedly a little crazy, but he could see the crowds outside their venue through the front windscreen.

"Everything will be fine. I'll be with you the whole way."

Mav stared into Douglas's crystal blue eyes, and everything inside him settled. At that moment, a song popped into his head—*You and I* by One Direction—and he smiled, saving it for later when he could sing it to Douglas. The car came to a stop.

"Ready?" Douglas asked.

"Yes."

The driver climbed out at Douglas's nod and opened the door for them. Douglas slid out first, the flash of camera lights bright even before he exited. Mav could hear them calling Douglas's name as he waved to them.

"Prince Douglas!"

"Your Highness!"

"What are your plans for the evening?"

"Have you brought a date with you?"

The last one brought Mav's head up, and he swallowed hard as Douglas presented his hand for Mav to help him exit the car. He held tight and stepped into the bright lights and barrage of questions. Douglas pulled him to his side and wrapped an arm around his waist. Mav was helpless but to do the same. He was thankful Douglas's bodyguard was with them.

Douglas leaned down. "Smile, sweetheart."

Mav glanced at him, catching his smirk. "Shut up," he said without moving his lips, except into a smile. He knew some people tried to work out what was being said by reading lips, so he knew to be careful.

They waved at the crowds, and Douglas made for the

entrance when Mav's gaze caught the few members of the public he could see.

"Don't you need to meet your fans?" he asked.

"No, we can go straight in. I know you want to get out of here."

Mav shook his head, stopping their forward movement. "Let's go meet them."

Douglas raised his eyebrows. "Are you sure?"

Mav dragged him over to the side with a smile. Douglas grinned back, then focused on the people who were waiting to see him. Douglas received several bouquets that he passed behind him to the assistant, who would take care of them during the event. Mav watched as Douglas crouched when he noticed a little girl with her face pressed to the barrier.

"Hello, sweetie. What's your name?"

"Annie."

"Hello, Annie. How old are you?"

"I'm seven."

"Seven! Wow, you're a big girl now."

"I want to marry a prince or princess when I'm older."

Mav's breath caught at the words, and Douglas appeared stunned for a second before regaining his voice. "I think you would make a wonderful princess, Annie. Wait there for a moment, okay?" He glanced at Annie's mother, who nodded.

Douglas moved to the assistant and whispered in her ear. She nodded and held the bouquets in front of her. Mav frowned as he watched Douglas choose several flowers from each bouquet, then smiled as he realised he was going to give them to the girl. When he didn't, Mav tilted his head and watched as Douglas weaved the flowers together. Douglas pivoted back to the girl and kneeled, presenting her with a crown of flowers, much to the girl's and mother's delight.

At that moment, Mav knew he'd lost all hope. He was irrevocably in love with Douglas, and nothing could ever come between them. A tear slid down his cheek as Douglas rested the crown on the girl's head and kissed her cheek.

"This is until you have your princess crown when you marry your prince or princess."

"Thank you, Prince Douglas."

"You're welcome, sweetheart." He turned to the girl's mother, pressing a kiss to her cheek. "Thank you for bringing her up, knowing she has choices. Have a wonderful day."

Douglas turned to him, frowning when he saw Mav's face. He stepped closer. "What's wrong?"

"Not—" Mav cleared his throat and tried again, "Nothing. It was…You're amazing."

Douglas cupped his face, wiping his tears with his thumbs. "You're not so bad yourself, my love." He dropped his head, their lips meeting in a gentle kiss that would be all over the media and across the entire world by midnight. Mav found he couldn't care less.

They held hands as they entered the building, and Mav noticed there were more cameras and people to greet before they entered the ballroom being used for the event. By the time they were finished with all that, Mav was exhausted.

"How do you do this each time?" he asked when Douglas passed him a glass of bubbly—he assumed it was champagne.

Douglas shrugged. "I'm used to it, I suppose. I've grown up in the public eye, and this is normal for me. I forget how overwhelming things can be for someone who has not done it before. Are you okay?"

Mav smiled. "Yeah, I'm good. This place looks fantastic."

Douglas glanced around. "They have done a brilliant job.

If you want to, there's a child-friendly event happening in a couple of weeks. You'd get to see how the children celebrate."

"That would be great."

Douglas leaned down.

"Now, now. Enough of this shit when I'm here."

Mav turned, Douglas's lips glancing off his cheek instead of his mouth, where he'd no doubt been aiming. "Katrina! What are you doing here?" He gave her a gentle hug, not wanting to smudge her makeup. She wore a red halter neck, floor-length dress, and she had swept her hair up into an intricate braid. "You look beautiful."

"Thanks, sweetie. Your other half thought you'd be eaten by the wolves if you were left alone, so he asked me to tag along. Free drinks all night? I'm in."

"It has nothing to do with the fact that you like Mav?"

Katrina pulled a face. "Whatever." She winked at Mav and gave a small smile. "We can sharpen our claws while everyone gets a view at the new power couple."

"Power couple?"

Katrina smiled. "I thought you read the news—"

"Well, I work on social media."

"It has highlighted you as the couple to watch and emulate."

"Seriously?" Mav wanted to check his phone or, better yet, his tablet, but he had things he had to do first. "They're not going anywhere," he mumbled.

"Sorry?"

Mav glanced up, shaking his head.

Douglas chuckled beside him. "Don't worry. He's most likely already making a list of things he has to check when we get home."

"Forget about it for now, Mav. Let's distract you with gossip, eh, Douglas?"

Douglas snorted. "Make sure the people you're talking about are not next to you, unlike last time I let you attend one of these." He sipped his drink, grimacing. "I need the bar. This drink never gets any better. Come on."

He rested his hand against Mav's lower back, helping guide him through the guests. Despite having several layers separating them, Mav was sure he could feel the warmth from Douglas's hand. As Douglas ordered them some fresh drinks, Mav studied the occupants of the room. If he caught anyone's eye, he smiled and nodded, receiving, mostly, the same back. There was the odd person who frowned and moved away. He knew they wouldn't please everyone, but he hoped those people were less vocal about it.

"Oh, shit," Douglas mumbled. He leaned into Mav's ear. "This won't be pleasant, and if I could get you away from it, I would, but I'm sorry in advance."

Mav frowned at him. "What—?"

He lost his words when a cloud of perfume enveloped them, a robust woman with long black hair standing in the centre. She appeared formidable with her jet-black ensemble and matching accessories. A dark queen of sorts, except her eyes gave her away. There was nothing pleasant in them at all.

"Douglas! How nice of you to attend. I'm sure your mother is ecstatic you're here."

The words, however nice they were, sounded the wrong side of sarcasm. As soon as he had the thought, he understood who this was.

"Aunt Charlotte, nice to see you again." Douglas made no attempt to kiss or greet her in any other way.

Charlotte glanced at Mav, raking her gaze up and down him, then moved onto Katrina as if Mav wasn't there. "Katrina, darling, it's nice to see you again. Are you planning on making an honest man of Douglas yet?"

Mav bristled, but a hand on his lower back had him taking a drink and closing his eyes for a brief second. He couldn't make a scene in the middle of an event like this. She would say her piece and leave, though it didn't make it any easier to bear.

Katrina smiled. "I think he's honest enough without me, Princess Charlotte."

"Don't leave it too long. I'm sure someone will snap him up in no time."

"I already have been, Aunt Charlotte. May I present my boyfriend, Maverick Houghton."

Charlotte didn't look at Mav. Instead, she glared at Douglas. "No, you may not. Enjoy the rest of your evening."

With that, she swirled away, her perfume going with her, thankfully.

"Fucking bitch," Douglas griped, throwing back his drink and indicating for another.

Mav turned his back to the room, keeping his head lowered and his voice quiet. "She's not worth it, Douglas. Thank you for the reminder to keep my cool. It's not easy when they say stuff like that about my boyfriend."

Douglas grinned. "Shall we give them something to complain about?"

Mav smiled. "If it's a small kiss. I don't want to trample all over this event. It's a good cause."

Douglas stared at him and shook his head. "How you keep me humble."

Mav lifted his head, their lips meeting. It took all Mav

had to stop from going further, but they had a charity to celebrate.

"Come on. Let's mingle."

Douglas offered him one elbow and Katrina the other, and they held their heads high as they worked their way through the guests.

29

DOUGLAS

Mav and he had spent the entire morning lounging in bed. They'd arrived at Douglas's apartment well after midnight because they'd stayed to ensure certain people didn't think they were running scared. They weren't. Aunt Charlotte was a force to be reckoned with, but she was also a small price to pay for being able to hold Mav's hand in public. Douglas wouldn't allow anyone to stop them from continuing their relationship now that they'd fought so hard for it.

"Would you like to come and meet my dad?"

Mav was curled against his chest, swirling a finger around his lover's stomach, and Douglas ran his fingers up and down Mav's back. Mav didn't tense up when he asked the question; therefore, Douglas knew he felt relaxed about it.

"I'd love to. You have lots to talk to him about, though. Are you sure you want me there?" Douglas nuzzled his nose into Mav's hair, inhaling the faint aroma of his shampoo from the evening before.

"Yes. I want Dad to meet you." Mav kissed his chest. "Besides, he's probably already found out who I'm seeing from the morning papers."

Douglas had persuaded Mav not to check social media before they went to bed and, so far, had distracted him enough to keep him in bed instead of working. He knew it wouldn't last, but he'd be grateful for every minute Mav lay with him.

"Sure. I'll let Eric know, and he can check it out before we leave." He quickly added, "Not check your dad out. I mean, check to see what's around there for security." Douglas sent a quick text to Eric.

Mav chuckled. "I know, Douglas. Don't worry. I also know they will check Dad out, and that's fine."

"I hate it can be so invasive sometimes. It must be awful to have your entire life rummaged through like at a car boot."

"You've been to a car boot?" Mav lifted his head to smirk at him.

Douglas grinned. "No, but I know what they are." Mav's tongue lapped over Douglas's nipple, then he kissed it. "You start something; we won't get to your Dad's house."

"I know, which is why…" He rolled to his other side and swung his legs off the bed, sitting up.

"Tease," Douglas pouted.

Mav's laughter floated back as he wandered to the bathroom. As tempting as it was to join Mav in the shower, he knew they'd be late. He refrained with difficulty, swapping places with Mav when he exited in a cloud of steam. They made a quick lunch of sandwiches and fruit while Mav checked in with his tablet, then travelled down the lift to the car park.

"Are you nervous?" Douglas asked.

"Not even a little. I'll drive."

Mav winked and strode to his car. Douglas followed and climbed into the passenger seat. Douglas's phone beeped, and he checked the message from Eric, saying he was ready.

"Let's go."

Mav drove through the streets of London with Douglas's gaze mainly on him, not where they were going. He couldn't resist. Mav was a beautiful specimen of a man, but it was his heart that mattered most to Douglas. Everything Mav did was with no expectations from anyone else. It was refreshing.

When they pulled up outside the little cottage nestled between bigger houses, Douglas was immediately charmed. The two-storey stone building was covered with greenery at the front, the windows, door and roof, the only things breaking up the mass of plants. The front door had an over-hang some would call a porch. The garden was filled with plants, flowers and bushes of types Douglas wouldn't be able to name. It reminded him of the house they used to stay in when he was younger when they holidayed in Scotland, just on a larger scale to this one.

Mav opened the front door and called out, "I hope you're not up a ladder again!"

Douglas closed the door behind them and heard, "What're you going to do about it if I was?"

A man with a lined face and whitening hair came into the hallway, drying his hands. Douglas knew Ronald was over sixty years old, but he appeared older like he felt tired. Mav's father stilled when he saw Douglas, then flicked his gaze to Mav.

"You could've warned an old man he was going to meet royalty."

Mav rolled his eyes. "Why? You don't need to act any differently around him. Today, he's just Douglas." Ronald gave Mav a flat look, and Mav chuckled. "Fine! I apologise. Next time, I'll send a telegram."

"You better believe it." Ronald stepped closer and held out his hand. "Ronald Houghton. Nice to meet you, Your Highness."

He bowed slightly over their clasped hands and stepped back, shoving Mav mildly before wandering towards the back of the house without giving Douglas the chance to say anything.

Douglas glanced at Mav with wide eyes, and Mav chuckled. "Don't worry. He's testing you."

"Hang on! You said nothing about passing tests!" Douglas complained as he followed Mav down the hallway, getting a glance at a younger version of Mav in several photographs lining the walls.

They entered the kitchen, and Mav dropped into a chair at the table, indicating for Douglas to sit next to him. "This is where we do our chats," Mav whispered.

"You have a lovely home, Mr Houghton."

"Thank you. I try to keep up with the maintenance of it because it's what Essie would have wanted. She loved this place."

Douglas realised Mav hadn't spoken of his mother, and he felt bad for not asking before. Mav gave him a small smile.

"Mum died from cancer nine years ago. It's been just us ever since."

Douglas rested his hand on Mav's knee and squeezed.

"Here you go. Tea of champions." Ronald placed a mug in front of each of them on the weathered table that had no doubt seen so much love and sat opposite them. "I'm assuming you got your head out of your ass and sorted things with him." He pointed at Douglas with a tip of his mug.

"Dad!" Mav rubbed his head and sighed. "Yes. We sorted things out. We're official now."

"Ooh, official." Ronald's eyes twinkled. "I know. I saw the papers, and you all decked out fancy-schmancy." He glanced at Douglas. "You look good together. Happy." He sipped his tea.

Mav smiled. "I am, Dad."

Ronald turned his gaze to Douglas. "You're going to take care of my son, aren't you, Your Highness."

A statement, not a question, though Douglas answered anyway, "Yes, with everything I am. He'll want for nothing. No one will hurt him. You have my word. And please, call me Douglas."

Ronald narrowed his eyes and stared at him for a few seconds, nodding once. "Good. Now, what's this I hear about you not working for Bert any longer?"

A quick change of subject, but Douglas knew they had his blessing, and it eased his tension. He'd wanted Ronald to like him, and it seemed like he did. At least until Mav explained his role in Mav losing his job if he was going to tell his dad about that.

"You know I wanted to start my own business. I thought it was time to try." Mav sipped his tea, and Douglas could see he was trying not to fidget, but Ronald's eyes narrowed again.

"Bullshit. You seemed happy there, Mav. Why the change of heart?" Ronald squinted at Douglas. "Does this have something to do with your new relationship?"

Mav grimaced, which gave away the fact he was hiding

something, and Ronald must've seen it because he pounced, aiming his question to Douglas, "Why does he need to not work for Bert if he's in a relationship with you?"

Douglas wanted to tell Ronald everything, but he knew Mav didn't want him to think badly about his best friend. "I support—"

"Okay!" Mav rubbed his forehead and pushed his mug away, crossing his arms on the table. Douglas knew how hard this was going to be for Mav and wrapped his arm around his shoulders. "Bert has been blackmailing me into staying working for him. Douglas sorted the situation out. Hence, I'm now working for myself."

Ronald slammed his cup down on the table, spilling the contents. "He's been blackmailing you? Why? With what?"

Mav exhaled. "A couple of years ago, I went to an event with him, and he believed I showed him up and made him look a fool. He sent me to work for Douglas as penance, and when I tried to hand my notice in," Mav glanced at Douglas and winced in what he knew was an apology, "Bert threatened your job unless I stayed working for him."

Ronald was quiet for several minutes, but his jaw was working beneath the white and brown beard. Mav opened his mouth to say something, but Douglas stayed him. Ronald needed to gather his thoughts. When the older man stood and shuffled across to the counter, Mav half-stood, but again Douglas kept him from going. Ronald picked up his phone, dialling, and Mav dropped into his seat, leaning his head in his hands as if he knew what was going to happen.

"Hey, Jeffrey. I won't be coming back to work." Ronald was silent as he listened and stared out of the back window. "No. I don't appreciate my son being blackmailed by your brother so I could keep my job. As of this moment, I no longer work for you. If you have a problem with it, take it up with your brother. I certainly won't be talking with him again." Silence again. "I don't believe you didn't know, Jeffrey, and I refuse to work for someone who could do that. I'll send someone for my things in the morning." He hung up.

"Dad, you didn't have to—"

"Yes, I did. No one, and I repeat, no one does that to my son and gets away with it. I've put up with many things from those two men over the years, ignored a lot of unacceptable behaviour I shouldn't have, but no longer. You're my son. I take care of you as much as you take care of me. It's the way it is." Ronald retook his seat, bringing a cloth with him and wiping up the mess before gulping his brew.

"What are you going to do?"

"I'll find plenty of things to do. I'll just retire early; it's only two years, after all." Ronald chuckled, though his face belied his anger. No doubt at the men, not the situation.

"I'm sorry, Dad."

"Don't you dare be sorry. I'll say this once and only once. You are not to blame for their behaviour. Get it out of your head now. Got it?" Mav nodded, and Ronald sighed, then changed the subject. "So, you're creating your own business. How is it going to work?"

Mav swallowed a few times before he spoke, "King Andrew has taken me on as a freelance social media manager for Douglas as we work well together." Mav smiled at him.

Ronald raised his eyebrows. "Does he know about..." He flicked his hands between the two of them.

"Yes, my parents know about us. Father opposed, to begin with, but he's come around and has given us his blessing."

"You'll be a lot busier than before." Ronald's brow lowered and puckered.

Mav reached for his father's hand, covering it. "I'll be here as much if not more than before." Mav frowned and glanced at Douglas. "We need to arrange something for my dad. The media will start harassing him, too."

Douglas nodded. "I'll have someone come and chat with you if that's okay, Mr Houghton? See if we can come up with something that would work for you."

"I'll be fine. I know how to ward off annoying pests."

Douglas and Mav argued with him for a few more minutes before Ronald caved and agreed to have a meeting with someone about his security. After they settled it, Douglas spent several hours getting to know Ronald better.

At six o'clock, Douglas said, "I'm sorry, but I have to go. I have dinner with my parents this evening." Heart racing, he stared at Mav. "I would like it if you'd join me."

Douglas watched Mav's eyes widen, and his mouth opened and closed several times.

"Yes, he'll join you." At Mav's glare, Ronald continued, "Get it over and done with now, and you can relax. I highly doubt they'll lock you in the Tower. Although if they'd met you as a child, they might have."

Douglas chuckled and stood. "It's okay. We can do it another day. When you're ready."

Mav sniffed and tugged on his earlobe. "I suppose it's not like I don't know them." He braced himself on his knees and stood.

"That's the spirit." Ronald rose with trembling arms. Douglas refrained from offering to help, although he wanted to. "Get off with you. I'm sure I'll see you soon. Now that I have more time on my hands, I can get more work done around here."

Mav whirled to face him, pointing a finger. "No climbing ladders without someone with you."

Ronald threw his head back and laughed. "Okay, okay."

Mav wrapped his arms around his father, and they murmured for a moment. Douglas moved closer to the door, not wanting to intrude. When Mav joined him, Douglas held out his hand.

"Thank you for having me, Mr Houghton. It was a pleasure."

Ronald took his hand in a firm grip. "I think we can get rid of the titles now, don't you? Call me Ron."

"Thank you, Ron. I look forward to seeing you soon, and I'll be in touch about the security."

Ron waved them off, and Mav drove towards the castle. "I can't believe I'm having dinner with your parents."

Douglas snorted. "It's not like you don't know them as you said."

"But this is different! Before, it was on a professional level. This time, it's personal."

Douglas slid his hand onto Mav's thigh, squeezing. "Mother loves you. Freddie thinks you're great. George told me to stop talking about you because you're too perfect. And Father…you saw how he was when I was released. He likes you, too."

Mav exhaled. "Well, I'm sure we'll find out."

They wandered through Windsor's corridors after parking the car, arms wrapped around each other and lost in their own world. In Douglas's rooms, Douglas kissed Mav with a desperation he'd not felt in a while. He rested Mav against the door, exploring his mouth while his hand covered Mav's eyes. His other hand unfastened both their jeans and, once they were free, encircled both cocks.

Douglas tore his lips away long enough to mutter, "Thrust your hips, Mav," and took his mouth again.

He kept his hand tight enough they both leaked precome, easing their movements. This would be fast because they were both worked up, and they had little time. A knock sounded behind Mav, and Mav stilled, pushing against the hand covering his eyes.

"Stop," Douglas whispered. "Colour?"

Mav inhaled shakily. "Green."

The knock sounded again. "Who is it?" Douglas asked as he began stroking them again. Mav's bottom lip was caught between his teeth, his hands clenched around both of Douglas's wrists.

"Freddie."

"Is it urgent?" Douglas pumped harder, and Mav whimpered.

"No," Freddie said hesitantly.

"Can it wait until dinner or after?" Douglas fought to keep his voice steady.

"Sure. See you soon." Now amusement ran through his voice.

"We'll be there shortly."

"I'm sure you will." Freddie chuckled.

Douglas grinned at his brother's words, knowing Freddie knew what they were doing. "Come for me, Mav," he whispered in Mav's ear.

Mav muffled his moan with his own hand as he came over them both, with Douglas following several strokes later. Douglas let his hand slide off Mav's eyes and burrowed his face into Mav's neck. They allowed their breathing to return to normal before Douglas pulled away and dragged Mav towards the bathroom. Luckily, Mav had left some clothes in his room the day before because there was no way they could wear their current outfits.

"I can't believe we did that."

Mav covered his face with his hands, cheeks darkening to a deep rose colour.

"Freddie doesn't care. He also won't tell anyone." Douglas divested them of their clothes.

"It doesn't matter. How embarrassing. I won't be able to look at him now."

Douglas chuckled and pulled Mav under the spray. "Come on. Let's get ready."

They didn't mess around in the shower, although Douglas washed and dried every inch of Mav.

"I've noticed you haven't had many headaches recently." It had been something that had been rolling around in Douglas's mind for a while, and he was sure he was right, and Mav hadn't been hiding them from him.

Mav frowned and paused in pulling on his trousers. "You're right. I've had the odd niggle, but no migraine."

Douglas smiled. "Good. Although we know how to fix them now." He winked.

Mav's mouth curled. "It's because the troublesome prince I usually have to deal with has gone on hiatus."

"Hey!" Douglas threw one of his socks in Mav's direction.

Suitably dressed, he linked their hands and left the room, tugging Mav's hand occasionally to keep him moving. He explained the few rules they had for the dinner table, and when they entered the dining room, everyone was already there. His mother rose with a smile and stepped closer, holding her arms out for a hug as she always did.

"Douglas, I'm glad you could make it." She kissed his

cheek and turned to Mav, enfolding him in her arms. "Maverick, I'm so happy you could join us. Come, let's eat."

"Thank you, Your Majesty."

"Oh, pfft. Call me Louisa."

"Um…Uh…"

Douglas hid his smile. "I think you broke him, Mother. He's strict with his manners. It might take him a while before he can do it."

She smiled and tapped Mav's cheek lightly. "You'll get there."

Douglas guided Maverick to sit next to him. "Relax," he whispered.

"I'm trying," Mav mumbled back.

"So, Maverick," Father said, "what did you think of the event last night? Any tips on making it better?"

And with that, Douglas knew his father had accepted their relationship and would fight for it as much as any other.

30

GEORGE

George hid his smile by stuffing food into his mouth. He could see how uneasy Maverick was, but he was glad the focus was off him for once. The repeated refrain of "what are you doing with your life" was something he was happy to brush aside for tonight.

He listened with half an ear on the conversation, keeping his quips to himself, and instead, focused on what had happened with Douglas over the last few weeks. He couldn't pretend he had seen the sparks flying between him and Maverick because the only electricity he'd seen was when they butted heads, but maybe that was what they needed and how their relationship worked. It wasn't for George to say what was right or wrong. He had no relationship to gather evidence from, so what could he say? He played hard with others at the club, but relationships? No.

Instead, he focused on being happy, upbeat, funny, and whatever else people needed to lighten the mood of his family. Being part of a royal family had more downsides than upsides, as far as he was concerned, but he could usually lift the load a little. Except when it came to Douglas being in jail. That had been a low point, and George hadn't been able to do anything to help.

"George?"

He blinked and stared at his mother. "Yes, Mother?"

Her mouth twitched, but she withheld her smile. "Your phone?"

It was then he noticed his phone buzzing and blaring its ringtone through the room. He winced and fumbled to remove it. "I'm so sorry. I'm sure I turned it off."

He finally silenced it and fixed an appropriately apologetic look on his face before glancing at his father. The king shook his head and refocused on Maverick. George exhaled and stared at his food. For some reason, it was the one rule at the dinner table that he always forgot. He didn't know why because it wasn't like the rule had ever changed.

Tuning in to the conversation, he ate methodically.

"Do you have plans to expand your new venture, or do you want to stay small and personal?" his mother asked Maverick.

"I think staying small and personal would be a good option for me to begin with. Once I get my feet under me, I could reconsider, but I'm only one person, and if I employ people, I will spend less time doing the work I love."

"That is an excellent point, Maverick. Doing something you love is vitally important," his father said.

George was sure there wasn't a dig at him in those words, but he spent many years being told he needed to find himself a job. What his father didn't know was that he *had* a job— two, actually—but neither would be regarded as fit for a prince if his father found out. Problem was, George loved every minute of both of his jobs, and he was good at them.

Thanks to his mother and their PA, Randall, George could do one of his jobs anonymously. The other job no one knew about because he controlled it over the internet. Nothing on his profile pointed towards him being a prince, and he was determined to keep it that way.

"Have you heard any more about the Talon debacle?" he asked.

As soon as he'd said the words, he knew he'd made a mistake because his father glared at him. "I hadn't planned on discussing that tonight because this is supposed to be a family meal."

"Sorry, Father. Forget I asked."

Douglas held out his hand. "No, it's okay. I think it's good to talk about it as a family." He gazed at George. "The last I heard, and correct me if I'm wrong, Father, was that Talon was still in jail, awaiting a court date. The police are collating all the information they have to ensure he doesn't see the light of day. Harvey is still missing, although they have found his ex-boyfriend, who had some information to give them. I don't think it will be long before we find Harvey."

"That's good. I'm glad they're going to get what they deserve," George said. That they could roam free was something George didn't want to think about. If they did, anything could happen to anyone.

His phone buzzed against his thigh, but he ignored it. At least it was silent now. He finished his food, and once everyone had finished theirs, he excused himself, kissed his mother and left. There was no need for him to stay when they began talking more business. He was only third in line to the throne, so he doubted he'd ever need to know most of it. It gave him a certain amount of freedom, which Douglas had often commented on. It was true. Douglas was the spare heir, and as such, needed to know as much as Freddie did. They would only need George if something happened to both his brothers as awful as that was to think about. They were strong, though. Nothing would happen to them.

George could live his life as he wanted.

31

MAVERICK
TEN MONTHS LATER

"Henry! I wasn't expecting to see you here?"

Douglas hugged his cousin with a back slap. Mav marvelled at how alike some of the cousins were and how different others were. The diverse and complicated results of genes had always amazed him.

"Yeah, I was told you needed some extra hands, and I had some time."

"Great, thanks. Mav, what needs doing?"

Mav checked the clipboard he had close by and ran a finger down the list. "The flowers?" He raised an eyebrow at Henry. "Would you mind?"

"That's cool. I help Mother in her garden, so flowers don't bother me. What needs to be done?"

Mav studied the room and saw who he needed. "Robert!" When the man turned to him, Mav waved his hand to get him to come over. When he did, he introduced the two men. "Robert, Henry can help with the flowers if that's okay with you?"

Robert was a slim, toned black man with short, curly hair,

a barely-there moustache and chin beard. He accessorised his look with jewellery and makeup that varied every time Mav saw him. Robert had been their florist for the last several events, and Mav hoped he would continue because he was the easiest man to get along with.

"Of course. Follow me, Your Highness. I'll show you the plans." Robert pivoted and sauntered back the way he'd come.

Mav frowned when Henry didn't follow.

"Everything okay, Henry?" Douglas asked before Mav could.

Henry started and glanced at them, his cheeks pinking. "Yes, sorry. Off in my own little world. I'll..." He indicated with his thumb in Robert's direction, then scampered off.

"What was that about?"

Douglas gave a small smile. "I think someone has a crush."

"Really?" He glanced at Robert and Henry again, not seeing whatever Douglas had. He shrugged. "If you say so."

Douglas slid his hand around Mav's waist, resting his chin on his shoulder. "I do."

Mav shivered at the words. Douglas had been dropping hints about potentially getting married at some point, but Mav hadn't been acknowledging them. He would love to marry Douglas, but he wouldn't make it easy for him.

"We have work to do. We can play later."

Douglas growled into Mav's neck, sending tingles down his spine, and pulled back. "You're right. The quicker we get this prepared, the better. Although, tell me again, why are we decorating this place when we have other people who can do it?"

"Because then we can see what's involved in creating

something this extravagant, and it'll help us with planning in the future."

Douglas rolled his shoulders. "All right. What am I supposed to do?"

Mav gave Douglas his job and watched him stride across the room to help the decorators who were stringing up lights and balloons. He knew Douglas didn't mind helping, especially as this event was for the children he'd been getting to know through the charity he supported. Over a hundred children had received handwritten—by Douglas—invitations to attend the party tomorrow night, and he knew Douglas would do everything in his power to make it a success. There were several types of entertainment: a magician, a company who brought weird and wonderful animals for them to see, several street performers, some small trampolines and a bouncy castle. It was a veritable wonderland for kids.

It hadn't always been plain sailing for them. The case against Talon had brought a few things to light about the club the royal family hadn't wanted known. Unfortunately, once they had acknowledged the information, despite it being deleted from the record, those who were there knew it. The result had been that Club Royal had received an astonishing amount of membership requests. The family had hired someone to take control of that aspect of the club.

As for Talon himself, he pleaded not guilty though there had been witnesses to what he'd done, and therefore, the court case had drawn out enough Kendal, Eddie and other subs had to go through the ordeal of sitting in front of the courtroom and having their lives exposed to all. Douglas and Mav had ensured they cared for each sub during and after the case, as had the king and other Monitors. When Talon had been given seven years in prison, they'd collectively let out a sigh of relief.

As the hours passed, Mav got more and more excited about what he and Douglas had planned for that evening. For the first time, he was going to the club. Douglas had offered to take him as soon as Mav was ready, and when they got home tonight, he was going to tell Douglas to take him. He was equal parts excited and nervous because Douglas had done his best to explain and describe what it was like there, but Mav wanted to see for himself.

He hoped there wasn't an event or anything to stop them from being able to go now he'd gained the courage.

"Are you ready to go?"

Mav jumped and spun around, hand on his chest. "You scared me."

Douglas frowned. "Everything okay?"

"Yeah, I was concentrating, that's all." Mav shuffled the papers he'd been working on, then picked them and his tablet up before turning back to Douglas. "Ready."

Heart racing, he inhaled and allowed Douglas to guide him through the room with a hand at Mav's lower back, as he always did. They said goodbye to the remaining staff and journeyed home. Mav found it difficult to believe Douglas's apartment was now his home, too. He'd let his own apartment go when the lease ran out two months ago, but it seemed strange when he entered the penthouse to find his own belongings intermingled with Douglas's, and especially his guitar, which now lived in the corner of the living room.

Mav placed what he was carrying onto the counter and turned to Douglas. It was now or never. "I want to go to the club."

Douglas raised his eyebrows, eyes widening as a slow grin crept across his face. "Seriously?"

Mav nodded. Douglas dashed across the distance separating them, and crushed Mav into a kiss. He knew he'd made the right choice, and he knew Douglas wouldn't let anything happen to him. The reason it had taken Mav so long to gain the courage to do this was that he was scared, and nothing would stop him from being scared until he took the leap of faith and went.

"We don't have to do anything. We can watch and wander around drinking beer and seeing what everyone else is doing. Oh, my god! This is going to be great. You'll like it; I know you will."

Mav was sure he would, but he was nervous. Douglas had introduced more sensation play into the bedroom throughout the months they'd been together, and they had also watched several BDSM videos—not the porn type, but with people who knew what they were doing—to get Mav used to what he might see at the club. Mav knew what to expect.

"When do you want to go?" Douglas cupped his jaw.

"Tonight?"

Douglas's eyes widened. "Are you sure?"

Mav shrugged. "Why not? We don't have plans." Plus, Mav needed to do this before he lost his confidence again.

"All right. Let's get ready." Douglas took his hand and pulled him towards the bedroom. "I have something special for you."

Mav's heart raced. "What?"

"Come see."

Douglas let his hands go and ventured into the room, rummaging through the bottom drawer. He brought out some black fabric and turned to Mav. "If you don't like it, it's absolutely fine."

Douglas's uncharacteristic show of uncertainty charmed Mav, and he drifted closer, holding out his hand. "Let me see."

Douglas passed him the item, and Mav shook it out. It was a black mesh shirt, which meant it was slightly see-through. Mav loved it. He dropped it on the bed, stripped off his shirt and held it up to his chest in the mirror. He didn't want to put it on before he'd showered, but it intrigued him. It wasn't easy to see, but he liked the idea. Throwing it back on the bed, he held out a hand to Douglas.

"Come on, shower time."

They showered in record time, and Mav laughed at Douglas's exuberance.

"Sorry, I'm excited to show you what it's like."

Mav put a hand on his chest. "It's okay. I know. Let's get ready, and we can go." Mav slipped some black trousers on, then pulled the mesh shirt on. He wasn't sure what the material was, but it was soft against his skin. Once dressed, he stood in front of the mirror, running his hand over the surface of the material. It was strange to see himself dressed like this, but it looked good. It was in keeping with his love of shirts with a collar and cuffs of solid fabric, but the rest of it...had holes.

Douglas wore black leather trousers and a black waistcoat, but he pulled a suit jacket over the top. "I'd be front-page news if I wore this in public, so I'm told." Douglas winked. "Are you sure?"

"Definitely."

It didn't take them long to get there. Douglas pulled into

the car park and held his hand as they entered the lift. As soon as they exited, a tiny woman greeted them.

"Good evening, Your Highness, Mr Houghton. I'm glad to see you."

Douglas chuckled. "Clarice is a stickler for titles like you are, Mav. Mav, this is Clarice, who keeps this place ticking over. Clarice, this is my boyfriend, Mav."

"Nice to meet you, Clarice."

"Likewise, Mr Houghton."

Douglas pressed his thumbprint to a sensor and indicated for Mav to do the same. He'd already explained this was how they could gain entry to the main club.

"Thank you. Let me save your details, Mr Houghton, and you'll be all set."

"Make sure he gains full access, Clarice. To my locker as well." Mav shot a questioning glance at him. "It gives you access to the Monitors' changing room, too."

"Okay. All sorted. Enjoy your evening."

"Thank you, Clarice."

Douglas guided him through a doorway and into what appeared to be a changing room, then took a right into another large room.

"This is the Monitors' room. You can use my locker for anything you don't want to take with you."

Mav withdrew his wallet, and Douglas slipped off his jacket, hanging it inside. Douglas turned to him.

"There is something I'd like you to wear. Subs often wear a collar to show they have a Master. It also tells other people you are not open to invitation. Would you be willing to wear mine?"

Mav's eyes filled. "I'd love to."

Douglas pulled something from his locker and held it up

for Mav to see. It was a solid circle of silver, with a small padlock at the front.

"You don't have to use the lock straight away. I don't want you to feel like you can't take this off."

"It's perfect. Will you put it on?"

Douglas's hands shook as he fitted the choker-style collar and clicked the lock into place. Mav turned to the mirror and smiled, brushing his hand over the lock. There was something soft and elegant about the collar that made him feel less rugged and more cared for.

"I love it." He whirled around. "I love you."

"I love you. Remember, we can take it off whenever you want."

"It's staying. Trust me."

Douglas rewarded him with a gentle kiss, then grinned and dragged him to the door. Mav's stomach filled with butterflies as they crossed to the main doors and stepped across the threshold.

The first thing Mav noticed was the noise, or rather, the lack of noise. It wasn't silent, but he'd expected the hustle and bustle of a nightclub environment, and although there were plenty of people around, there was soft music and gentle conversation. There were also moans and groans, but he put it aside for the moment.

They stood a few steps inside the door, and Douglas slipped his arm around his waist. Douglas had already told Mav the rules, so when another Master approached, Mav lowered his gaze, though he didn't let go of Douglas.

"Master Douglas, nice to see you."

"The same to you, Master Frederick."

"I see you've brought your sub for his first visit. How are you finding it so far, Mav?"

Mav didn't raise his eyes but answered, "Intense, sir."

"I can imagine. Well, remember, if for any reason you need help and Douglas isn't around, find one of the Dungeon Monitors or someone you know from the other side of your life. No one will hurt you on our watch."

"Thank you, sir."

"Take it easy on him now, Master Douglas. We want him to return."

They chuckled, and Douglas pressed his lips to his ear. "Well done. Let's check out what's around."

Mav lifted his head a little to study his surroundings as they wandered, but he lowered his gaze if he needed to. He didn't want to cause Douglas any problems.

They stopped in front of a window, and Mav glanced in to see a man strapped to a bench of some sort, with another man pounding into him from behind. Mav's breath caught, and he couldn't look away.

"We call this a fuck bench," Douglas whispered in his ear after he stood behind him and wrapped his arms around Mav's waist, linking his fingers in front. "The recipient can't get away and has to take everything given to him."

Mav watched as the Master raked his nails down the sub's back, and the only movement Mav could see was the slight lifting of the sub's head and the clenching of his fingers and toes. Mav felt his cock stir at the vision.

"They know we can see them, but they can't see us. It means they don't know when someone is watching," Douglas continued, his fingers sliding under Mav's shirt and scratching gently at his skin. Heat flooded Mav's body, and he rested back against Douglas. "See how the sub wants to squirm and buck but can't. They are at their Master's mercy."

Douglas lowered his free hand and covered Mav's groin,

Mav bucking to gain friction, his eyes locked on the two men through the window. Within seconds, Douglas moved his hand away, and Mav whimpered.

"Would you like someone to see how beautiful you are when you're writhing beneath me?"

Mav's heart skipped a beat. He hadn't thought he'd like the idea of people watching such an intimate act but seeing these men had Mav thinking it wouldn't be so bad, especially if he couldn't see who watched. He nodded.

"Words, Mav."

"Yes, Sir. Please."

Douglas caught Mav's earlobe between his teeth and grazed the skin as he pulled away. "Your wish is my command."

Douglas guided Mav away from the window and led him to a room. He closed the door behind them and engaged the lock, then pressed a button by the door before facing Mav.

"Strip."

Mav immediately went to work on his clothes, laying them across the back of a chair, then stood before Douglas naked. His body trembled, both with nerves and the need to do everything Douglas asked him to.

"Get on your back on the bed."

While Mav situated himself, Douglas wandered around the room, gathering some items. As he approached the bed with a trolley, Mav saw a blindfold, some fabric, some wax and some other items he didn't know.

"We've spoken about wax play before, haven't we?"

"Yes, Sir."

"Are you ready to try?"

"Yes, Sir."

Mav knew there was likely some pain involved in this; it

was, after all, hot wax. He wasn't certain he'd like it, but he'd agreed he'd be willing to try when they'd discussed several aspects of sensation play, and it was what they were apparently doing tonight.

"Safe words?"

"Green to continue, yellow to slow down, red to stop."

"If at any time you are not enjoying this, say red. This should be an enjoyable experience. Do you understand?"

"I understand, Sir."

Douglas brought the fabric up and tied Mav's hands to the headboard and his ankles to the bottom of the bed. He pulled the blindfold over Mav's head to his forehead, leaning over and kissing him soundly before pulling it over his eyes. All at once, Mav's senses went into overdrive as they did every time they covered his eyes. His hearing picked up every small sound: the clink of a jar, the din of metal, his own breathing.

"I'm going to rub oil over your stomach, which is where we will try the wax to begin with."

Mav heard the click of a bottle and the sound of something rubbing together. He jerked when Douglas's hands rested on his stomach and began kneading the oil into his skin. He remembered the conversation they'd had before about needing oil to stop the wax from sticking to the hairs on his body as much. The oil would make it easier to remove the wax at the end.

The hands disappeared.

"Ready?"

"Yes, Sir."

Mav inhaled roughly when a spot of wax landed above his belly button, and he jerked against his bindings. It was painful for around two seconds, then a gentle heat seeped into his skin. He repeated the same response when another drop hit his lower stomach. A similar sensation happened. Each time the wax touched his skin, he flinched but arched into it. It was as if he was being warmed from the outside in.

He hadn't expected his cock to get excited at the sting of pain, but was it the pain, or was it the warmth afterwards? Either way, his cock was hard, and he needed Douglas.

"Please, Sir."

"Colour?"

"Green, Sir. I need more."

"What do you need?"

"You." Mav heard movement, then the sound of a zipper, and he moaned and arched, wanting Douglas inside him. "Please, Sir."

Despite the urgency, Douglas prepared him well before pressing inside and making Mav groan at how right everything felt. He knew he wouldn't last long, but he had to wait for his Master's permission first.

Once Douglas was fully seated, he leaned forward and whispered in Mav's ear, "Come whenever you want. Everyone will see how responsive you are to me and only me. You're mine."

Douglas pulled back and slammed back in, his grip on Mav's hip firm. It was only as he crested that he felt another splash of heat hit each of his nipples in succession, and he exploded. Mav couldn't hear anything other than the rush of air through his lungs as his body convulsed.

Seconds later, he fluttered his eyes open and saw Douglas leaning over him, beaming at him. "You're fucking amazing, Mav. I love you so much."

"I love you always."

They sealed the deal with a kiss.

Did you enjoy this book? Why not find out why Henry appeared so lost and tongue-tied in the final chapter by pre-ordering Secretive Royal? It will be delivered to your kindle on Nov 4, 2021

Sign up to my newsletter to get a free prequel from Club Royal called Royal Firsts.

ABOUT ELOUISE EAST

I am Elouise East but feel free to call me Elli. I write sweet and steamy connections in gay romance. I also touch on taboo stories under the name Elouise R East.

Books that tell the stories where friendship and family are the focal point - be it blood family or chosen - is very important to me. That's why I include a variety of personalities, talents, ages, situations and abilities as I believe a story needs, or a character needs. I want my characters to be real, to be relatable, to be free to have whatever views they tell me they have. And trust me, most of the time, I do not have *any* say in the matter!

My characters come to life on the page for me as well as my readers. Their stories unfold in front of me, and I have very little input into how they want to be shown. Just like real life, the lives of my characters change with every choice, every interaction and every conversation. And I wouldn't have it any other way.

I write books that are emotionally realistic, even if liberties are taken with other aspects of my stories. I don't know any other way to write. It comes from deep inside.

Who am I? A single parent to two children who make life worth living. An avid reader who still devours every book she can get her hands on. A student of learning about any subject that takes her fancy. An author of books she would read herself. And a romantic at heart who loves anything cheesy.

Who's in?

DADDY

Love Me, Daddy

Soothe Me, Daddy

Spoil Me, Daddy

DARK & DIVERGENT

A Biker Make Three

Forbidden Temptation

Too Many Secrets

STANDALONE

Treehouse Whispers